A Countryman's Creel

The *remarkable*, the *heart-rending*, the *intriguing* the *almost unbelievable* short stories of

CONOR FARRINGTON

Illustrated by Joseph Shepherd

Merlin Unwin Books

First published in Great Britain by Merlin Unwin Books, 2011

Text © Conor Farrington, 2011

Merlin Unwin Books Ltd
Palmers House
7 Corve Street
Ludlow, Shropshire SY8 1DB
U.K.

www.merlinunwin.co.uk
email: books@merlinunwin.co.uk

ISBN 978-1-906122-35-5

Designed and set in Bembo by Merlin Unwin
Printed and bound by TJ International Ltd, Padstow, England

Contents

For Mama, Papa, Sinéad and Claire

Pallas quas condidit arces
ipsa colat; nobis placeant ante omnia silvae.
VIRGIL

The Unseen Hook

IT WAS an odd kind of cast he made that sunlit afternoon on the Laver, with the gut looping and bellying-out in a manner quite unlike the straight-line method I had been taught by my father before the War. I didn't think much of his choice of fly, either – one couldn't catch anything on a Greenwell's Glory at this time of year. On the other hand, Atholl had told me the night before that Myerscough was considered rather a swell in the sporting line at his Club, and that he had put in a lot of time on the Ifjord plains. I didn't know much about Norwegian fishing in those days, and I thought that perhaps he had picked up some outlandish techniques from the old førers that, I'd been told, you can find up on the Jakobs.

Regardless of what the chaps at the Carlton thought of Myerscough, I must say that he had an unlikely appearance for an outdoorsman. He was pale and gaunt, with protuberant eyes and a drooping moustache that gave him a gloomy, hangdog look. His bony elbows and knees stuck out of his ill-fitting Lovat three-piece like chicken legs, and I saw him walk out on the Tuesday morning sporting an Ulster that a destitute crofter would have declined. His whole demeanour had a rather unwholesome air that reminded me of a travelling salesman, and he seemed as out of place on Atholl's riverbank as a clergyman in a Clydeside brawl.

But then I am always meeting men who look unlike their preferred occupation. In Aden I befriended an Egyptian bookseller who reminded me of a horse dealer I know in Clonakilty, and when I was with the Guards in Mesopotamia in 1919 I kept coming across a local official who was the very image of my housemaster at Eton. Heavens, I didn't much take to Atholl when I first laid eyes on him. We met in a rackety train on the line that runs north-east from Cape Town to Pretoria, and his bronzed skin, muscular physique and hard, jutting jaw led me to take him for a cattle ranger rather than a Scottish laird. (It was only when I realised he was wearing a Merton College tie that we struck up a conversation.) So perhaps I was judging Myerscough too harshly. But still there was something about him that I couldn't take to.

Atholl, too, seemed to have reservations about the fellow. Perhaps I should explain that Atholl – for so he is known to his intimate associates, although you will find him listed as The Eighth Baron Laver in Burke's – had become a good friend of mine out in the Cape, despite our rather hesitant rendezvous. We were both young men then, before the fields of Verdun matured us, and that was the time to be a young man in Africa. Together with Roylston and Boling-broke - you may remember him from the Lloyd's affair in '20 - we got into the mining business up near the Drakensberg hills, and all four of us made respectable piles (although Atholl was already as rich as Croesus).

We rushed home when a dust-up looked imminent, and since Atholl and I were in different regiments we didn't meet again during the war. We came across each other quite by chance outside his London residence just two months ago, and as we were both at a loose end we agreed to set up in business again together. The idea was to get into aviation, which seemed to offer plenty of scope for adventure. Atholl had some madcap scheme for flying tourists from London to Paris, and back again if they wanted.

In fact, it was in connection with this scheme that

Atholl had invited me up to the Laver estate. He had recently got to know this chap Myerscough – funnily enough, they had also met in a railway carriage – and thought that he might make a useful third in our commercial venture, since he had been in the Royal Flying Corps during the recent festivities. (Another unlikely line of work for a chap who looked like a dyspeptic milkman.) Atholl seemed unsure about the man's character, however. His telegram last week ran: "Concerned about M's credentials. Think best to have a second opinion. Come to Laver from Monday for week's sport. L." Of course I packed up my things like a shot; Laver's fishing and shooting was of wide repute, and furthermore I relished the prospect of a week spent in Atholl's company. I got the morning train from King's Cross and was at Laver Lodge by twilight. The laird himself met me at the door – a signal honour that amply compensated me for my long journey.

'Ah, Mountbank,' he said. 'Glad you could come. No, no, leave your things in the car – Williams will get them out for you.'

He was looking at me quite curiously, almost frowning, as he said this. Perhaps I seemed a little taken aback by the intensity of this examination, for he remarked, 'As a matter of fact I have been wondering how you were – I heard yesterday that you hadn't been feeling yourself.'

'I don't know who could have told you that, old boy,' I replied. 'I'm as right as rain, and raring to have a go at those trout of yours.'

'Quite,' he said. 'Well, come on in. Sandy Duncan is here, and Tiggy Broughton, and Edward Neville, whom you might remember from Eton? No? Well... Charles Nichols – Lord Apperley, that is - is here too, and his divine sister, Barbara – oh, and Myerscough,' he added in a lowered voice. 'I want to see what you make of each other this week,' he went on as we passed through a rather grand entrance hall. 'He could be a useful addition to our little endeavour, but I'm not sure – well, I'm not sure if he's quite the thing, if you take my meaning.'

'Yes, of course, Atholl,' I replied. 'I will watch how he

performs on the river. Always an infallible guide to a man's character.'

With this we reached the smoking-room. Atholl turned the door-handle and together we entered the snug little chamber, decorated with assegais, knobkerries, and many other wonderful things that Atholl had collected on his travels. I at once apprehended that Nichol's sister, Lady Barbara, was not among those present, and felt slightly disappointed – but then, I reminded myself, this was the smoking-room in a country house, so one would not normally expect to find any women there. Duncan and Broughton, whom I had met in France, were standing by the fire; they nodded a greeting to me.

Three other chaps had arranged themselves in various postures on Atholl's enormous leather easy chairs. Two of them looked ordinary men enough – Atholl introduced them to me as Neville and Nichols. But the third was this chap Myerscough, and as I have already mentioned I didn't much like the look of the fellow. His handshake was a limp and half-hearted affair, and I had to hide my shudder of distaste. Fortunately I didn't have to talk to him much that first night, as Neville, seeing my Eton tie, buttonholed me with a lot of talk about old schoolmates and masters. Oddly enough, we didn't seem to know any of the same people. In fact we couldn't work out how we hadn't come across each other, as I had only been there a couple of years before him.

I soon had the doubtful pleasure of conversing with Myerscough, however, for he made a point of sitting by me at table the next morning. Unfortunately for him, he succeeded in getting on my wrong side with his very first remark – quite an achievement, for I'm usually as amiable as an alderman.

'Aren't you hungry, old ch-ch-chap?' he stammered, looking at my empty plate with a curious smile. 'It's just that you haven't f-f-fetched yourself any b-b-b-breakfast.'

'Ah yes – of course – I'm used to being waited on at breakfast, you see,' I replied. 'I got used to it in Africa, so I have my man wait on me these days as well. Frightfully uncivilised, I know! But didn't you find it hard to get used to serving yourself again at breakfast?' – this to Atholl, who mutely shook his head, however.

I started up to get some eggs and bacon, and knocked my knee painfully on the underside of the table. It was all too ridiculous, but I found my face going red; it's a habit I have when I get angry. Worse luck yet, Lady Barbara – Nichols' sister – chose that moment to walk into the room, accompanied by Nichols, Duncan and the rest. I hadn't met her before, so her first impression of me was that of a clumsy, red-faced fool, upsetting tables and careering around the breakfast room with an empty plate. If you haven't had the honour of making her acquaintance, you won't quite understand how galling this was to me – but if you have been in Society at all, you will certainly have taken note of her startling beauty, which has made her the darling of gossip columnists and the centre of attention at even the most dazzling parties. Doubtless there are men for whom the accompaniments of such parties – a painted face, an expensive frock, and a lot of affected chatter – formed an essential part of Lady Barbara's charm and attraction.

But for me that morning, with the soft grey light streaming through the breakfast room windows, her unadorned face and plain attire made her the very picture and perfection of womanhood. Of all those on whom I had hoped to make a favourable impression that week, Lady Barbara ranked very highly indeed. Consequently, my annoyance with Myerscough for causing my discomposure in the first instance was very great.

However, resolving to put a brave face on things, I walked up to Lady Barbara and offered her my hand. She seemed slightly surprised – unaccountably so, indeed, given the careful graciousness of my manner. Perhaps the plate I still held in my left hand disconcerted her, although I have always been given to understand – that is, I have always found in experience – that the ruling classes take less stock of such trifling matters of form than the bourgeoisie. She appeared to recover her sense of courtesy after a short interval, although I noticed that when I attempted to shake her delicate hand, she deliberately held it still in a manner which was quite new to me.

At this point Atholl remarked, 'Oh, do sit down, Mountbank – we don't stand on ceremony here.' I think that perhaps he was embarrassed at Lady Barbara's infringements of the laws of polite society. At any rate, our host's interjection helped to ease the atmosphere somewhat, and the remainder of the meal passed over pleasantly enough. We mostly talked about Atholl's explorations in Tanganyika, punctuated by Duncan's interesting recollections of similar endeavours in the Far East. I kept my end of the conversation up pretty well with some reminiscences of big game shooting in the north of the Cape.

Myerscough's contribution to the discussion was somewhat less edifying (though doubtless I say it as shouldn't). He limited himself to boring the company with a tedious anecdote about the time he visited his cousin Algernon, who was a District Commissioner in the Gambia. I noticed that he had an odd way of talking, with a curious accent and a hesitant manner of speech that (as I have already observed) was practically a stammer. I also noticed that Nichols caught Duncan's eye while Myerscough was talking, and was gratified to see that they were both smiling discreetly – no doubt they also found Myerscough little to their taste.

After breakfast, Atholl mentioned that he had to see his Factor about some tiresome tenant farmers, but that he planned to return for luncheon. He suggested therefore that we amuse ourselves during the morning, before making a concerted assault on the Laver in the afternoon. Lady Barbara announced that she had some letters to write, but that she hoped us chaps would venture out of doors so that (as she charmingly put it) 'at least some of the party would be getting their exercise.' To this we all assented.

Atholl had told us the night before that there was some very pretty scrambling to be had on one of the nearby crags, and as hill-walking is a passion of mine I voiced my desire to spend the morning in making a circuit around two of the nearest summits. To my surprise and annoyance, however, Myerscough was the only member of the party who indicated willingness to join me. The others wanted to have a look at Atholl's yew and Scots pine plantations, which, on Duncan's account, were coming along very well. My dislike of Myerscough had become so strong that I would have given pounds to accompany Duncan *et al* to the plantations. I judged it would be bad form to back out now, however, so – yet again – I decided to make the best of things.

Soon thereafter Myerscough and I left the Lodge and struck out towards the nearest crags. As we walked up onto the heather, grouse (some black but mostly red) and large numbers of ptarmigan rose everywhere, and using my field-glasses I observed some very fine bucks over the lip of a distant corrie. The muted but lovely scent of a fine Highland moor came to us from every quarter, and when the sun began to peep through the clouds to illumine the *Calluna vulgaris*, the conditions for a perfect day on the hills were fulfilled.

For me, however, the mood was entirely spoilt by Myerscough's presence. I was still seething with the man over his infernal rudeness at breakfast, but to this outrage he added fresh irritations at every moment. His myopic eyes seemed incapable of identifying correctly the species of anything, flora or fauna, upon which they rested, while his clammy fingers kept fingering his weak moustache, as if the blessed thing might suddenly fall off. He was perspiring freely beneath the weight of his foul Ulster. And all the time he kept yammering a lot of nonsense in that strange voice of his, half-speaking and half-stuttering. I cannot recall now what it was he talked about, but I remember realising that his voice reminded me of Atholl. He had the same habits of speech, the same inflections; but it was a curiously distorted version of Atholl's manner of talking. In fact, it was just the sort of accent you might expect if someone with quite a different voice had deliberately set out to imitate Atholl's speech.

It was then that the secret behind Myerscough's odd behaviour – his rudeness at breakfast, his strange manner of dress, his curious accent – dawned on me. He was playing a part, acting as if he were an artist upon a stage – but his audience was a group of the biggest men the Kingdom could furnish, and his wages were not the actor's honest shilling but the chance of taking part in a business venture on equal terms with Atholl and myself. It became as clear as day that his whole personality was nothing more than a monstrous and pitiable pretence, and that he was no more a gentleman than I am a Frenchman.

Such a man should no doubt be pitied. Pity him? I should say I did! – But I also despised him, for nothing makes my blood boil more than pretension, the silly acting of the middle classes that is really the worst kind of sycophancy. I became enraged at his audacity at attempting to treat with men like us on an equal level. One thing was certain, I told myself – he should never become part of our venture into aviation.

I could walk beside such a man no longer, and I turned back with some excuse about an old war-wound that occasionally made walking difficult. He said that he would carry on and do his best on the peaks. I fear I only grunted in reply; but what more do dishonest men deserve?

I resolved to apprise Atholl of my conclusions regarding Myerscough at luncheon. Until then, I decided to pass the time smoking in my room back in the Lodge. As it happens my room could only be reached by walking past the Library on the first floor. I suppose my stockinged feet made little noise on the wooden staircase, so that those in the Library did not hear my advent. In any event, the door was slightly ajar, and I could hardly help overhearing snatches of the conversation taking place within. Lady Barbara was talking to Atholl, who had evidently finished his business with the Factor. As far as I could make out, Lady Barbara was discussing one of the guests.

'Well, I think you're probably right, Atholl darling,' she was saying. 'Although it might be as well to be certain before you say anything.'

'I quite agree,' the laird replied. 'I've a pretty good idea how things stand already, but perhaps you could have a talk with him today to make absolutely certain? You're simply wonderful at wheedling things out of people...'

I didn't wait to hear any more. It looked as Atholl and Lady Barbara were of the same mind as myself about Myerscough. Indeed it seemed that I hardly needed to talk to

Atholl about him, although of course as he had asked for my opinion it would only be courteous to provide him with it.

When the luncheon hour arrived, however, I was delighted to find myself taken up by Lady Barbara, who so monopolised my conversation that I found it quite impossible to be alone with Atholl. I imagine that she regretted her slight discourtesy earlier that morning and had decided to make amends, although goodness knows I'm not the sort of fellow to bear a grudge. In any event, she was charm itself, and I was so taken up with her that I hardly noticed my surroundings (although I did note that Myerscough failed to show).

At first we talked about Oxford. It turned out her cousin had been at my college, Pembroke, though neither his name nor those of his friends were known to me. Once this became apparent, Lady Barbara began to talk about the previous Season, dwelling in particular upon the scandalous adventures of the Countess Ogilvy and the Hungarian count, Mihály. There I was on firmer ground, for I often read about such things in the papers, and we had quite a merry chat together. Indeed we sat perhaps too long at table, for I suddenly realised that the other chaps had left the room and were doubtless preparing for the afternoon's expedition to the Laver.

Hastily I made my excuses to Barbara (for so she had insisted that I refer to her henceforth) and headed for the gun-room, where my equipment had been temporarily lodged, to make my own preparations. I had a silk cast to dress, and I wanted to look out several new flies tied by an old fellow who works at my outfitters in Pall Mall. There wasn't much time, but I managed to throw everything together and dash downstairs in order to accompany the chaps to the Laver. Broughton had cried off, complaining of a headache (although I suspected rather a desire to ingratiate himself with Barbara), but the rest of the men were gathered by the Lodge's magnificent portico with an impressive array of fishing gear. My pleasure in joining the company was lessened only by the sight of one particular moustachioed visage, from which a pair of vacant eyes assailed me with an ardent querulousness.

'M-M-Mountbank!' he exclaimed, as we set off

towards the Laver. 'I thought you were s-s-suffering from your war-wound.'

'Ah yes, well, I took a very refreshing dip in the lake this morning, followed by a long soak in the tub. That always does the trick. I feel as right as rain now.'

'I'm d-d-delighted to hear it, old m-m-man,' he said.

'Did you have a good time on the peaks?' I asked.

'Yes, indeed,' he answered. 'I could hardly t-t-tear myself away from them. I'm sure you noticed that I was absent at luncheon.'

'Oh, really?' I said. 'I don't think I did, as a matter of fact – but then I was very taken up in conversation with Barbara.'

'Yes, B-B-Barbara is such d-d-delightful company,' he replied, with a pleasant smile, but with a slight emphasis on her name that made me suspect that he was mocking me. I felt my temper rising once again, and in order to avoid making a scene of any kind, I forged ahead to the front of the party, where Atholl was walking alongside Nichols. We fell into step, and I joined in a most interesting conversation concerning a new arrangement of the butts on Atholl's grouse moor. Thus engaged we arrived at the Laver, which flashed and sparkled in the sunlight as it flew over its rocky riverbed. Among the whorls and sun-flecked ripples darted dark fingerlings, vibrant brown trout of the very finest stamp. Here was sport fit for a king, and here were the fellows to enjoy it and appreciate it as few others could.

On the way to my spot I stopped for a few minutes to watch Myerscough at work. I believe I have already mentioned the unappealing aesthetic of his technique, which seemed all of a piece with his strange, affected manner of speech and unorthodox patterns of behaviour. As I predicted, his Greenwell's Glory failed to produce the desired result, and when I left him he had failed to bank a single fish. I disingenuously wished him good luck, lit a cigarette plucked from my monogrammed case, and proceeded further downstream to take up my station.

As the afternoon progressed I had my share of luck with

the trout, and also landed a jaded but still well-conditioned out-of-season grayling. At four o'clock we had arranged to meet at Atholl's station and pop open a few bottles of Bollinger, which was simply divine when taken with Atholl's hothouse strawberries. I was surprised to note that Myerscough was not among those present, and remarked upon his absence to the company at large.

'I say, where's Myerscough? Don't tell me he's given up!'

'He's gone back to the Lodge,' replied Atholl. 'He said that an old war-wound was playing up.' As he said this, I noticed that he caught Nichols' eye, and that they exchanged a conspiratorial smile. For a frightful second I wondered if they were making a joke out of me, but then I realised that Atholl must have taken Nichols into his confidence about Myerscough. I must confess I was a little taken aback, but perhaps Atholl was considering taking Nichols into our venture rather than Myerscough. Of course I would have preferred that Atholl had let me know beforehand, but then I had hardly had a moment alone with him since my arrival. And if we must have a third, Nichols would be infinitely preferable to Myerscough. In addition to Nichols himself being rather a noble fellow, I relished the prospect of the further intimacy with Barbara that would undoubtedly ensue from his involvement in our venture.

After our little champagne party, we fished on for an hour or so, lighting endless cigarettes in a largely fruitless attempt to repel the innumerable midges. Their persistence was so wearing that I felt quite relieved when the chaps began to think about packing up their rods and calling it a day. We slowly gathered up our things and wondered back to the Lodge in that supreme mood of content that always follows a day of excellent sport spent in good company.

When we came within sight of Atholl's stately residence, I caught sight of a familiar form with a noticeable sinking of my spirits. Myerscough was hanging round the front lawn, clearly waiting upon our return. As soon as he saw us, he broke into an awkward half-trot that roused my hackles with its scarcely-concealed enthusiasm.

'Oh God, look at him,' I murmured to myself, but loud enough for those around me to hear.

'Yes, he's quite a piece of work, alright,' replied Broughton, sotto voce. There was no time for any further conversation, however, for he was upon us.

'Atholl, old ch-ch-chap,' he stammered, 'I have discovered something of g-g-great interest to you in the Lodge. I think it is t-t-time for the party to meet in the Library.'

'Certainly,' replied Atholl decisively. He then turned to look at me. 'You might find this of particular interest, Mountbank. I hope you chaps will also come along,' he added, addressing Duncan, Nichols and Neville. 'It won't take long, and I think you'll find it a rewarding experience.'

The chaps all smiled with anticipation, but I felt rather left out of things. Were they talking about some kind of pre-prandial entertainment, traditional to Laver Lodge? That would be all very well, but I couldn't understand why Atholl had not seen fit to apprise me of the event beforehand. Still, at least he had singled me out as likely to find whatever it was of particular interest, a mark of distinction that I valued greatly. Dwelling on these matters, I followed Myerscough and the rest up the stairs to Atholl's palatial library. Barbara was already there, seated in a comfortable chair by the bay-window, with Broughton standing by her side. Myerscough walked across to the large table in the centre of the room, and turned to face us.

'Atholl, old m-m-man, a week ago you asked me to look into certain affairs on your behalf. Specifically, you were c-c-oncerned about a man with whom you were thinking of g-g-oing into business, and about whom you had some concerns as to his standing as a g-g-entleman.'

'Wait a minute,' I interjected. 'Are you saying that you are a private detective?'

'Private detective? I should say not!' snorted Atholl. 'This, my dear Mountbank, is the Twelfth Earl of Lindon.'

Then transpired the most remarkable transformation I have ever had the privilege of witnessing. Myerscough – or Lindon, I should say – plucked off his moustache, which

I now saw to be an imitation. His figure straightened, and seemed to somehow fill out and become more substantial: having previously appeared thin and bony, he now presented a fine, muscular figure of a man. His suit, which I had thought ill-tailored, now fitted him like a glove, and could only have come from Savile Row. But most remarkable of all was his face, which seemed to dissolve before our gaze before knitting itself into the strong, handsome physiognomy known in every corner of the land.

I had been right to call him an actor; but his acting was of quite a different kind from that with which I had associated him. Here was a master of disguise, a man whose fluidity of appearance was as good as a diplomatic carte blanche, and I knew instinctively that he could pass for a Mexican peasant or a Prussian nobleman with equal ease. But I was still unclear as to his purpose. Whom could he possibly be investigating? Had Atholl indeed been contemplating another, different commercial venture, perhaps with Broughton or Duncan? For my part I had always thought of them as excellent fellows. I put the question to Lindon.

'May I congratulate you on your astounding abilities, old man! But who on earth are you investigating? We are all gentlemen here.'

Lindon smiled, a dagger glinting in the sunlight. 'Don't you recognise these, old man?' he asked me. His words, uttered in a clear and pleasant baritone that, I now realised, must be his natural speaking voice, were surprisingly derisive, and I think that that was the moment when I first realised I was in trouble. When I saw the three volumes that he had picked up from the table, my heart missed a beat. For in one hand he held my copy of *Burke's Peerage, Baronetage & Knightage*, while in his other hand he held Debrett's *Correct Form* and my *Guide to British Heraldry*, with its supplement on College and Regimental Ties and Shields. I knew in that instant that Lindon had been in my room during luncheon, had discovered the false bottom in my case, and had laid bare all my schemes. I was undone.

As I looked around the room, I felt Atholl, Duncan and the others close ranks, excluding me forever from their company. Lindon's face was merciless, and behind him I saw Lady Barbara's eyes glittering with cold amusement.

'We have all been watching you, old chap,' Lindon continued, ruthlessly. 'Your strange behaviour at table and elsewhere has betrayed your unfamiliarity with gentlemanly ways. Your pretence of having attended Eton and Pembroke was laughable. Your casting technique revealed you as a bounder of the worst kind. And your manner of speech, with its hideous imitation of our own, has turned all our stomachs.'

'I suspected it all along,' said Atholl. 'But one notices these things less when travelling overseas, where one's own standards become of necessity so relaxed. But here, on my own territory, I would never willingly entertain such as you. I saw you hanging around my London residence for days and days before I chose to meet you and, having guessed your purpose – to pay off your debts by hanging on my coat-tails – I determined to be your undoing. I hope now that you will leave this house. I know that none of us wishes to set eyes on you again.'

'But Atholl,' I stammered. 'Don't you remember our times in Africa? When I saved you from the lion's charge? When I nursed you after your bout of malaria?'

'That was in the wild; this is not,' he replied. 'We do things differently here, old man, and your face doesn't fit. I think it best if you leave now. Your things are packed, and a car awaits you. I advise the evening train to Glasgow, an hotel there, and thence a train to the South tomorrow morning.'

I looked around the room in silent appeal to my erstwhile friends and companions in war and sport; but I could see it was hopeless. Their faces were set against me. I turned to leave.

I left the library, my eyes smarting and my cheeks aflame; but I held my head high, my jaw firm, and my shoulders upright, as I had learned to do when striding across the African veldt. I left them like a gentleman; I left them as an Englishman. What did it matter if I left my heart behind?

To the Point

MY NAME, unfortunately, is Oliver Thorogood-fforbes-Wynstanley, and when I am not riding I am a salaried partner at a smallish solicitors' firm in Islington. My triple-barrelled name is less of a difficulty than it might have been in other professions; indeed, clients in search of legal expertise seem to find it reassuring, as if each moniker were some kind of qualification, rather than the mere historical accumulation of stubborn family pride and (decidedly minor) dynastic marriages.

My colleagues at the firm were, inevitably, less impressed – most of them had two surnames apiece themselves, and of course one can hardly move in the legal profession without encountering firms practically groaning under the weight of their chosen appellation. (Tyacke, Falkingham, Pitt, Jolly and Grimble is my personal favourite in terms of ridiculous length, but for quaintness few can beat the Cambridge house of Pleasance, Hook, and Nix.) There was still a bit of ribbing about my name, however, and the trainees had recently printed out a photo of a triple-barrelled shotgun and taped it on my office door. I took it in good part, and didn't tell them that my grandfather had commissioned that very gun as an expensive joke.

'A barrel for each name,' he used to say to me whenever he got it out of the cabinet; and as I got older he began to add: 'And perhaps you'll add another name when you get married, one of these days. I'd wait until you're a full partner, though, if I were you – four-barrelled guns don't come cheap!' He had passed on some years ago, still waiting in vain for me to add another name (and another barrel). Probably I was a source of some regret to him; I was told once by my father that the old man had longed for great-grandchildren, to make up for the disappointment of his children and grandchildren.

Nevertheless, and in spite of familial urging, my life increasingly took on the patterns and habits of confirmed bachelorhood, with long hours at the office filling the gaps between hunting and point-to-pointing in the winter, and cricket and coarse-fishing in the summer. In the short intervals between work and sport I ate and slept in Knightsbridge, where I shared an expansive flat with my friend Seb Ryland, a surgical registrar at one of the London hospitals. We had been at University College London together, though we were of course in different departments and might never have met if we hadn't both turned up to a fancy dress party in full hunting regalia. We nodded and touched our whips to our hats, and after doing the rounds and paying our respects to the host by getting on the outside of a decent amount of cheap plonk, we inevitably gravitated to each other.

There was none of the usual (and rather dull) university conversation – what do you study, where are you living, where did you go to school, &c. Seb simply asked me where I hunted; I told him. Then he lit a cigarette and said that he hunted with the Bicester when in town, and the Quorn when at home. This was just after they introduced the law against smoking indoors, or in public places, or whatever it is, and soon an earnest young man with floppy hair ran up to us and told Seb that he couldn't smoke here – it was banned, and, besides, it would make the sofa smell. In response, Seb puffed out a great cloud of smoke, looked at the chap with half-lowered eyelids, and drawled: 'I don't much care for bans.'

I loved him for that, of course, and it wasn't long before we became inseparable. In our third year he asked me to share his flat in Knightsbridge – his family owned the building, so it would be rent-free. Naturally I agreed like a shot, and once I had moved my things out of my dingy student room we began sharing phone bills and dinner parties. We went on holiday together countless times, including one memorable visit to Amsterdam – well, I say memorable, but in fact I can only remember the outward journey – and a polo tournament at Shandur, in Pakistan. We even kept our hunters at the same livery yard near Egham, and as we were both of a competitive nature we tended to compete in the same races at point-to-points.

Looking back, it would have been amusing to film our behaviour on the day of a point-to-point. We would rise early with an excess of good spirits brought on by the excitement of the day ahead, but by the time we got into Seb's Merc to drive to the yard we would have calmed down somewhat owing to the realisation that we would soon be racing against each other; and by the time we had got our hunters into our respective horseboxes our conversation would have dwindled to monosyllabic grunts. We would nod when we left the yard, and would barely utter another word to each other until the day was over. Then we would return to Knightsbridge and go out to a local bar, celebrating the day's success or submerging its disasters in a river of champagne cocktails. This behavioural arc would probably have appeared very strange to an observer, but it seemed perfectly natural to us.

As it happened, most racing days found me privately rejoicing in my triumphs while outwardly consoling Seb about yet another catastrophe. He was, and had always been, inordinately successful in every area of his life save one – racing. He had swept through school and university with effortless ease, seeming to collect beautiful people and glittering prizes left, right, and centre, and all this with an air of assured nonchalance, as if he could drop it all and walk away.

I had my moments (and had had my own share of prizes), but I couldn't quite boast of Seb's social skill; nor had I come top of my year at UCL three years in a row. I had never been invited to a house party in Monaco by Rachel Weisz, and the President of the Law Society did not solicit my opinions on challenges facing young practitioners (as the head of the

Royal College of Surgeons appeared to do with Seb).

On the credit side, however, I can ride. I have a good seat and good hands, an intuitive sense for positioning and jumping, and most of all I have Qualia, my seven-year-old dark bay gelding, of sixteen hands. There's a rather complicated story about why I called him that name, and an even more complicated story about how I found him in the first place – but to keep things short, I gave him his name because qualia describe the way things feel, like landing a salmon or looking at a sunset; they're completely subjective and as such we can't be in error about them. (At least, so I was told by a friend who was studying philosophy at the time.) And indeed my Qualia is seldom, if ever, in error – I never met his like for instinct when jumping, or deftness when landing.

I found him (never mind how) in a little Irish yard near a house where I was staying in County Leitrim, his mane and tail sorely in need of untangling and his coat in need of brushing. He looked terrible, in fact – but he had good legs and a stocky, butty kind of look underneath the dirt, and I saw straightaway he had potential in spades. I spat on my hand and sealed the deal there and then, and have never regretted it since – John Warde of Squerries could scarcely have gloated more over Blue Ruin than I have over Qualia. I occasionally make mistakes when racing, as we all do, but Qualia somehow knows when I've misjudged a jump or set the wrong pace, and does all he can to set me right. Together with my own reasonable level of skill, this priceless attribute has ensured a pretty decent level of success, and I'm considered among the best point-to-pointers in the region (and certainly in my Hunt).

Poor Seb lacked a Qualia of his own, however, and was always changing horses in a vain attempt to find a hunter with whom he could establish some kind of connection. One year he even went to Ballinasloe Fair in Ireland, seeking, I think, to replicate my stroke of luck and pick up a hidden gem. He came back in triumph with a fine-looking chestnut mare, but I was worried about the length of her pasterns. I didn't say anything to Seb, but sure enough the chestnut developed tendonitis, and was sold on as a hack. Since that debâcle, I believe he went through at least eight further hunters - a chaotic assortment of mares, geldings, and entires of all shapes and sizes, high-withered and low-withered, in-bred and out.

But whatever horse he was mounted on, success consistently eluded him. He would be caught napping at the starter's post, or his horse would bolt away from him outside the paddock; perhaps he would fall at the first (or the last); or maybe his mount would start at some imagined threat, and throw him off.

On one memorable occasion, Seb failed to check that his girths were tight, with the result that he gradually but inexorably slid round his horse, finally disappearing underneath just before the first jump. But whatever the precise reason on any given day, the simple fact was that it was unusual for Seb to get round a course in one piece. Indeed, I had lost count of the number of times I had seen him come off in one way or another (assuming he actually got to the starter's post), and had also lost count of the subsequent trips I made to the A&E departments of local hospitals. He was a popular rider with the crowds — his falls were usually fairly spectacular affairs — but he had also built up an impressive reputation with the clinicians at several regional hospitals, and I understood that one of the orthopaedic surgeons had seen Seb so frequently that he published a paper in *The Lancet* examining the risks of point-to-pointing, using Seb as a case-study.

Despite the rather public nature of these humiliations, I must say Seb took his riding failures in excellent humour. 'It's good for me to be bad at something,' he would say, often adding that it must be good for me *not* to be bad at something, for a change. (I never rose to this.) I also admired the fact that the severity and frequency of his falls seemed to affect neither his pacing and positioning (which were those of a successful and ambitious thruster rather than a dangerously unlucky amateur with a penchant for calamitous mishaps) nor his enthusiasm for point-to-pointing generally, which of late had so eclipsed his original interest in hunting that he was perpetually at risk of failing to fulfil his required number of days. Whenever I reminded him that he would be unable to enter point-to-points if he did not also hunt, he would say, 'Well, the thrill of the chase has gone now, hasn't it? Not much fun hunting a trail. No, give me point-to-pointing any day of the week – that hasn't changed, at least.'

He was right about that, of course: very little had fundamentally changed in point-to-pointing for a hundred years or more, despite the advent of sponsorship and dedicated facilities; and as I thundered up the hill amidst a packed field in the Men's Open at a windswept Hackthorn, Cambs, I hoped fervently that it never would. The furious jostling of men and horses moving as one, intent only on winning; the distant sounds of spectators urging on their particular favourites, mingling with the echoes of the commentator's voice and the barking of the hounds; the thunder of hooves on firm ground; and above all the wind rushing against one's face - what could be better? At times like this, when I was struck by the vitality of racing and the sheer joy of being mounted on a hunter like Qualia, there was a definite risk of losing my concentration and suffering the same fate as Seb – so I pulled myself together and started to think about my position. I had started off on the inside, as I always try to do, and perhaps two-thirds down the field; Qualia liked to save his energy for the latter half of the race, and could pull very strongly indeed towards the finish, so I usually tried to avoid tiring him out too much in the early stages.

Usually Seb took the opposite approach, as I mentioned, and was likely to be well towards the head of the field by the second or third jump (assuming he got over them). Today, however, I was surprised to see that so far he was riding a steady race, and was in fact hardly any distance ahead of me (although he was on the outside). On the drive to Egham, I had hinted that perhaps he would do better to conserve his mount's energy and be a little more strategic; it amused me that Seb might have finally decided to take my advice, and I remember smiling to myself as I jumped the fourth. I think Qualia sensed I wasn't completely focused, and shook his head in annoyance; duly rebuked, I buckled down and set my sights on moving up to half-way by the sixth.

This I achieved, but with some shortness of breath – unusual for me, as I keep myself in pretty good condition. As I started up the hill again I also became aware that my eyes were streaming despite my goggles; but it wasn't until I felt the itchiness on my cheeks and neck, and began to feel as if I needed to sneeze, that I realised I was having an allergic reaction, and a bad one at that. My various allergies had been rather a nuisance when I was at school, and several times I had been rushed to hospital with an alarmingly puffed-up face and a chest so congested that I could barely speak to the doctor. Eventually the medics diagnosed severe allergies to cats and latex surgical gloves; thus was I removed from the ranks of scientists and cat owners. Since then I had avoided said items like the plague, and as I didn't generally suffer from hayfever (and certainly not on a cold February day in Cambridgeshire), I couldn't understand what was going on. In any case, as I was doing rather well in the race, I decided – unwisely, as it transpired - to carry on regardless.

I think it was near the top of the hill, where the wind blew most strongly, that things started to get much, much worse. My vision began to narrow and my breathing became more constrained; I remember that as we approached the top fence I was drawing in great heaving gasps just to keep going. I made a complete hash of it, as you might expect in the circumstances, and I remember seeing Seb's red and yellow quartered jersey flying past as we made a clumsy landing. (Despite my predicament I was pleased that he was still on board Pavane, his most recent equine acquisition, and gave him a feeble cheer.) As we set off down the hill for the last time I hung on with all my strength, but I was fighting a losing battle. I was told later that I fainted and pitched off before we had gone a hundred yards.

—◦—

A voice punctured the darkness.

'What's his BP?' it said.

'82 over 58, but rising,' said another voice. 'No tachycardia, before you ask.'

'What's he on - epinephrine?' said the first voice.
'Yup. Listen, you got the note about gloves? His records say he's latex hypersensitive.'
'Yes – look, unpowdered gloves, as ordered.'
'Good job he's a jockey and not a doctor.'
'I'm not a jockey,' I croaked. 'I'm a solicitor.'
'Oh, you're awake,' said the first voice. 'Can you open your eyes?'

I tried, and just about managed to create a chink of light before the very same light sent my already splitting headache into neurological overdrive. I yelped in rather an unmanly fashion, and put my hand over my eyes.

'Never mind,' said the first voice, as I descended into a sea of pain. 'Just take it easy for now. You've had a fairly severe allergic reaction, and as you were in the middle of a race at the time and subsequently fell off your horse' – she made it sound as if only an idiot would have done this – 'you also sustained some substantial bruising. How you managed to avoid breaking anything is beyond me.'

'Relaxed muscles help,' I groaned, with my hand still covering my face.

'Yes, well,' said the second voice – a man's voice. 'You were very lucky, all the same. How on earth did you get near latex in the middle of a race?'

'Search me,' I said. 'I'm allergic to cats as well, by the way.'

'You sure you aren't allergic to horses?' said the first voice.

'Um, pretty sure,' I said. 'I've been riding for twenty years.'

'Allergies can change, you know,' said the male voice. 'You may have developed an allergy to horses.'

'In the course of a week?' I asked; and then, sensing that further explanation was required, added: 'I rode at a point-to-point last week with no problems. I won two races, as a matter of fact.'

'Well, you'll have to be tested anyway,' said the first voice. 'Your GP can refer you to an allergy clinic – I strongly recommend you get that done before you go near a horse again. Now you'll have to excuse us, I'm afraid, Mr Thorogood - '

'Thorogood-fforbes-Wynstanley,' I said, automatically.

'Yes, that,' said the first voice, making me smile (and then wince with the pain of my headache). 'We'll be back to check on you later on today. I'm Miss Skeaping, by the way – I'm a consultant; and this is Dr Mildmay, a registrar here.'

'How long will I be in for?' I asked. I had a long list of important clients to meet the following day, and I knew it would be carnage if I couldn't make it.

'Until tomorrow, for observation – and you'll be off work for a week,' they said as they left, and I uttered a heartfelt sigh. I would have to get a nurse to call the office tomorrow morning and let them know. 'Damn, damn, damn,' I said to myself.

'Is it as bad as all that?' said another voice, brightly. This time I didn't attempt to open my eyes; and in any case I knew to whom the voice belonged.

'Seb!' I said. 'Good of you to come.'

'Well, it's only polite,' he said. 'God knows you've come to see me often enough, although I must say, Ollie, I generally look a damn sight better in hospital than you do right now. I mean, yes, I have a sling or two, and maybe a plaster cast if things have gone particularly badly, but my God! You look like you've run into a bee-hive and then gone swimming in a patch of nettles.'

'What a coincidence – that's just how I feel. Except that I also have an incredibly bad headache and aching ribs, and other maladies too numerous to mention.'

'What on earth happened – do the medics know?'

'Yes and no,' I said. 'It's my latex reaction again, just like at biology in school – remember? But what they don't know, and nor do I, is how the hell I got anywhere near latex in the middle of a point-to-point!'

'It's a mystery, is what it is,' said Seb. 'Not like you not to finish a race in the top three!'

Suddenly I remembered my precious horse. 'Qualia!' I

croaked. 'What happened to Qualia – is he OK?'

'Relax, relax,' said Seb. 'I've taken care of it. He was fine, and I boxed him up and drove him back to Egham myself; I got a friend to drive Pavane back.'

'Thanks, Seb,' I said, and meant it. 'That's a relief, at any rate.'

It occurred to me then that I should probably ask Seb how he got on in the race – a question that usually amounted to asking how near he got to the finish, rather than where he was placed. But it had to be asked, all the same.

'So, what's the bad news?' I asked. 'Did you walk in here on your own two feet, or did I hear the dulcet tones of crutches?'

'Actually, I managed to stay on this time,' he said, after a pause. 'In fact, I did rather well.'

'You did what?' I cried, wincing as a jet of pain shot through my head. 'You did what?' I whispered.

'I stayed on – and not only that, I was third. Or rather Pavane was third; I just about stuck on, and earned the accolade. But it was all down to Pavane. I think I've finally found my Qualia!'

'Third…' I lapsed into an unbelieving silence. The only time Seb had ever come third in a race was in 2003, and that was in a running race rather than a point-to-point; and even then we had only pretended he came third. It was the night England won the Rugby World Cup, and to celebrate we had raced Seb's classmates Carl Fernandes and Aubrey Smith down Wimpole Mews, near Marlborough High Street. Strictly speaking Seb didn't finish, as he fell at the last fence (i.e. the green wheelie bins). He looked so pathetic lying there unconscious that we had pity on him and told him the next day that he had just pipped Aubrey to the post before running into the wall.

'I'd say that I'm wounded by your incredulity,' said Seb, 'but given my form…' He began to laugh, and added: 'Anyway, I'm organising a party to celebrate – at the flat, on Friday night. God knows I've waited long enough! Hope you'll be back to normal by then? Don't want you scaring off the ladies! You do look quite a sight, you know.'

'Oh, well, I'm terribly sorry, Seb,' I said. 'I promise I'll stay shut into my rooms if I don't look better by then.'

'No, that's no good,' he said. 'We're going to use your bed for the coats! Hang on – back in a sec.'

His mobile was ringing, and of course he answered it – he never paid much attention to rules. 'Don Carleone! Yep – yep. No, I'm just at the hospital. I know! Look – I'm just coming now. See you at the pub. Let me just say cheerio to Ollie and I'll tell you all about it.'

'Cheerio, Ollie,' he said. 'You're in overnight, did they tell you? I'll pick you up tomorrow, if you like – they'll let you go about lunchtime, I should think. Give me a bell and I'll be here. Got to dash – Carl wants to hear all about the race! Ciao for now!'

And as he left I heard him walking down the corridor, still talking away on his phone: 'I know! He looks awful, I've taken a photo of course – it'll be up on Facebook before the night's out...'

—◦—

The photo duly appeared online - several photos, in fact, that publicised to a wide circle of friends the unforgettable sight of my face, not much of an oil painting at the best of times, but now red, swollen, and enlarged to a truly monumental degree. I strongly suspect that a desire to see the hideous sight in person was a key factor in the 100% attendance rate for Seb's celebratory party, which kicked off at a surprisingly early hour on the Friday after the race. I think it was around four in the afternoon (I had taken the week off work, as the doctor ordered) when the doorbell rang to announce the arrival of the first guest.

'Sinéad!' I said as I opened the door. 'You're - ' glancing at my watch – 'ridiculously early.'

'Just let me look at you,' she said, stepping forward and peering at my (by now almost completely recovered) face. 'Oh. You're alright. What a shame, after Seb's rabble-rousing! Come and see Ollie's pumpkin head, he said, and help me celebrate my win.'

'Win? What win?' I asked, as I poured us a glass of wine apiece. (Might as well start as you mean to go on.)

'Well, that's what he said, but I agree - coming third is hardly a win, is it? And now that your head is back to its normal potato-like shape, I'm almost sorry I made the effort. I had to postpone some rather interesting work I'm doing.'

'Tracking down the Higgs boson, I suppose?' I asked. 'Or creating a black hole to swallow us all up?' (Sinéad, I should explain, is a particle physicist at the CERN accelerator in Geneva.)

'Ideally both,' she replied. 'Though judging by how Seb was going on, it'd be an impressive black hole that could have swallowed you up a couple of days ago. I'd hoped to get a photo to put up in the lab - what a disappointment you are!'

—— ⚬ ——

Sinéad's air of aggrieved discontent set the tone for the majority of those who followed in her footsteps. Aubrey and Carl, Seb's surgical colleagues, subjected me to a more searching examination than most, as did my old friend James McAulay, a paramedic from St George's who had been at Westminster School with me; but their manifest dissatisfaction at my recovery was shared by my fellow solicitors Mike, Adam and Nick (whose unusually single-barrelled surnames would nevertheless have made a respectable firm: Govind, Scragg, and Ferro). Together with a later batch of lawyers, with names too lengthy to repeat here, these chaps had clearly turned up in the hope of capturing more photos to 'share' at the office.

My botanist friend Catherine and her partner Matty (also a plant-lover) were the last to arrive – a last-minute emergency with some plant or tree or something had delayed them – but they seemed no less keen to postpone dinner by discussing my downfall and its possible causes. (Catherine, herself a dedicated showjumper, seemed particularly amused at the possibility that I might be allergic to horses.) Indeed, my sadly deflated face became the focus of so much debate on the part of our guests that I wondered if Seb might become a little jealous – he was notoriously keen on being the centre of attention, and he had after all organised the party as a celebration of his third place at Hackthorn.

Seb was a tall, good-looking fellow, and had even been dubbed 'The Angel' by the girls on the third floor of my student digs at UCL (I'm not quite sure what name they came up with for me); but at times like this, when he sensed that people found others of more interest than himself, a slightly petulant look spread itself over his features and he became rather acid in his remarks. It wasn't my favourite of his characteristics, but in the interests of social harmony I decided to direct some attention towards Seb's 'victory'.

'Look, you're embarrassing me,' I said. 'Let's have something to eat, and then Seb can tell us about what happened in the race on Saturday. I'd tell you myself, but I was out cold.'

'Not exactly an unusual state of affairs with you,' said Adam. 'Though I'll admit it's more often due to a few too many beers than to bad horsemanship.'

'It wasn't bad horsemanship!' I said, before I realised he was pulling my leg. 'Well, laugh all you like' – this to the company at large – 'but I'll have my revenge, in this life or the next.'

'I'll admit I haven't seen Gladiator for a few years,' said Sinéad, 'but I don't seem to remember Russell Crowe looking quite as haggard as you do – and surely you aren't casting Seb in the role of Commodus?'

'Of course not,' put in Nick. 'Commodus was a cheat, but Seb got his third fair and square.'

'Just like Ollie's degree result at UCL, then,' said Mike; and of course everyone laughed again.

'Quite right, Mike,' said Seb. 'Come on - let's have some supper, and I'll tell you all about my brilliant success. I know Ollie's ridden a lot of winners, but he never says a word about them afterwards. I'll be better value for money, I assure you. To dine!' And with that he sashayed his way through the flat towards the dining-room at the back of the building, pausing only to light a cigarette from a candle and to pour himself another measure of whisky.

Seb had spared no expense, hiring in a private catering firm complete with butler, sommelier, and waitress, and as a result supper was fairly spectacular – caviar and champagne, of course, and the standard array of courses, but topped this time with an exquisite confection of foie de gras and butterflied chicken served as a sweetmeat, and dominated physically by a truly stupendous ice-sculpture of a horse jumping a fence, that Seb had commissioned from an ice studio in Primrose Hill. (Judging by the jockey's face, I strongly suspect that Seb had asked the sculptor to model it on his own.)

In such a context, conversation could hardly fail to focus on point-to-pointing and on the recent Hackthorn race in particular, and it wasn't long before Seb held the floor with a richly detailed and, I have no doubt, highly-coloured version of what transpired in the race after my departure from the world of consciousness.

I'm certain he exaggerated the length of time I was dragged along the ground by Qualia – apart from anything else, Qualia, as I have already mentioned, is a wonderfully intelligent animal – and I very much doubt that Seb was capable of outwitting Martin Denison by the rails, as he claimed; probably Martin, a fine rider and a great racing strategist to boot, had been so astonished by Seb still being in his saddle half-way through the race that he had let him through in sheer amazement, rather than any particular brilliance on Seb's part. But Seb was an old friend; and after all, who was I to begrudge him his joy? God knows I'd ridden enough winners in my time - mostly thanks to Qualia, of course – but I had found the thrill of victory to be an enduring delight, undimmed by repetition.

In a nod to the smokers present in the party, dessert (a fluffy prosecco sorbet) was served in buffet fashion, allowing us to stand or sit on the balconies, or stay in the dining room, as desired. I had some Montecristos that I wanted to finish, so I took these out with my sorbet and a fresh bottle of champers, and offered the box around to my fellow smokers James, Adam, and Aubrey. (Seb normally jumped at the offer of a cigar, but was busy chatting up the waitress – who, it emerged, was moonlighting in order to pay her tuition fees at RADA; and Seb loved actresses.)

'Looks like he's found someone to admire him for the evening,' said James.

'Sure does,' said Adam. 'I'd bet a large sum he's telling her all about the race – probably with even more exaggerations than last time.'

'Agreed,' I said. 'Or maybe one of his surgical stories – they seem just as far-fetched to me.'

'No, you're wrong there,' said Aubrey, drawing on his cigar. 'He really is a miracle-worker in the OT. He's done things that nobody can do – nobody except him, that is. He'll be a Sir one of these days, or a Lord...'

'Isn't he already something like that? The Honourable, or something?' said James.

'Well, no,' said Aubrey. 'But his father's a baronet – hence all this,' waving his cigar at the flat.

'None of that matters these days, anyway,' said Adam. 'Sir, Lord, Mr, Dr – it's all the same.'

'That may be true metaphysically,' said Aubrey. 'But it's not at all true in reality. Look at the NHS – founded as the embodiment of the welfare state, we're all equal, etc, etc. But it's probably one of the most hierarchical organisations on the planet. Think of all the different types of doctor – and then there's all the different kinds of nurses, and all the different kinds of managers, and so on, ad infinitum. Having a 'Sir' or 'Dame' in front of your name means a lot, believe me. Maybe it shouldn't, but it does.'

'Still, third place or no third place, Seb won't earn any knighthoods from his riding,' I said.

'That's for sure,' began James; but then he noticed that Seb had come out onto the balcony, and (I later realised) had been standing behind me when I made my remark. Seb's face clouded over, and he said, 'Thanks, Ollie,' before turning on his heel and marching off to his rooms (and slamming the door when he reached them).

'Trouble in paradise?' asked Catherine, who had just come out on the balcony with Sinéad.

'Honestly, you're like an old married couple,' said Sinéad. 'Well, you'd better get after him, and make it up!'

This was excellent advice, and I wasted no time in following it. He wouldn't let me in at first, but after a while I gained entrance and persuaded him that I had only been joking, and that I thought he was an excellent point-to-pointer, and a great thruster in the field (which was true, if your definition of a thruster revolved around enthusiasm rather than staying in the saddle). It struck me then, as it often had before, how odd it was that this up-and-coming surgical genius should care so much about his riding and, especially, his racing, and also that he should care so much what I thought of him. I suppose I put it down to immaturity – to a general childishness that expressed itself as much in caviar and ice-sculptures as in his competitiveness in racing (and surgery, for that matter). At times like this, pleading with a grown man not to be offended about a passing joke, I almost wondered why I bothered maintaining the friendship – but then I had been raised to consider loyalty as the defining virtue of friendship.

Anyway, we came to an amicable arrangement after a while, and rejoined the party. It was already late by then, and after an hour or so our guests began to leave in ones and twos, citing long weeks and Saturday morning activities by way of excusing themselves. After the last couple left, Seb and I bade each other good night and retired to our respective sets. As I closed the door to my rooms, I saw the butler and the waitress packing up the remains of the supper. (Seb had already got the waitress's phone number, of course.) The ice-sculpture had begun to melt, with the horse and rider metamorphosing into a shapeless mass; and I wondered at the energy and care that went into crafting such an ephemeral art-form. But then, I reflected, wasn't winning a race rather like that? I mean, who remembers the winner of the Men's Open at Hackthorn last year, and the year before? But then I realised that I had won both of those races, and knew that I would always remember them, even if nobody else did. The thrill of victory is evergreen.

Three days after the dinner party I got the results from the allergy clinic – confirmed positives for allergies to latex and cats, the letter said, but nothing else had showed up. I definitely wasn't allergic to horses. Seb didn't show much interest in the news.

'Well, of course you're not,' he said. 'How could you ride as much as you do, and not have noticed it before now, if you were? I reckon you just got a hint of something in the breeze – hay, for example.'

'Or a cat in a hot-air balloon made of latex?' I suggested.

'Or, as you say, an airborne cat,' he replied. 'You should write to the Master of the South Cambridgeshire and suggest they impose a no-fly zone over Hackthorn.'

'It's not Hackthorn I'm worried about,' I said. 'It's Waterfield. It's only a few days before the point-to-point there, and I don't much fancy waking up in the local hospital again.'

I hesitated before giving voice to a thought that had recently crossed my mind with disquieting frequency. 'You don't suppose – well, you don't suppose it could be something about Qualia himself, that makes me react badly?'

'What – you mean, could you be allergic to Qualia, and no other horse? Don't see how that's possible; you've been riding him for years.'

'But how else can I explain it?' I replied. 'You don't just get a reaction like that from something floating around on the wind – you're a doctor; you know that it just doesn't happen like that.'

'No, I know,' he said. 'Well, look, there's an easy way to find out whether it's Qualia or not – just go down and ride out for a few hours, and see what happens. Tell you what, I'll come with you – how about Wednesday morning? I presume you're still off work for a few more days to come?'

'Yes, until Thursday. I was going to go back sooner, but the boss insisted I recover properly. He was so solicitous (if you'll pardon the pun)' – Seb groaned – 'that I almost wondered if you'd emailed him the photo from the hospital.'

'Would I do such a thing?' said Seb, innocent-eyed.

'Hmmm...' I said. 'Anyway, I've been planning to go

down and see Qualia soon, to make sure he's OK after my fall, and not spooked, or anything.'

'He seemed fine when I took him back after Hackthorn,' said Seb.

'Thanks again for doing that. I wouldn't have trusted him to anyone else, especially after a fall like that.'

'No problem at all,' said Seb. 'I'm sure he'll be fine, and glad to see you back on your own two feet. Right – I'll ring the yard and tell them we'll be down on Wednesday am. Better get onto the hospital too – I don't want any minor inconveniences, such as operations, getting in the way of our leisure activities.'

⎯ ◦ ⎯

And so Wednesday morning saw us wending our way once more to the livery yard, where the head groom met us with her usual blend of unwilling courtesy and bluff indifference.

'Morning,' she grunted, putting down a bucket and wiping her nose (which was unmistakeably flecked with manure). 'Don't often see you down twice in a week, Mr Ryland' – this to Seb, of course. This was news to me, but as I turned to look at him with an air of mute enquiry, he solved the mystery by explaining that he'd thought that he'd left his mobile here when he dropped Qualia off following the Hackthorn fiasco, and had come back to look for it.

'And did you find it?' I asked.

'What? Oh, no – it was under my bed all along. But as I was here, I rode out on Pavane, and gave her and Qualia a good groom while I was here, didn't I, Jackie?' – this to the head groom, who nodded and said: 'You did a good job, alright. A lot of owners in part-livery don't bother with that; they just leave it to us. We get a lot of that.'

'Well, you can't get to know a horse properly without taking an interest in all its aspects,' said Seb – rather to my surprise, as he'd never shown much interest in that kind of thing before. But the head groom broke in on my thoughts.

'You'll want to ride out today, then?' she said, quite briskly; I got the strong impression that she had had enough of social chit-chat for one day, and was keen to get back to work. So we went ahead and saddled up, and before long we were trotting down one of the pretty lanes surrounding the yard.

I had been paying close attention to my breathing and general state of wellbeing throughout, of course, but apart from a slight tickling in my throat when I first walked into Qualia's box, I had no adverse reaction at all.

'I'm relieved, but puzzled,' I said to Seb as we drove back to London. 'Thank God I can carry on riding Qualia; but what on earth went wrong at Hackthorn?'

'Who knows?' said Seb. 'I don't suppose you'll ever know. Just forget it – put it down to a freak accident, and focus on the next race.'

'I suppose so,' I said. 'But I think I'll have to – hey, what are you doing?'

We had just been drawing up to the garage under our building, but at the last minute he put his foot down and pulled out into the street again. I caught a glimpse of a figure standing outside the entrance to the building – a thickset man, dressed in black and wearing a baseball cap – and as we drove to the end of the street and turned into the square I asked Seb again to explain what was going on.

'Oh, don't worry about it,' he said. 'It's just – well, it's a chap I'm not particularly keen to see, although he's very keen to see me. It's about – it's about his girlfriend, you see.' And he smiled at me rather shamefacedly.

'For heaven's sake, Seb...' I began; but it was no use. This kind of thing had happened before, and he knew how much I disapproved of it; but it never made any difference to what he did. So this time I contented myself with rolling my eyes and sighing expressively, and (quite demurely) allowed Seb to drive me to a little place we know in Islington, which does the best steak and kidney pudding in London. We had supper there, and returned home around eleven. To Seb's obvious relief, a quick reconnaissance from the end of the street revealed an absence of would-be assailants, and we pulled into the garage without incident.

'Was it the waitress?' I said as Seb parked the Merc.

'Was what the waitress?' he said, rather obtusely. Patiently I said: 'Was the waitress at the dinner party the girlfriend of that guy outside the flat?'

'Oh – yeah, sure,' he said, rather distractedly. Then he seemed to pull himself together somewhat. 'Yes, that's right. Odette – studying at RADA. Wonderful girl!' But his enthusiasm seemed rather forced, and I noticed he looked rather pale in the glare of the garage lighting. It was all very odd.

The oddness continued and even intensified over the days leading up to the Waterfield point-to-point, with all manner of strange happenings contributing to my vague but definite impression that something was going on. The phone would ring in the middle of the night, but nobody would answer; and sometimes when I answered the phone during the day (as I was still off work), a gruff and rather uncultured voice would ask for Seb, and then hang up when I said he was at the hospital. Seb took to keeping rather unconventional hours, and also started coming in the back door, a highly inconvenient point of entry that required an extra trip of some five hundred yards. He was avoiding the baseball cap, of course, whom I often saw hanging around the entrance to the flat. I got rather sick of his menacing presence, and once I picked up the phone to call the police; but Seb practically knocked the phone out of my hand. I looked at him in astonishment, and with a reddening face he said:

'Sorry, old chap – I don't want the cops involved. It would be embarrassing – for Odette, I mean. I'll deal with it, don't worry. It'll be fine, soon.'

'I hope so,' I said. 'I'm getting tired of seeing him every time I go out for a pint of milk. Are you and Odette still together, anyway? I haven't heard you on the phone to her for ages.'

'Look, Ollie, it's a bit complicated,' he replied. 'Just leave it, will you?'

So I left it, and him, by retiring into my rooms and closing the door. It wasn't often that we disagreed, or at least it *hadn't* been often that we disagreed; but he was becoming so impossible to live with that for the first time I considered looking for another flat.

On the day before the race at Waterfield, however, he seemed to realise that he was being a pain in the neck, and exerted himself to make amends. I had gone back to work on the Thursday and so hadn't been around the house as much, but when I got in on Friday evening I realised I hadn't seen the baseball cap for a couple of days; perhaps this was what had elevated Seb's mood, but for whatever reason he seemed in much better spirits. He breezed in with a brown paper bag full of delicacies from the local deli, and cracked open a bottle of champagne, apologising for having been gloomy and proposing toasts to our success at the Men's Open on the following day.

I wasn't quite sure how to react: certainly I welcomed a change from the morose and strange character who had possessed Seb's body in recent days, but then again this flushed and energetic persona seemed rather forced. I couldn't quite put my finger on it: Seb was never the kind of man who sought to play any part other than being exuberantly himself, but there seemed something unreal about his current behaviour, as if he had somehow been artificially stimulated. Seb, I knew, had nothing against the occasional use of illegal substances, but this seemed different. I got nothing out of him, however, when I asked him if everything was alright; he just grinned and said something about an operation that had gone well at the hospital. So I shrugged my shoulders and drank his champagne. (I resisted the gourmet luxuries, however; staying below twelve stone was a perpetual struggle for those of my build, and I didn't want to scupper my chances with unnecessary calories.)

The next day saw the two of us rising long before dawn, blinking away the debris of a long week's work (for Seb) and two long days' work (for me) and, after a hurried breakfast, embarking upon the familiar drive to Egham. I still felt somewhat at odds with Seb after the past few days, and as a result our conversation was muted as we led Qualia and

Pavane into their respective mobile homes and set off on the long drive north to Waterfield. When we arrived we parked away from each other, as usual, and prepared for the race more or less in isolation, as we both preferred.

I was paying more attention than usual to my breathing and the state of my skin. Although my conscious mind was quite convinced that I was not allergic to horses in general, far less Qualia in particular, there was clearly still a part of me that urged caution: I didn't worry much about the physical risks of falling, but I feared another such blow to my pride as I had sustained at Hackthorn. (All the more so today, as I knew Sinéad was coming to Waterfield for a day at the races, and I hate making a spectacle of myself in front of friends.) However, I noticed no discomfort of any kind while getting Qualia ready, and indeed I felt pretty good – it was a bracing morning with bright spring sunshine, and I could tell that Qualia, too, was raring to go.

The day seemed to shoot by – I always find that time speeds up, somehow, towards the start of a race – and it was no time at all before I was weighed in and mounted on Qualia in the paddock. Seb came over to wish me luck, as he often did, and to give Qualia a pat on the neck. As he did so, a man in a waxed jacket took a flash photo right next to us, making poor Qualia start and back away in surprise. I gave him a good telling off, of course, but really there'll be no end to that kind of thing until they have an X-ray machine at the entrances to racecourses, and destroy everyone's cameras on the way in. Poor Seb was butted sideways, and had to hang on to Qualia's mane to stay upright; he looked as annoyed as I did.

There wasn't much time for any more remonstration, however, as the Master of Foxhounds sounded his horn just then, and it was time to set off up to the starter's post. I waved hello to Sinéad, who was standing nearby, and began to canter up the low hill to the racetrack. It was just as I breasted the summit and turned onto the course that I began to feel unwell again: my breathing began to come in ragged spurts, I felt an incredible itchiness all across my face and neck, and my legs seemed to lose their ability to hold me up. A ringing sound filled my ears, and Qualia's neck, still jerking up and down as he cantered towards the starting line, began to go in and out of focus. I think I gave out an indistinct call for help, and I remember seeing the nearest rider's face looking at me from ten yards or so away, his arm gesticulating wildly and his mouth opening and closing; but I heard nothing. I saw the sky tilt and the sun dancing amidst the clouds, before the view changed to a belt of trees and finally Qualia's hind-quarters as he raced on without me. I remember thinking how beautiful he looked; then I passed out.

The situation was tediously familiar: the swollen face, the lack of eyesight, the splitting headache irritated, rather than soothed, by the steady beeping of the hospital's various machines. Also familiar, but infinitely more welcome, were two well-known voices: Seb and Sinéad. After the usual (and by now tiresome) jokes regarding my appearance, Seb told me how one of the stewards had captured Qualia after I came off and led him to the side of course until after the race. He then told us how he fell off himself at the seventh – which, I should note in fairness to Seb, is notoriously difficult. Finding himself still in one piece, he then boxed Qualia up and took him back to Egham before coming on to the hospital. A friend of his took Pavane (unhurt as before) back to the yard later. He shrugged off my commiserations and thanks with an airy contentment that seemed quite at odds with his bad luck in the race, and when he left I said as much to Sinéad.

'Yes – and I think I know why,' she said. 'I was there at the paddock before the race, and I saw something – something rather disturbing.'

'What did you see?' I asked. Then she told me.

Seb's unusually good mood lasted for the next week or so, during which I was off work once more. My continued absence caused some dismay at the firm – not owing to any irreplaceable brilliance on my part, of course, but simply because my clients were apparently becoming rather restive. One of the (full) partners honoured me with a phone call on the third day I was at home; the subsequent exchange was both apologetic (on my side) and apoplectic (on hers), and left me with the distinct impression that I needed to think carefully about where my priorities lay.

'If you're allergic to horses,' she said, 'then stop bloody riding!'

'I'm not allergic to horses,' I protested.

'Well, what are you allergic to?' she asked; and then sighed when I didn't – couldn't – answer. She sighed again, then said:

'My advice to you is this: get it sorted out. Either that, or join the ranks of the great unemployed. Your choice.' And she rang off.

I was annoyed, but I saw her point; spending three weeks out of four away from the office hardly qualified me as a candidate for Employee of the Month. I thought for a moment or two, then picked up the phone and rang Valerie, the HR manager at the firm. I asked her to put my sick days down as annual leave – or, as we used to call it, holiday. 'That should keep the wolves at bay for a while,' I told her; she laughed, and did as I asked.

After that I got on the phone to Catherine; I had a particular favour to ask of her, a favour to which she kindly agreed. Lastly I called the livery yard and had a word with Jackie – I had something to ask of her, too.

I had just put the phone down when Seb came in. As I have already mentioned, he had been on unusually good form since well before the race at Waterfield – to such an extent, indeed, that his continued exuberance had begun to get on my nerves. That evening, however, it seemed that the pendulum had swung back the other way again: Seb's face was white and drawn, and he barely acknowledged my greeting.

'Bad day at the hospital?' I asked.

'Something like that,' he said, sinking down onto the sofa. His pocket buzzed, and he drew out his mobile. He read a text message, and spent some time answering it. Suddenly he looked across at me again.

'Are you feeling any better?' he asked.

'Getting there, thanks,' I said. 'Much the same as last time. But you look worse than I feel, as a matter of fact. Why don't you have something to eat?'

'I'll be fine,' he said abruptly. 'So are you thinking of riding at Ramsholt?' – this was the next point-to-point we had planned to race at, down in Surrey.

'Well, I don't know,' I said. 'The last two times haven't turned out so well, have they? I still can't work out what's up with me.'

Seb was silent for a moment or two. Then he said: 'You know, Ollie, I've been thinking… What if it's something to do with the changing rooms? Asbestos, or something like that? They're very old, some of those places.'

'Could be,' I said doubtfully. 'But why would there be a problem now? I've been getting changed in them for years, and no harm done.'

'Oh, I don't know,' said Seb, with some exasperation; but he collected himself, and went on: 'Probably building work at Hackthorn and Waterfield – I think they've been renovating their facilities. But look – that's great news!'

'It is?' I said.

'Well, Ramsholt have built brand new facilities – just completed. Colonel Heronby told me – you know, the chap from the Jockey Club; we met him once with my father.'

'Really? That's good news, regardless of the allergy issue – the old facilities were a bit antediluvian. Rather like the Colonel, in fact.'

'So you'll race, then?' Seb went on, with something approaching his old enthusiasm.

'Well, I suppose I might. If I'm well enough to ride out on Qualia by this weekend.' (The race was the weekend after that.)

'Oh, I'm sure you will be,' said Seb.

'Why are you so keen for me to race?' I asked.

'Oh, I'm not, particularly,' he replied, unconvincingly. 'But it'd be a shame to break our record – three seasons in a row, racing in every major point-to-point in England...'

'True,' I said. 'Well, we'll see how it goes.' And with that he had to be content.

— ∘ ◦ —

A few days later I was feeling somewhat better, and so I told Seb that I would indeed be racing at Ramsholt. He was suitably pleased (although he still looked rather haggard). When he left for work, I got on the phone again to Catherine and Jackie, to make sure all the arrangements were in place – nothing too complicated; just a few ideas to improve my chances in the Men's Open. I told Catherine where I'd meet her on the day, and let Jackie know my plans for Qualia. They both agreed to everything, and I rang off with some satisfaction. After that I hit the sack for a while; if anything was certain, it was that I would need my strength back.

— ∘ ◦ —

The days seemed to drag as the point-to-point at Ramsholt approached, and Seb didn't help matters by getting more and more irritable and anxious as time wore on. I half wondered if he might be losing his nerve, and told him reassuring things about Pavane and the unusually gentle fences at Ramsholt; but it didn't seem to help much, so I shrugged my shoulders and got on with my preparations for the race. I was absolutely determined that I was going to finish the course this time, and possibly even return to my winning ways. Apart from anything else, I was sure that my successive falls must have led to a catastrophic slump in my stock with the racing public (and with some of the bookies); and despite being contentedly anonymous in most respects, I had a strong aversion to losing the esteem of people I admired and respected myself.

As such, my preparations were detailed and exhaustive; but that didn't stop me from feeling more than usually nervous on the morning of the race. Seb and I followed our usual routine: rising early, a hurried breakfast, the drive down to Egham (with decreasing levels of conversation), and boxing up our mounts at the yard before setting off to the racecourse.

It took me a little longer than usual, and after a while I called out to Seb to go on ahead. He called out his assent, and soon I saw him driving out of the yard with Pavane. I followed soon afterwards, and by eleven or so I had parked my lorry near Seb's at Ramsholt.

The Men's Open was up second, so there wasn't a lot of time to get changed, weighed, and so on. Once I had got Qualia sorted out, I left him with the groom whose services I'd hired for the day, and grabbed the rucksack containing my racing silks. As I did so, however, I realised that this wasn't my bag but Seb's; and sure enough, there were his characteristic red and yellow silks inside. I sighed deeply; then I dashed over to his lorry to see if he was still there. I saw him coming out to meet me, smiling and holding out my rucksack.

'Guess we mixed them up this morning,' he said. 'My fault, probably! Here you go – see you inside.' And he turned back to his lorry.

I set off for the changing rooms then, pausing only to say hello to Catherine (who was standing around near the Tote) and to pick something up from her.

'Thanks!' I called back as I hurried off. 'See you afterwards, I hope!'

'Try to stay on this time!' she called back.

'Just watch me!' I cried; then I was in the men's changing room. The other chaps gave me some wry looks, and one or two of them even seemed to shrink from my presence, as if they might catch my allergy, or perhaps just my bad luck. Even Seb seemed unwilling to meet my eyes properly, but I reckoned he was probably keyed-up about the race. I'm sure I would have been, too, in his shoes (or rather boots).

One odd thing happened in the changing-room: one of the riders asked me if I was happy with the new facilities.

'Yes, of course,' I said. 'Why wouldn't I be?'

'No reason,' he said; but his face betrayed some internal hostility that I couldn't quite understand. Then he said, 'Especially as my dad's company built it,' and I understood. I turned to look pointedly at Seb, who must have told some of them his theory about my allergic reactions to changing-rooms; but again he avoided my gaze.

Regardless of all that, I still felt pretty good as I finished weighing-in and hopped up on Qualia in the paddock. I noticed that Seb didn't come over to wish me luck, as he often did. I also noticed a distinct lack of flash photography, for which I was profoundly grateful. I think Qualia was, too; at least, he seemed very happy to be out and about, and showed a proper liveliness as the groom walked us around the paddock. Soon we were released from the public gaze – the paddock always makes me feel like a goldfish in a bowl - and cantered down to the post in small groups of twos and threes (although I rode alone). The going was good to firm, which suited Qualia perfectly. He was steady and confident under me, and as I looked at the firm swell of his neck and his powerful trunk muscles I felt certain that we would have a good race.

At the post I checked the girths and generally made sure everything was as it should be. Soon we began the familiar circling and jostling for position; I preferred to start on the inside, as did most riders, but as I was happy to start in the second rank I generally got what I wanted. Seb was on Pavane, of course, wearing his familiar red-and-yellow silks and looking over at me from time to time; he seemed to be trying to start only a little farther ahead than me, and more on the outside. This was unusual for him, as he usually tried to get away on the inside, and right at the head of the field. Perhaps he thought Pavane would do better jumping from the left-hand wing; or perhaps he had something else in mind.

In any case, there wasn't much time for reflecting on Seb's tactics: within a few minutes we were under Starter's Orders, and soon the Steward's flag went down; we were off. The track at Ramsholt is a figure-of-eight, which you go around twice. The figure-of-eight undulates across two little hillocks, so you have a lot of very complicated jumps (including two water jumps and an open ditch) with gradients, inclines, cambers - the whole shooting match. I had to concentrate pretty hard on getting the approaches right, and was over three fences before I remembered to think about whether my breathing was OK. I realised then that I was breathing easily

– not a trace of an allergic reaction. I had expected this, but even so I was filled with an unreasoning exhilaration: I was functioning perfectly, firing on all cylinders; fantastic. Now all I had to do was to win the race!

I like to think that Qualia sensed my new-found exuberance; certainly I seemed to feel a response from his bold spirit, from the great heart beating beneath me and driving us forward with such boundless energy. At the fifth a horse refused in front of us – his rider had shown him too much daylight; I would have ridden him in the middle of the field and come upon the fence suddenly – but Qualia responded to my suggestion and stepped neatly around to take the jump from the right-hand wing. At the sixth I employed a little trick I know to discomfort Ben Howard, one of my closest rivals in previous races. I knew that his mount, Urhan, was slower-paced in the air than Qualia, so I held Qualia back just a trifle and fooled Urhan into taking off at the same time as us. I didn't overdo it – I liked Ben, and didn't want to see him pitched onto the ground – but all's fair in love and war, and I fairly rejoiced when I saw Urhan lose a length in the air. We left them behind, struggling in our slipstream.

On the second lap I realised that Seb was riding closer to me. Initially I was impressed that he was keeping his head and not letting Pavane run away with him, but then I realised that he was veering towards me on the approach to the water jump – firstly in a minor way, just a presence on the edge of my vision, but soon coming closer and closer until Pavane was practically running into Qualia. I shouted and waved him off, trying simultaneously to concentrate on getting Qualia lined up for the water jump – no easy task, with half a ton of bone and muscle about to crash into you from the side. We managed it, but only just; and I shouted at Seb again as we landed. He shouted something back – it sounded like 'sorry', but I couldn't be sure.

His repentance was insincere, however, as he did the same thing at the very next jump. It was a normal fence rather than a water jump, but even so I didn't appreciate his crowding in on me in the last fifty yards or so. He rode so far across my line that I thought I might even go over the wing; I shouted and waved my whip, but to no avail. By then it was a choice between doing something more drastic or breaking my neck, so I waited until he was about to take off for the jump, and hit him hard across the ribs with my whip. He jerked with the impact, and Pavane, feeling the change in rhythm, took off late; they crashed into the fence, and as I landed I looked back to see Seb rolling on the ground.

I was shaken, and my hands were trembling; I hadn't thought he would take it so far. But I had to get on and finish the race if I could – I owed myself, and Qualia, that much. Ben, on Urhan, had made up a lot of ground owing to Seb's antics, and I had my work cut out keeping him out of the frame as we came up to the last fence. But Qualia pulled out all the stops on the home strait, and we just beat them to it. Ben's face was a picture at first, but he was gracious enough after a minute or two, and reached over to shake my hand as we pulled up.

'Good race,' he said between breaths; it had been an energetic finish. 'But what on earth happened to Ryland? I thought you two were pals.'

'I don't know,' I said; but I lied. I knew what had happened to Seb – more or less, at any rate.

I couldn't see him anywhere as I trotted back to the unsaddling enclosure, and hoped at least that his fall was not too serious. I jumped off to the applause of the spectators, and after unsaddling Qualia (and being weighed again) I shook a good many hands and enjoyed once more the elation of success – or at least I would have done, if I hadn't had Seb to think about. They told me his fall hadn't been catastrophic, but it had been fairly serious all the same, and one of the medics had taken him off to hospital to have him checked over. Of course I felt pretty bad about that, regardless of the circumstances, and as soon as I had received the little trophy and left Qualia with Catherine I borrowed a Steward's car and dashed off to the hospital.

Seb was sitting up in bed with a neck brace and his right arm in a sling; he also had bruising around his left eye, which looked all the more livid owing to the paleness of his face. He was staring at the wall opposite him.

'Seb,' I said.

He didn't look surprised to see me – didn't even look my way. He just said, 'Hello, Ollie. Sorry about the race.'

'Which one was it?' I said.

'What are you talking about?'

'Which bookie? Oh come on, Seb,' I went on, moving round the bed to make him look at me. 'I know what you've been doing.'

He looked at me then, but with a defiant air. 'No, you don't,' he said.

'Yes, I do,' I replied. 'You've got into debt – no, don't deny it, I know you have. You bought Pavane, but you couldn't afford him – not really. Then there are the parties, the champagne, the cars, the drugs – it all costs money; a lot of money. Your family's rich, but not that rich. Sooner or later you were bound to run out of money, but in your case it was sooner.

'OK, so you're out of money. What do you do? You can't sell Pavane – you'd do anything but that; you love racing too much. Sell the Merc? No chance; and you can't get rid of the house, either – your family wouldn't allow it. So – you need some money, ready money. What do you do?

'Then you think of the races – you think of them from a different perspective, not the view from the horse's back, but the spectator's view; and then, the bookie's view. What if you found some way of making money from that perspective? Betting on races would be too uncertain – you know that, of course, better than anyone. But what if you could fix races?'

'Ollie,' Seb began, but I cut him off. 'No! Let me finish. You decided to fix races, not by throwing them yourself – you never win, so that wouldn't work – but by making sure that I wouldn't win. You get a bookie to give me excellent odds to get the cash coming in; then I would crash out of the race, and you and he would split the money.'

'Ollie, this is crazy!' he said. 'How could I get you to crash out of races – you're a far better rider than I am!'

'Maybe,' I said. 'But I'm not a great rider when I can't breathe – when I'm falling off Qualia because I can't even see. When I have allergic reactions to latex.

'I know, Seb. I know what you did. You know that I'm allergic to latex, so you got hold of a box or two of surgical gloves at the hospital – nothing easier, for a surgeon! – and spread their dust coating over Qualia's mane before the race at Hackthorn – that's why I had a reaction at the top of the hill, when the wind blew the dust into my face. So I fell off and didn't finish, and your bookie pal cashed in; and so did you. You were overjoyed at coming third, but perhaps even happier that you'd won yourself a lot of money, very easily. Some of that money went on the ice-sculpture of yourself, I'll bet – very nice, but very expensive; too expensive.

'Perhaps you felt guilty after that, and wanted out – but that wasn't going to happen, judging by the heavy-set bouncer the bookie sent to intimidate you around our flat. Or maybe he was one of your creditors, looking for his money back. Either way, you knew you had to do it again – so you did. You took me down to Egham to convince me that I was fine and that I could ride Qualia in the next race; and you knew that there would be no problem riding out, because you'd already been down earlier that week, to clean all the dust off Qualia – Jackie practically said as much when we visited the yard.

'Your mood seemed to get a lot better on the Friday before the race – maybe you'd managed to convince your creditors to wait until the week after, or perhaps you'd been in touch with the bookie again, to set up the weekend's scam. And the scam was pretty clever, I'll admit: you got the bookie to take a flash photo in the paddock at Waterfield, and in the confusion you threw some more dust into my face while I was looking the other way. And don't deny it, please, Seb – Sinéad saw you do it. You cashed in again, and paid off some debts, perhaps – that's why you looked so happy, despite falling off yourself. That used to make you miserable for days.

'But the good times didn't last long, did they? One day you came back looking like death warmed up, and I knew that they'd got onto you again – your creditors, of course, looking for more money. Again you encouraged me to race again – you even spun me a yarn about an allergy to old changing-rooms, so that I'd feel happier in the new facilities at Ramsholt. You spread a rumour that the only problem I had was an allergy to asbestos, or whatever, in old facilities; I wondered why at first, but then I realised you were worried about the punters losing faith in me. You wanted to restore their confidence so they'd put their money where you wanted – straight into your pocket.

'I knew you'd try again today. To give credit where it's due, you tried to get me in a different way, by swapping our rucksacks over, and putting the dust all over my racing silks.

'But what you didn't know is that I took a few precautions before the race. On Wednesday I drove Qualia over to Reading, to stay with Catherine for a few days; she brought him along here this morning. The horse in the box at Egham was a similar-looking gelding that I borrowed from one of Catherine's friends, in case you decided to put any more dust on his mane during a secret – and, doubtless, solitary – outing to the yard. I didn't think you'd try the flash photo trick again – too risky, and perhaps I'd get suspicious if it happened the same way twice. But I wondered if you'd try to sabotage my silks – so I sent some of my gear to Catherine, who brought that along today, too; I took it from her before the race. When she opened the rucksack you gave me – I didn't dare, myself – she said that even she began to feel a bit short of breath, there was so much latex dust inside.

'Nevertheless, I escaped; and when I cantered down to the start, you must have realised the game was up. But you didn't stop there, did you – you didn't give up. You were overcome with fear about what the bookies (or your creditors) would do if I finished the race, or worse still won the race; and so you decided to make sure I didn't finish, even it meant knocking me off Qualia yourself. But you didn't quite manage it – Pavane is tremendous, and if it weren't for him you wouldn't even have got close; but your horsemanship just wasn't up to it, I'm afraid.

'And so here I am, and here you are – and you're

damned lucky we're both still alive, after the stunts you tried to pull.'

Towards the end of my Hercule Poirot-style denounce-ment, Seb seemed to collapse inwards like a dying star; his shoulders slumped and he dropped his gaze from the wall opposite to his good hand, sitting motionless in his lap. He sat there in silence for a while, just breathing; then he raised his head, very slowly, and said to me:

'It wasn't just the money, you know. It was more than just the money.'

'What was it, then?' I said.

'It was the winning – or rather, the lack of it. Look, you always win, or at least come second, or third, or even fourth. There were weeks when I would have killed to come fourth, Ollie – and it was all so easy for you, with Qualia. I could never find a horse like that, myself.'

I had to challenge this. 'What about Pavane? One of the finest jumpers I ever saw.'

'Yes – but not as good as Qualia. And I had to pay through the nose for him – far more than I could afford.' And he went back to inspecting his hand.

I hate to say it, but I began to feel sorry for him. I had always been struck by how much Seb had – his surgical career, his family, his wealth – but now I saw him in a different way: I saw him as a schoolboy, upset over his omission from the First XI; or as someone slighted by an adored lover. I saw him as a venal, petty man, willing to betray his friends, and even himself, for the sake of a few little trophies. It was pathetic, but it was so pathetic that I couldn't be angry with him, and soon I asked him:

'How much?'

'Eh?'

'How much are you in hock to the bookies? I finished the race, so they must have lost a lot of money.'

'Oh, I don't know,' he said. 'A few grand, I suppose. Maybe twenty or thirty. More than I have to give them, anyway. Not the nicest chaps, some of them, Ollie.'

I refrained from saying that it had been his choice to

get involved with them, and merely nodded. I got up then, and turned to go, but as I left I turned and looked at him.

'I don't think you should race any more, Seb,' I said. 'Just sell Pavane and buy a chaser to go hunting with. You needn't worry – I won't tell anyone about all this. You might want to tell the police, though, if they keep sending bouncers round to put pressure on you.

'I'll be gone when you get back,' I went on. 'And don't try to call me. We're finished. It's a damn shame, but there it is.' And with that I walked out.

I cleared my things out of the flat that same day, and moved them into a friend's place while I found somewhere to live. I left my keys on the dresser by the entrance to the flat, together with a cheque for ten thousand pounds, made out to Seb – the last token of a broken friendship. He cashed it three days later.

As far as I know he took my advice and gave up racing; at any rate I never saw him at point to points anymore, although I do see him occasionally at hunt meets. We nod and touch our helmets with our whips, as we did so long ago at that party in London; and every time I see him I wonder if he feels the same pang of regret that I do.

The thrill of victory is evergreen, I said; and winning a point-to-point still gives me the same fierce pride and delight as before. But afterwards, when I drive home alone, I think of Seb, and become very aware of his absence; and the champagne cocktails never taste quite as good as they used to. Perhaps it is time to add another name to the escutcheon, and commission that four-barrelled shotgun – but if I do, I will make one stipulation: that she doesn't ride in point-to-points. One fool per household is more than enough.

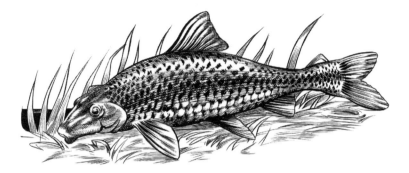

Sharpe's Story

IT WAS at Farlow's, in Charles Street, that Richard Penrose and Douglas Sharpe accidentally renewed their friendship.

'Penrose!' said Sharpe.

'Sharpe!' said Penrose. 'Wonderful to see you, old man! What are you doing here?'

'Come in to look at a new Express – you?'

'Rod tip repair, if you can believe it. I tripped over the blasted thing in Wiltshire last week – at Buffy's. You remember Buffy Porson?'

'Remember Buffy Porson!' cried Sharpe. 'I don't see how I could forget him, seeing as he landed me in quod for a week on Boat Race night in '28. How is he these days?'

'Oh, pretty much the same as ever, you know – it's a mystery how he manages to put one foot in front of the other, yet he can come out with the most brilliant things given enough time, and enough claret. But I say, it's funny I should run into you like this. Buffy and I were going to look you up at your Club – White's, isn't it?'

'That's right,' said Sharpe. 'Planning a reunion, are you?' – Penrose, Sharpe and Porson had spent their formative years together at the University.

'Of a sort,' said Penrose. 'I'm glad to see you are still

a sporting man, in any case, for the thing we have in mind is of a sporting nature... Did you know that Buffy's uncle was Lord Methven? Nor did I – but when old Methven passed on, Buffy found himself the master of a superb park, five miles of Wiltshire's finest chalkstream, and a goodish-sized patch of excellent rough shooting. He's in a sportsman's paradise, and he knows it – but the trouble is, he has no-one to gloat over it with.'

'He didn't get married in the end, then?' said Sharpe.

'No, Alice chucked him over for a chap going out to Hong Kong – can't say I blame her, come to that, although I wouldn't have Buffy know that for the world. But it's not just that. His Wiltshire neighbours are dry old sticks, and most of the Brasenose men he knows opted for postings overseas, so he's positively crying out for company and the chance to lord it over us mortals who have to scratch around for our sport.'

'I imagine I could find it within me to relieve him of his misery, by spending a month or so in Wiltshire,' said Sharpe. 'Of course, if I took such a long vacation, the Permanent Secretary would be beside himself - thus conveniently filling my vacated spot.'

'How magnanimous of you!' replied Penrose. 'As a matter of fact he said he was going to invite you himself, when he comes up to town for the King's Speech. But that isn't what I was going to say. You see, Buffy wants to start a dining society, for blackguardly chaps like us who want to boast to each other about our exploits in the field. His notion is to ask a different member in turn to tell a sporting tale over the port, with the tale to be taken from personal experience. And if the tale is dull, or incredible, or unsatisfactory in any other way, then the teller is sconced.'

'Sconced?' cried Sharpe.

'Sconced,' said Penrose. 'If a chap offends his company in some way, then he is handed a silver vessel, containing at least three pints of ale, and he must drink it all down – don't you recall sconcing from the Varsity?'

'Yes, of course I do,' said Sharpe. 'Avery once sconced me twice in a row on Annunciation Day – I'd like to see a fellow erase that from his memory. I was merely expressing my surprise that you would wish to inflict the practice on grown men - sober, useful members of society...'

'To whom are you referring?' interrupted Penrose. 'I was talking merely about you, myself, and Buffy. And such other men as we might see fit to invite – Hickson, for instance, and Henton... Brudenell too, and possibly Harry Trevithick as well, if he could be prevented from talking about his blasted polo ponies. And Buchan, of course, although he is always so confoundedly busy now that he's an MP...Are you in?'

'Well, I suppose I had better come along, if only to keep you and Buffy out of mischief. What's the society to be called? We ought to have a name, for decency's sake.'

'Well, Buffy came up with a large number of college-related suggestions, as you can imagine. "The Brazen Noses" was his first suggestion, followed (some bottles of champagne later) by "The Brozen Nazes". I will spare you the rest of them. Suffice to say that common sense eventually prevailed, and we stuck on "The Sconcing Society".'

'It has the virtue of simplicity. When is the first meeting?'

'Buffy wants to meet us a fortnight next Monday, at the Savoy.'

'Good-oh. I look forward to it.'

'I'll leave you to it, then. And Sharpe? You'll be telling the first tale!'

———◦———

April was more than usually mercurial that year, and so it was with some degree of irritability that a drenched trio of youngish men foregathered under the expansive canopy afforded by the entrance to the Savoy. 'Spring weather be damned' was the tenor of their conversation for some considerable time, until at last good manners returned and Buffy shook Sharpe's hand with vigour.

'How good it is to see you again, Sharpe! It must be years and years since last we met – at the Deb's Ball, if I don't mistake... Wasn't Diana Montague a stunner! But listen, let's not moulder out here any longer – I can hear a steak and a bottle of Burgundy calling to me from the Grill.'

'I'm with you, old man,' said Sharpe. 'Absolutely,' added Penrose; and with that the party repaired within, to a world of gleaming silver and spotless linen. The dinner was everything that could have been expected – Buffy particularly remarked upon the Tournedos alla Rossini – while the sommelier positively outdid himself with a noble Domaine Leroy, an excellent Sauterne, and a truly matchless Garrafeira. When the decanter had gone round two or three times, Buffy and Penrose lit their cigars, settled in their seats, and gazed at Sharpe with a benign air of expectation. He took the hint – it was tolerably obvious – and lit his own cigar with a gesture of resignation.

'Well, I see the time has come to find out if I can entertain you,' he said. 'And if I fail, I suppose we shall discover if I can still drink three pints of ale down in one go.

'My story begins nearly four years ago, when I was staying with friends in Berkshire – the Greenhalghs – I think you may know them, Buffy. The son was running for Parliament at the time, and in a weak moment I agreed to help him with his campaign. I paid for it with many dreary days treading dusty lanes and by-ways – but I won't go into all that now, as it doesn't come into the rest of the story.

'After what felt like weeks of hard work – it was probably only a few days – Greenhalgh was obliged to go up to town for a meeting with the party bigwigs, and I had a precious few hours without any canvassing to be done. Immediately I put up a rod and line and headed for a nearby stream where I had heard of great things in the coarse line. (The one and only benefit of electioneering is the time spent in public houses, listening to the old boys' sporting wisdom.)

'But although I set out enthusiastically enough, I soon found that I was dragging my steps – and I'll tell you why. If you spend enough time with a fellow, sooner or later you will hear a litany of complaints about things he hasn't achieved in the field. Perhaps his hook came loose when he had an enormous salmon on the line, or his stalker sneezed at the last moment and affrighted a sixteen-point beast. Maybe his chance at a Macnab was foiled by damp cartridges, or his hunter pitched him off over a noble hedge just before the kill. Whatever the particular complaint, the country is full to the brim with men who bewail their sporting misfortunes – who never miss an opportunity to carp about their rotten luck.

'Well, that wasn't my problem at all. In fact, my difficulty was pretty much the precise opposite: at the age of twenty-six, I found I had pretty much achieved everything I wanted to in the sporting line. For consider: I had banked a thirty-four pound salmon from the Tay, and an eighteen-pound cannibal trout from Loch Ness. I had bagged a couple of woodcock, left-and-right, and three of the highest pheasants the keeper had ever seen at Beaulieu, not to mention the eighteen-point buck I took at Glamis. And for good measure I had caught fine specimens of all the coarse species – carp, bream, tench, barbel, and roach. Indeed, for a short time I held the national record for rudd, with a fine Norfolk fish of 2lb 3oz, that I hauled out of Blackhorse. I wept like Alexander, for there were no more worlds to conquer.

'But although my enthusiasm was lacking on that hot day in Hampshire, I pressed on nonetheless – one has to play the game – and within half an hour or so I came to the spot I had been told about. It was a curious stretch of stream, overhung by serried rows of willows and overlooked by a tall arcade of cypresses, planted long ago to mark the boundary of a ruinous estate. The cumulative gloom of these stately guardians cast a heavy shadow on the waters, which meandered softly – I might almost say meditatively – beneath the waving tendrils of salix. So little light penetrated the walls of this living fortress that to gaze upon the surface of Glymbrook – that was the stream's name – was merely to encounter a ghostly reflection of oneself, a pale likeness of a face held up in a shimmering, changeful mirror.

'Yet while the depths were lightless, they were by no means lifeless. Sudden, unexpected waves and dim flashes of gold and silver attested to the presence of numerous underwater denizens – chub, I made no doubt, with perhaps a deep-chested barbel or two thrown in for good measure, and probably some grayling in the winter months. My appetite for the pursuit was sadly lessened, but I thought of Horatius at the Bridge, and, sighing, began to unburden myself, laying out my creel, net and rod on the verdant bankside. Soon all was ready.

'It was just as I cast my line – 4x gut to a size 16 hook, with a piece of cheddar on the shank – that the old man spoke. It gave me such a start – I thought I knew something about stalking from my time with Macarthur in Galloway, but even he couldn't hold a candle to this chap.

'"Bain't no use looking for chub 'ere," he said.

'When my heart steadied, I replied – somewhat hotly,

'"What the devil do you mean by creeping up on me like that? And – dash it – I distinctly saw the flash of a chub's tail. There! Can't you see it?"

'"I can see it, or'right," said the old fellow – Johnson was his name, as it turned out. "But they'm no record fish in there – and that's what you're arfter, ain't it – Mr Sharpe, if I don't mistake?"

'And I'm blowed if the old man hadn't seen my photograph in the sporting papers, when I caught my record rudd. He must have had an uncommon good memory, and sharp eyes besides, for it was no kind of a likeness. Photographs rarely are, I find – the lens always makes my complexion look so bleached.'

'Oh, get on with it, Sharpe!' cried Penrose suddenly.

'Yes, for heaven's sake – how you do go on!' put in Buffy. 'Pass the port, Penrose, there's a good chap. And get ready to tip the wink to the waiter for the sconcing vessel – I feel that my credulity is about to be stretched well beyond breaking point.'

'Shut up, Buffy, there's a good chap,' said Sharpe. 'You put a fellow off his stride. Now, where was I? Oh yes: Johnson – the record rudd – the absence of record chub. Et cetera.

'Well, he was probably right, of course – it was a fairly slim river, and chub often like a bit of space, you know, to get really deep and broad. But it was all too ridiculous, having this old fool tell me my business, and I confess I got rather hot under the collar. I reeled in violently and began to pack up my gear. But he laid a great spade of a gnarled hand on my arm, and spoke again.

'"Now, now, young feller," he said. "Bain't no need to go gettin' all haughty wi' me. I'm just by way of suggestin' that you might want to fish a bit finer, like, and go for a real record fish – the biggest small fish nor ever you seen, if you take my meaning" - I absolutely didn't – "for I swear by my old missus's pitchin' fork, there's a record gudgeon in there."

'"A record what?" I said.

'"A gudgeon," he said. "Ain't you never caught one? It's a prime fish, prime – small, mark you, not much over a few ounces at most – but sleek and fast and well-lookin' enough, in 'is own way, is the gudgeon."

'At this point he pulled a scruffy tobacco pouch out of his pocket, from which he produced a yellowed cutting, much crumpled and put about, but still legible. It read: "COAL MAN CATCHES SMALLEST FISH", and narrated how Johnson, having entered a village fishing competition some years before, had won a wooden spoon for landing the smallest fish in the competition.

'"But see, they got it all wrong," he said, looking at me earnestly, almost entreatingly. "They did, I tell you. This worn't no mere tiddler; this here's a prize gudgeon" – tapping the cutting so that bits of tobacco fell off it – "as I live and breathe. Over five ounce if it's a dram, I'll swear to it, and I'd have the British record now, if it worn't for the vicar's daughter, Mary, that sneaked the fish out of my net and gave it to 'er cat, when my back was turned, the little hussy..."

'He then subsided into a clearly well-worn set of grievances, to which I barely gave ear. To tell the truth I was somewhat taken with this agèd country relic and his picaresque notions. A record gudgeon, forsooth – a fish I had never even heard of before today... And yet, this would at least be a challenge, of sorts – not to catch the biggest, but rather the very smallest, of the river's denizens... Surely my blasted streak of luck, my unwonted and inescapable good fortune, could hardly help (or rather hinder) me here, for it would in the nature of things be bad luck to land a gudgeon, prize weight or no... My mind was soon made up; I would take Johnson's word for it, and go after a prize Glymbrook gudgeon. The prospect of two national records was rather alluring, after all.

'But then it struck me to ask why this old man was telling me to make a play for the fish? Surely, if there were such a paragon of watery virtue to be had, he'd keep it as quiet as possible, rather than broadcasting it to all and sundry.'

'Just what I was going to say,' broke in Buffy.

'Veering dangerously close to the incredible,' added Penrose.

'Just listen, will you, and all will become clear,' said Sharpe with a touch of asperity. 'So as I say, I asked myself why Johnson wasn't going after the miniature monster. And after I had asked myself, I asked him.

'"Why, that's simple," he replied. "I would go arter 'im in a second, was my luck a little better. But no sooner do I touch line to water, this past ten year, than all 'ell breaks loose – never was an unluckier wight, is my belief. Once a swan attacked my float, and then turned on me, directly; and just last Candlemas I stepped on my own gin-trap while out poachin', and was laid up for a month."

'"No, sir, my fishin' days is over – I know when I'm beat. But you – I can see you're a likely feller – why, anyone can see it, to look at you. You catch my gudgeon, and I'll stand 'ere and watch you, and that'll be good enough for me. My name's Johnson," he added, shaking my hand. " – And now old Mister Johnson'll be off 'ome, for he's bin expected this past 'alf-hour and more. But I'll be back tomorrer, at three sharp – mark you, three sharp, Mr Sharpe!"

'And with this the old man pottered away, still chuckling to himself over his execrable joke.

'Well, this decidedly one-sided arrangement put me in a difficult position with young Greenhalgh, as I had promised to accompany him to a Women's Institute meeting on the following day. The good ladies of the WI notwithstanding, however, my clear duty was to keep my engagement with

Johnson, and have a crack at that gudgeon of his' – 'Hear, hear,' said Buffy and Penrose – 'and so, following a decidedly uncomfortable scene in which Greenhalgh made painfully clear his disbelief regarding my sudden need to visit a long-lost aunt in nearby Stonely Parva, I once again made my way to the shady grove through which the Glymbrook flows.

'There was no sign of Johnson when I arrived – I was a few minutes early – but I decided he wouldn't mind if I got started without him, and soon my line was in the water. I chose to trot the finest of tackle – 8x gut and size 24 hook, with a single brandling worm – under the prettiest light Avon float you ever saw. I got it at a little shop in Market Sudbury one day – the proprietor makes them himself, and I never go anywhere else.

'Fishing a float on that particular stretch, which was heavy with overarching branches, called for some careful casting. My apprenticeship on the upper reaches of the Avon served me well, however, and it wasn't long before I had a nibble – I struck, but a little too late – nothing on the line, and when I reeled in the brandling had disappeared.

'Quick as a flash, I put another one on, and re-cast. The bright orange tip of the float twitched as it caught on a floating reed – steadied again – accelerated towards a likely-looking eddy – dipped, stopped, dipped again, and then disappeared from sight. I struck.

'I won't say it felt like a good fish, as it didn't – it felt as if I'd hooked a small, a very small, lump of weed. Nevertheless I felt that old, familiar, yet long-missed thumping of the heart that attends the fulfilment of a sporting goal. I had looked gudgeon up in the village library that morning, and as the tiny fish reached the surface I saw the mottled brown flanks and the single pair of barbles that mark out the species. And my word! What a specimen it was! Exactitude is difficult to obtain in these things, but I would swear the fish was eight ounces at least – a record, without a doubt. What a sharp old file Johnson was, to guess the existence of such a fish!

'But here my blasted good luck – for want of a better word – got in the way again. As I reeled the gudgeon in, splashing and jumping on the way, a jack pike loomed from the depths and closed its cavernous maw neatly around my prize.

'How can this be good fortune?' broke in Penrose. 'Surely you must have lost the gudgeon? Even a jack pike would make short work of your 8x gut!'

'Your impatience is your undoing, Penrose,' replied Sharpe. 'It was always thus at Fives, and I am sorry to see that it continues to this day. All will become clear!

'Where was I? Oh yes, the pike. Well, you will doubt-less be surprised to hear that the pike did not bite through the line. Whether it was because it was unusually good quality – it was Cheethams, an excellent brand – or because the line fell between Leviathan's teeth, or for some other reason, I cannot tell – all I can say is that after a short (and fairly violent) tussle, both the pike and the gudgeon lay on the bankside, the former having released the latter as soon as he felt my net close around him.'

'What – you landed them both?' cried Buffy. 'Really, Sharpe, you ask too much of us!'

'Not at all,' said Penrose. 'That has happened to me as well, when fishing for perch – although in my case neither pike nor perch were anything to write home about.'

'Thank you, Penrose,' said Sharpe. 'A helpful interjec-tion, for once! So – both fish lay on the bank. I didn't take much account of the pike – I never have, since my thirty-six pounder, from the Camlough in County Armagh. But the gudgeon – why, he measured a full three inches, with vibrant colouring and a fine, deep flank on him – a suitable fish for a new national record.

'Suddenly I jumped, for a voice called out, "You did it! Oh Lor', as I live and breathe – my record fish – you caught 'im!" It was old Johnson, of course. He ran up to the bank and stood over his precious gudgeon, gloating over its comparative immensity as it flapped around on the grass.

'"Oh, 'e must be eight or nine ounce, at the least, Mr Sharpe – what a champion! He must be stuffed and put up on the wall of the Royal Oak – but first 'e must be weighed. Just you wait here, sir – I've a scales in my satchel. We'll see how much that fish breaks the record by!"

'He rushed off to find his bag, which he had presumably left with his bicycle in a little clearing some thirty yards off; I had left my bicycle there as well. Meanwhile I got out pipe and tobacco and began to fill the bowl; I felt that I deserved a celebratory smoke.

'But here our fortunes converged, good and bad – my good luck secured the pike as well as the gudgeon, and Johnson's bad luck guaranteed the loss of both. For no sooner had I taken my eyes off the gudgeon (to attend to my pipe) than the pike, which had been jumping into the air every now and then, indulged in a particularly energetic convulsion, landed next to the gudgeon, opened its jaws and engulfed the smaller fish whole, leapt into the water, and was away into the depths before I could say knife.

'I stood there in some confusion for a while, until I realised Johnson had returned and was standing at my side, his scales in his hand. To me the loss of the gudgeon was a petty irritation; to him, surely, it would be a crushing blow. But to my surprise his face was philosophical.

'"Don't you be worritin' about me, Mr S," he said after a while. "I've had disappointments enough afore this - didn't my Mabel show up to the church on time after all? – and I can put up with this one as well. Now did you say you're a feller who likes his chub? There's a pretty spot just over in the next valley..."

'And after he had told me where to go, he went off and got on his bicycle, and I never saw him again. And that's the end of my story.'

'Bravo,' said Buffy, applauding. 'Hear him,' said Penrose, doing likewise. 'Not bad, not bad at all. Quite believable, I'd say – wouldn't you agree, Buffy?'

'Oh yes, I think so. No chance of a sconcing there, I think,' said Buffy. Sharpe sat back in his seat with a sigh of relief and lit another cigar with a decidedly relaxed air.

'Thank heavens for that,' he muttered to himself.

'Although - ' said Penrose ruminatively.

'Although?' said Sharpe, suddenly alarmed.

'The float...' mused Buffy.

'The float,' said Penrose, nodding.

'We've been to Market Sudbury, old chap – we were there for the cricket tournament, just last year. As it happens we popped into the fishing shop there – you know, the one you said you get your floats from,' said Buffy.

'And the old fool that runs it couldn't make a pot of tea, never mind a beautiful Avon float,' continued Penrose. 'A good story, Sharpe, no doubt – but we have found the weak link in your chain of deceit. I believe a sconcing is in order!'

'Oh, I say, this is preposterous! He does make his own floats...' said Sharpe, but he spoke half-heartedly; he knew his goose was cooked, and when the waiter brought the silver flagon, full to the lip and indeed brimming over, he accepted the inevitable with good grace.

'To old Mr Johnson, then! I always wished I could have had a drink with him, to thank him for his angling wrinkles – and by the way I caught some superb chub in the spot he advised – but this will have to do. Bottoms up!' he cried, and raising the vessel to his lips he drained it in one draught.

Beyond the Pale

I

'AREN'T YOU going to finish that?' he said. Then he plucked the half-full glass clean out of my hand.

I was, frankly, astonished. My travels on Company business had left me with few qualms about etiquette – you don't bother much about Ps and Qs when you are sharing goats' milk with a Bedouin Chief, or, for that matter, when you are painting the town red with the top man in a Texan oil concern. And it wasn't as if we were sipping sherry back at the Varsity, or at an Embassy bash. No – there I was, stuck for a fortnight in a godforsaken corner of Mozambique that looked as if its last coat of paint had gone on in the year dot.

So you don't expect much – you don't expect the waiter to come rushing over with the gigot the minute you polish off the fish, and you don't expect the Scotch to be anything but caramel water and hooch. But I'm blowed if I expected this old man to get started on my gin before I had so much as got down to the ice-cubes.

'What the devil – ' I began, but the waiter positively shot across the room (he was quick enough that time) and placed a restraining hand on my arm. I shook it off angrily, but the old man – well, he wasn't so old, really, but the drink – they can't all take it, you know, and this particular specimen had a face like a pickled cabbage. Anyway, he had already turned away and begun to hobble off, and I'm damned if I didn't start to feel sorry for the fellow. I'd noticed he had bandages on his feet, you see, with filthy toes sticking out of the ends. So I let him alone.

I saw him again the next evening, though, and this time he seemed quite a different man. There was a bit of life in those bloodshot eyes, and something about his bearing – was it good breeding, or some trace of residual pride? Perhaps it was just the Portuguese gin trickling out of his system. In any case, my curiosity was by now thoroughly roused, and when he sat down at my table on the veranda I didn't protest.

'Eduardo tells me I owe you an apology, sir,' he murmured in well-modulated tones, nodding at the waiter polishing glasses behind the counter. 'To my shame I cannot remember what transpired yesterday evening. It – it must have been the fever. It gets to me every now and then, when the weather is damp; has done since I came here in '31.'

And as if to demonstrate the severity of his illness, he broke into a fit of coughing. I wasn't quite convinced at first, but then I saw the blood on his handkerchief; that convinced me all right.

'I say,' I volunteered, when his paroxysm had subsided. 'I really think you ought to see a medic. I hear there's an English doctor up at Vilanculos, here on a fishing trip. I'm sure he would see you.' And now the old man astonished me all over again.

'Fishing?' he said, his face darkening. 'Don't talk to me about fishing! It's a waste of time, it's a waste of money, it's – it's – it's the ruin of half the youth of England!'

And so saying he swept crockery, cutlery, and glass-ware, the whole shooting match, off the table and onto the floor, and took himself off into the night.

The waiter again came running over – the old man had one friend in the place, at least – and cleaned up the mess, entreating me 'not to mind the old fellow, please, Senhor – not to mind' – as if I would do him any harm. He looked as if one good tap with a walking-cane would send him into the grave.

The third time I saw him – it was also the last – was two days after that. I had just had a very successful audience with the local Commissioner, and it looked like my baggage would finally be granted passage to Maputo on the following Tuesday. This was heaven-sent news, and I was celebrating my imminent departure with a few nips of Eduardo's execrable gin when a familiar footfall sounded on the wooden steps leading up to the bar. Yet although the old man's awkward gait was the same, his face was different again: neither sozzled to the nines, as on the first occasion, nor soberly watchful, as on the second, but possessed of an infectious, if vacant, jollity – a bit like an English Bacchus, full of wine and goodwill, but who doesn't quite know which end of his donkey is the one that bites. Once again he found his way to my table.

'My dear sir,' he said warmly, 'I don't believe we have met.'

'Er – no, indeed,' I replied, for nothing about this man could surprise me now. 'My name is McKean.'

'And mine is Leveret,' he said, shaking my hand. 'Rudyard Leveret, to be precise. And what brings you to the good town of Inhambane, Mr McKean? We don't see many Europeans here, except for the Portuguese, of course.'

I refrained from observing that the only good thing about Inhambane was the fact that I was about to leave it, and told the old man something about my work. I talked mostly about the oil side of things – I didn't mention the Danish Legation, for fear he might blab about it to someone unsavoury. I couldn't have that, for Johansen didn't know I was in Africa. Anyway I soon realised he wasn't listening; he had the air of someone nodding politely and waiting to put a question; and when I paused he asked me:

'And when were you last home, Mr McKean? How is the Old Country? Are – are the leaves turning yet?'

I answered him as best as I could, but of course the Warburg case had kept me from England for nearly a year. However, Barrett had told me in a letter that there had been a delightful Indian Summer this year, so I told Leveret that I supposed autumn would just be coming on now. When I said this, his jollity evaporated like mist, and a curious look came over his face – a look of weary yearning, combined with something I divined as sorrow. It was pitiful to see.

'When were you last home?' I asked presently.

'Oh, not for many years now, I'm afraid,' he said heavily. 'You see,' he went on, 'I had rather a strange experience there at one time. I couldn't very well stay there once I had – well, I couldn't stay.'

We sat without talking for a while after that, the heavy tropical calm broken only by the soft whirring of the ceiling fans and the occasional throaty cry from the nearby beachfront. The fishermen were coming in from the sea; and as they came they sang, singing (so the waiter told me later) of the sea and the stars, now hanging suspended like great globes of light over the darkened ocean.

I lit a cigarette, the smoke drifting slowly into the night.

'We've got the whole evening in front of us,' I said. 'Would you like to tell me about it?'

II

Rudyard Leveret is the only child of Martha and Edwin, who both died in 1905 in a motor-car accident in Brompton – it must have been one of the earliest in this country. After the funeral, Leveret went to live with his uncle, Sir Charles Leveret, Bart., and Sir Charles's son, David. Sir Charles's second wife, Victoria, had died some years before of tuberculosis, so the young Rudyard was deprived not just of his parents but of female company altogether, a fact which may be significant.

David was only a year older than Rudyard, and although the boys were at first wary (on Rudyard's part) and inclined to be resentful (on David's), they soon discovered common interests that brought the boys into that intensely close companionship which belongs only to youth. Their passions were many and varied: cricket in the summer, rugger in the winter; the stories of G.A. Henty and the ballads of Rudyard's eponym, Kipling; tree-climbing and apple-filching, model railways and air-guns; and a host of others too various to name, indulged and encouraged by the generous, if occasionally irascible, Sir Charles. In time the two boys became a familiar sight in the lanes and by-ways around the Leveret demesne, the one tall and spry, dark-haired and pale – this was David; and Rudyard, stocky and fair, ruddy-cheeked and blue-eyed. They fought often, but made up oftener, and proved their loyalty to one another in many a schoolyard scrap. In later days Rudyard would look back on his childhood as the summit and pinnacle of human happiness, with delightful memories, painful by comparison, of rainfall and mists, sunny days and frost.

One spring Sir Charles sat them down by the drawing-room fire and placed two long parcels on the table, one in front of each boy.

'Now, boys,' said Sir Charles, 'you are getting older, both of you' – he was fond of stating the obvious – 'and of an age to wield a fly-rod without disgracing the name of Leveret' – he could also be a trifle pompous.

'Oh, Father!' cried David, his face alight with joy. 'Are these the salmon rods you promised us?'

'Yes, David,' replied his father. 'One apiece, together with 'Perfect' reels, from the House of Hardy – only the finest will do! Now open that carefully, Rudyard' – this to his nephew, who had begun his to tear the brown paper from his rod with wild abandon. 'It cost pounds and pounds, you know!'

'Yes, Uncle – sorry, Uncle,' said Rudyard. 'Oh – thank you, sir, thank you!' he said, eyeing the brand-new rod with something approaching religious ecstasy. His delirium was further heightened by the feel of the beautifully-machined reel and the colourful sight of a hundred salmon flies, delicately arrayed in a Cherry wood box.

'You had better start getting your kit packed, boys,' said Sir Charles, to a rapturous reception. 'We're going to the Tay for a week of top-class sport, this very Saturday!'

The boys awaited the coming of the appointed day with an almost unbearable fervour. They had often heard Sir Charles speak in glowing terms of his sporting adventures north of the border – for reasons unfathomed he scorned to fish in his own country, whose rivers and lakes he derided as fit only for milksops and weaklings – and the boys had long yearned to emulate him in casting a line for salmon and sea-trout. Now that the dream was about to be fulfilled, it somehow seemed further away than ever.

Eventually, however, the Saturday in question arrived, and saw the three of them seated comfortably in a first-class carriage, travelling north by the dawn express. No fishing was possible that first day, of course, but they managed to get to water's edge just before nightfall, and spent a happy half-hour there prospecting their beat, and planning their line of attack.

'Stoat's Tail and Munro's Killer will be best, I think,' remarked Sir Charles, puffing on the Meerschaum that always accompanied him on fishing expeditions. 'And now to bed – but the river awaits on the morrow!'

And so it did: sleek and gleaming silver in the grey morning light, murmuring with powerful currents and filled with dark pools that spoke eloquently of the king of fishes. As soon as Rudyard set eyes upon it in the light of day he felt its pull, the weight of its waters and their imponderable, moving mass; but also he could not shake off a strange sense of foreboding. The river seemed so great, so majestic; how could he tame it, conquer it, with rod and line? The rod had seemed so huge in his uncle's drawing-room, but against the Tay's smooth expanses it seemed ridiculously puny. Beneath the overhanging bank on which he stood there were bare rocks and deposited boulders; the water gargled and splashed around them, and in their notes Rudyard heard a distant voice of menace; a hidden music, cold and ancient, that threatened him with ill-will for daring to challenge the river's might with his little wand.

Suddenly Rudyard was afraid; he blinked, and stepped back from the edge of the river. Into his mind there came unbidden an image of warm sun and quiet water, a lily-fringed pond with soft green depths, benevolent and rich. Its contrasted stillness soothed the boy, but his reverie did not last long.

'Come on, Rudyard!' cried David, already wading enthusiastically into the water. 'What are you waiting for?'

So Rudyard pulled himself together, and shouted to David, and waded into the river, and began to fish. In that week he caught his share of Tay springers – fine fish they were too, glistening and fresh from the sea. But he could not forget the voice of the river, distant but hostile; and he lay awake at night, thinking on its quiet insistence, and shivering. He was glad to return to England at the end of the week.

Three years after the boys' fishing trip, David left his father's house, and went up to Cambridge to read law at Trinity Hall. Rudyard, being a year younger, was obliged to stay behind. The young men were both bereft, but neither would admit it, David throwing himself into College rugger and the Union, and Rudyard falling in with a group of local boys from the village. He got into some scrapes thereby, and Sir Charles had several times to mollify enraged gamekeepers, orchard wardens, and schoolmasters, and, on one occasion, never to be forgotten, the local Constabulary.

Yet Sir Charles's justified anger on these occasions was as nothing compared to his rage when he caught Rudyard dapping for chub with Albert Thompson and William Everest. Shortly before this unfortunate encounter took place, war had been declared on Germany and her Kaiser, and David had immediately written to inform his father that he had volunteered, and had (on the recommendation of his Tutor at the Hall) been appointed to an Intelligence Unit in London.

In this he had gone against Sir Charles's wishes, and Sir Charles was, predictably, furious. At least the boy would be safe in London, but he, Sir Charles, had not paid for the boy to go to Cambridge so he could run off at the first opportunity and get involved in a war that looked set to cause a lot of trouble. Also at stake was the pride of the Leverets – how could David be called to the Bar without finishing his studies at the Hall? Two Leverets had been Queen's Counsels, and Sir Charles's cousin, Lord Walmisley, was relying on David to continue this distinguished tradition now that poor, raving Villiers had had to be committed. For these and other reasons, David's letter had occasioned little joy in the parental breast, leading to a general darkening of mood and a prevailing northerly wind.

As a consequence he was somewhat draconian in his treatment of Rudyard in the dapping incident. Sir Charles had come unexpectedly upon Rudyard as he sat barefoot by the river, holding a long stick with a piece of string tied to the end, and on a rough approximation of a hook, a lobworm, dangled enticingly on the water's placid surface. His new companions, the offspring of the tinker and the coal merchant respectively, were likewise occupied. Upon seeing Rudyard, he had hauled him upright by the scruff of his neck, ordering him home at once and marching beside him in a glowering silence that boded ill for the future. Once inside the house he let his anger loose, and it flowed out of him like a river in spate. He made it very clear that gentlemen do not associate with ragamuffins from the river; that gentlemen do not sit like vagrants at the side of muddy streams; and that gentlemen do not, under any circumstances whatever, fish for chub, roach, carp, or any other species of the coarse variety.

'Sitting at the side of a pond, staring like a simpleton at the orange tip of a float, waiting for it to disappear – why, it's not cricket!' he said, going a nice shade of puce in his rage. 'And for what? To land some fat lump of a carp, twenty pounds of him, I'll grant you, but fit for a gentleman's table? I rather think not.' And so it went on.

But Sir Charles's angry words had quite another effect from that which he had intended. Rudyard had never heard of float-fishing until that moment; nor had he envisaged the possibility of catching a coarse fish that had grown to such a monstrous size. As on the fishing trip to the Tay, he began once more to lie awake at night, only this time he dwelled not on the malevolent tones of a great river but on the bright orange tip of a float, suspended amongst clouds of bubbles released by leviathan grazing silently in the sunless deeps. The float twitches; it shifts to the side; it disappears; and now, with heart racing, the strike; and the first, sudden, irresistible rush of a weighty fish as he powers into the depths... Rudyard sighed in anticipatory delight, his face bearing a gentle look of rapture.

'I will find such a pond, with such a fish,' he would say to himself, 'and catch him on the float, like any grocer's son! Then I'll stuff the beast, and mount him on the mantelpiece, and the pride of the Leverets be damned! And how David will laugh to see that fish in uncle's drawing-room – when he comes back from London.'

⸺ ∘ ⸺

At around this time tragedy befell the Leveret family, with the consequence that Sir Charles became both more irascible and more withdrawn, alternating unpredictably between moods of violent anger and long periods of dark depression. Thus Rudyard had good reason to take himself away from the house more and more frequently, scouring the surrounding country-side for a lake that might hold the fish he sought. At first, he did so in company with Albert, William, and some other boys from the village. Before long, however, they seemed less willing to accompany him, and in any case he increasingly desired solitude. So he shed his erstwhile companions and took to wandering the countryside alone, frequently purloining his uncle's antiquated bicycle to aid his solitary journeys along lane and track.

These expeditions came to a sudden and unfortunate end, however, when the front wheel of the bicycle came off several miles from the house. Once Rudyard had staggered to a nearby public house and begged the use of their telephone, Sir Charles duly appeared in his Bentley and carted home his bruised but unrepentant nephew.

After a brief and (on Rudyard's part) particularly unpleasant interview, the bicycle was thrown into a nearby rubbish tip, and that was the end of that. Worse still, Rudyard was banned from leaving the estate until further notice.

The need to search far and wide for a place to fish was soon obviated, however, owing to a conversation with the sole remaining gardener, a wizened old man named Jukes, whose father had fought in the Crimean War. Jukes, Rudyard, and David used occasionally to sit together in Jukes' little potting-shed during the long afternoons, when the gardener had finished work for the day, and listen to Jukes' far-fetched accounts of the countryside and its history. Now that David was gone, Rudyard did not go to see Jukes so frequently; it reminded him of the gap, the seat without an occupant. But on this particular day Sir Charles had asked Rudyard to lend the old man a hand with moving some turf, as both the footman and the ostler were down with influenza. Once the last piece of turf had been laid, Jukes straightened and wiped his hands on his shirt. He looked at the young man, and said, 'I hear tell you're looking for a place to fish.'

'Yes, I am – but how on earth did you know that?' said Rudyard.

'I heard in the village that you'd been searching all around. Bain't no secret as far as I can tell. But see, you've missed a trick. There's a pond right here on your uncle's land, where he used to fish when he wasn't much older than you are now.'

'Here? Where?' cried Rudyard. 'There's no lake on this estate!'

'Nor I didn't say lake, did I? I said pond. There's a pond, all right. It's in the Old Wood.' The Old Wood was an area of wild shrubbery and trees, surrounding by brambles so tightly woven that not even David and Rudyard had ever ventured within.

'Not as how it mayn't be silted up by now,' Jukes went on. 'And I'm not saying I'd go there at night. Emily – that is, Sir Charles's first wife – well, there was something happened there – a long time ago. That's how your uncle came to stop going there, and stopped the gardeners looking after it, and planted the brambles all around it. But what I'm telling you is, there's a pond in there, and there were carp in it, too, once upon a time. I should know – I put them in there, with my old Dad, the year afore he died.'

'Oh, thank you, Jukes – thank you! I will go as soon as I may. I'll let you know if I catch anything!' he shouted back over his shoulder, for he was already hurrying up to his bedroom to prepare for a night-time expedition to the Old Wood. He had hardly heard Jukes' warning not to go at night, and in any case what did he care about that – the main thing was that there was a carp pond right here, in this very estate!

Jukes looked after the boy as he ran. 'Well, I wish it may do him some good, the poor lad,' he said to himself. He shook his head and sighed.

＊

Rudyard was all agog to explore the Old Wood, and awaited the coming of night with scarcely concealed impatience. He was not forbidden to roam the estate, of course, but from what Jukes had said, an expedition to the Old Wood would not go down well with his uncle. In any case, there was no point in taking unnecessary risks. So as soon as Sir Charles retired that evening, Rudyard carefully lifted the sash of his bedroom window and crept silently across the eaves. A helpfully situated drainpipe aided his descent, and soon he was running eagerly across the grass, moist and fresh and generously strewn with fallen leaves.

The air was intoxicating: cold and clear, with the faintest tang of distant wood-smoke. There was no moon that night, but the constellations above shone the brighter, creating soft shadows with their dim radiance, and lighting the path sufficiently to allow him to preserve the batteries of his electric flashlight, a birthday gift the year before from his uncle.

In time – for his uncle's estate was not small – Rudyard found himself standing on the rough land whose boundary marked the end of the gardeners' domain. Beyond lay the Old Wood, tangled, brooding, and darkly impenetrable – or so it seemed. But before many minutes had passed Rudyard's torch had found the vestigial remains of a path leading into the undergrowth. With determination aforethought the young man had brought his father's old cavalry sword with him; it now proved its worth in spite of ten years' rusting in Sir Charles's study, cutting through the entwined greenery in a manner that warmed Rudyard's heart; for every hard-won foot of progress would surely take him a foot nearer his goal. And indeed, less than thirty minutes' hard sword-work later, Rudyard found himself standing upon wet ground, his feet sinking into black and odorous mud. But Rudyard paid no more attention to the mud than to his rent clothing and innumerable cuts and bruises, for he must now be near the lake.

With an inarticulate cry of delight he jumped backwards, out of the mud, and began searching for firmer ground. Soon he found a small tract of land that would support his weight; underfoot were more traces of a long-forgotten path, and in a somewhat less overgrown area Rudyard's torch lighted upon the decaying remains of what must once have been a summer-house, with what looked like a ladies' parasol resting on a rotting bench. Pressing on, he cut his way through a mass of hawthorn and emerged at last, bleeding, hot, and dishevelled, but victorious, on the overgrown edge of a hidden lake.

Rudyard switched off his flashlight and stood for some moments waiting for his natural vision to return. Soon he saw a wonderful sight: a pond, roughly oval in shape, studded with water-lilies and the sharp pinpricks of a thousand reflected stars; their collected light, faint but clear, shimmered on the water's surface and danced in Rudyard's shining eyes. He breathed a great sigh of content: here at last was his hidden lake, in a corner so removed from the world that he could stop there forever, and no-one would be any the wiser. He did not mean merely to linger there, moreover; tomorrow night he would return with rod and line, home-made float and weight, and a jar filled with worms and gentles, to tempt the great fish that, he hoped and believed, still haunted the depths below. And then his joy would be complete.

He prepared to leave, casting one final look around the pond – but suddenly he froze with shock. Was that a man standing there – there, beside the willow-tree? Had he seen the shape of a hat, the glint of an eye, an arm resting on the willow's trunk?

'Who's there?' he called out. There was no reply.

His heart pounding madly in his ears, Rudyard slowly,

unwillingly, switched on his torch and raised his arm until the beam was pointing at the willow.

There was nothing there. Rudyard laughed aloud in relief, the sound echoing around the hidden lake. But then he was angry: he had made a fool of himself. He would have to hold his nerve more firmly than this, if he was to return and catch a carp. It had just been a trick of the dim starlight, a faint shadow falling in an awkward manner on a willow branch. Or so he told himself; but as he returned to the house his knees were trembling.

Consequently it was some days before Rudyard worked up the courage to return to the lake, and when he did so it was at the first sign of dawn rather than at midnight. Red streaks of light had already splashed the sky with colour when Rudyard set out with creel and tackle, and by the time he had forced his way through the undergrowth for the second time the October sun had pushed his heavy rim above the horizon. The chances of Rudyard's absence being noted in the house now increased with every minute that passed, for his uncle was a poor sleeper, especially of late, and was rarely to be found abed after eight in the morning. And of course Rudyard had to go to school every morning, while weekends were spend under strict supervision. But, with a bit of luck, one hour of fishing could be snatched before school each day, and Rudyard was determined to use them well.

Thus he approached the lake with care, treading softly lest his step alarm the fish. When he reached the pond, he pushed his way gently through the undergrowth until he reached the willow-tree; for there he would be less visible to the fish. It had crossed his mind that this was also the spot where he had thought to have seen a man, but an examination of the ground revealed no footprints, and in any case the wan morning sunshine dispelled any such fears. The pool bore an entirely different aspect from that which it had shown on his nocturnal visit, now glowing not with the silvery radiance of the stars but with a yellow light shot with the green of the lilies and softened by the dull white of their dying flowers. Around the water, Rudyard now saw, were trees and bushes of diverse species, some with leaves bright ruby and crimson, others verdant still, and yet more whose branches were nearly bare with the onset of autumn: the water danced and shone with their various reflections. But Rudyard had no eyes for scenery: with all his being he tried desperately to force his vision beneath the surface, down, deep down to the lake's obscured depths, to seek out their scaled inhabitants.

For five, ten, perhaps fifteen minutes he looked in vain, peering eagerly around the pond for signs of watery life, but to no avail. Surely the carp had not died out, poached by cormorants or swallowed by the encroaching silt?

But wait – something stirs in the depths – a ripple appears on the surface – and then, joy of joys, a wave is thrown into existence by the thrust of a mighty tail. Rudyard, vigilant and wary, maintained his hunter's silence; but he sang for joy within, and his young and recently sorrowful face now expressed a rare and heartfelt delight. Carefully he eased back from his observation point under the willow and began to reach for his rod.

'About fifteen pounds, I'd say,' remarked a familiar voice.

Rudyard shot backwards from the sound and nearly fell into the water, only saving himself by hooking his arm around a low-hanging willow branch. He pulled himself back from the brink and stood facing his interlocutor.

'David!' cried Rudyard, his face white with shock. 'What the devil are you doing here?'

'Hang on,' said David, smiling. 'Can't a fellow come and say hello to his cousin once in a while?'

'Well, yes – but you're – that is, I thought you had – I mean, aren't you in London?'

David smiled again. 'That's right, old chap,' he said softly, 'in London. But I wanted to come and see you, before – well, before I have to go back.'

'How long do you have? And why – why are you wearing cavalry dress?' For David was indeed attired in The 10th Royal Hussars's blue and gold. 'I thought you were in Intelligence,' went on Rudyard. 'I mean, I know that you weren't – well, you know what I mean.'

David smiled and nodded. 'I'm not sure entirely how long I have – but until the end of autumn, at any rate. And never mind the uniform – you know us Intelligence chaps, we often need disguises!'

'Well, it's wonderful to see you!' replied Rudyard. 'But how on earth did you know I was here? Are you staying in the area? Why haven't you been to see Uncle? He will be terribly upset to hear you haven't been to see him.'

'I just knew you would be here. And don't worry about Papa. The time isn't right now – but when it is I'll go and see him.'

'What do you mean? Why can't you see him now? It might cheer him up – at least, I hope it wouldn't upset him – but I can't see why he wouldn't...'

'Don't worry, old chap – it will all be fine, you'll see. I can't explain what has happened. But it's important that you don't worry.'

David placed a hand softly on Rudyard's arm as he said this; it felt very light, and Rudyard suddenly noticed that David was looking pale and thin.

'You need feeding up. Here, have some of my breakfast – I pinched it from the kitchen last night.' And he revealed half a fish pie, wrapped in a greasy handkerchief.

'Maybe later,' said David. 'That fish pie doesn't look very appetising to me. And anyway, speaking of fish, aren't you supposed to be trying to catch one?'

'Yes – that's right. You can help me! I wish we'd tried for carp here before. Why didn't we? Anyhow, at least we can do it now.'

'Come on then,' said David. 'Cast a line into the water, and let's catch the blasted thing! That is, if you haven't scared them all off with the racket you made earlier.'

They cast a line to where the fish had been seen, but without much hope of a bite. And whether the carp had indeed been spooked by the noise, or whether a choice bunch of gentles simply failed to entice them to feed on a cold October morning, the float remained stubbornly immobile until it was time to wind in and head for home.

There was a point in the Old Woods at which the remains of the path reached a fork; Rudyard now saw that David must have come to the pond along the second path, which led away from the house.

'Where are you staying? Is it with the Radens? I always knew you liked Janet,' said Rudyard.

'No – not at the Radens. Don't enquire too deeply – Intelligence work, remember,' said David.

'Fine, fine,' said Rudyard testily. 'Be mysterious. Just don't blame me when Uncle finds out!'

'Same time tomorrow?' asked David.

'Same time tomorrow,' replied Rudyard. And they headed their separate ways.

As October drifted on and turned into November, the cousins met almost daily at the pond. They fished intently, but without success save for a handful of tiny dace and a gudgeon or two. Often they talked, exchanging stories and fond reminiscences; but sometimes they merely sat and watched the falling leaves as they detached from the branches and drifted slowly on the air, side to side and downwards, before landing with sad, gentle finality on the pond's surface. Rudyard noticed that David watched the leaves intently, his eyes following their descent with an almost hungry look. He also noticed that David was looking even paler and thinner, if that was possible. He wanted to ask him why; he wanted to ask many things, but David had become so enigmatic, and Rudyard felt that he didn't like to be questioned any further. So he did not ask.

Towards the middle of November, Rudyard missed three days' fishing in one week owing to Sir Charles having suffered from an unusually bad bout of insomnia. For three whole nights, Sir Charles had walked the house, distressed, at all hours of the night and into the morning in a vain search for sleep and consolation, before finally collapsing in an exhausted heap in his study. The doctor was called, and prescribed a mixture of aspirin, whisky, and bed-rest for seven days in a row – a prescription that suited Rudyard to the ground, as it took his uncle out of the equation for a time. David had said he would have to go at the end of autumn. There weren't many leaves left on the trees; autumn was nearly gone. Well then, thought Rudyard, now was the time to push on and catch one of the carp before he disappeared again. There weren't many leaves left.

The morning after the doctor's visit, Rudyard gathered together his tackle and rushed out of the house, narrowly avoiding a collision with two of the maids, who had arisen early to wash the dining-room linen. The elder of the two tutted, and turned to her companion.

'If you ask me,' she said, 'it's Master Rudyard who needs the doctor. He's as white as a sheet these days, and ever so feverish.'

'He gives me the creeps, with those staring eyes of his,' said the younger maid. 'He wants watching, he does.'

But at that time the only thing Rudyard wanted was to get to the pool as quickly as possible. Rudyard had had no way of communicating to David the reason for his absence over the past few days, and he had been worried that David would have given up and gone away. But no – there he was, perched on a low branch and quietly smoking a cigarette.

'There you are, Rudyard!' David whispered. 'Where on earth have you been? – Well, it doesn't matter – you're here now. And I've seen the monster. Put a worm on your hook and cast to that bed of lilies – there, where the bubbles are. I saw him there not five minutes ago. As broad as a Labrador, with his sides flashing gold and bronze.'

In a delirium of haste Rudyard did as he was told, and soon the float nestled gently between two great lily-pads. The two cousins watched it as if their lives depended on it, and Rudyard soon became mesmerised by the orange-tipped peacock quill. A minute passed, then two, and Rudyard, his whole being projected onto the slender float, began to believe that it would hang, suspended and immobile, until the end of the world. With every fibre of his being he entreated and willed the float to move – and at that precise moment, at long last, it did. First it jerked to the side, the movement causing a cascade of infinitesimal (but infinitely welcome) ripples – then it dipped, once, twice, a third time – then, longed-for sight, it slowly and inevitably sank beneath the surface of the hidden lake.

Rudyard struck.

A second's pause, endlessly prolonged; then all hell broke loose. The huge fish convulsed with titanic strength, forcing a great mass of water aside; he jumped clear of the lake's surface, the morning light glistening on his muscular flanks; then he dived deep, deep into the darkened depths, pulling Rudyard's split-cane rod round to its utmost extent. The fight was long and hard, the carp striving first this way, then the next, in a desperate attempt to seek safety and freedom in the tree-roots that buried themselves in the lake on all sides. Many times Rudyard believed the fish must be lost; but each time he somehow fought him back, driving him with every ounce of strength and coaxing him nearer the bank, until finally, after nearly an hour of almost unbearable suspense, the great fish toppled his bulk over Rudyard's net and was lifted onto the bank.

Rudyard unhooked him then, and cleared the fish's sides of the weed and detritus they had gathered in the journey from pond to ground. Rudyard held the creature up, to see him better; and never was a better fish taken, he thought: a pure thoroughbred, from tip to tail, abounding in vitality and beauty and strength: the fish of a lifetime.

'Better than any salmon!' said David. Rudyard smiled a smile of great joy, and nodded his agreement; words were beyond him.

Rudyard had intended to keep the fish and have him mounted, but now that he saw the creature up close he could not bear the thought of killing him; and soon he stooped, and placed the carp in the water once more, and allowed him to swim slowly, powerfully, into the waters whence he came. Rudyard then turned to David, as if to justify his action, but David checked him without a word, and in his eyes was a look of understanding and love.

Yet Rudyard's joy turned to concern when he saw David's eyes narrow and his face darken with sorrow. His cousin's gaze had moved beyond Rudyard's excited face to look upon a tree at the far end of the pool. From this tree, a single, red leaf – the last leaf to fall – silently and reluctantly detached itself from the bough, and fell, twisting, to the quiet waters below.

III

The old man had been silent for some minutes, his eyes bright with unshed tears. I was reluctant to interrupt his narrative, but feared I would never hear its end unless I prompted him. So I asked him: 'And did you tell your uncle about the fish?'

He didn't reply immediately, but after a minute or two he turned his face to me and said, in tones of inexpressible weariness, 'Why would I? Fishing – it's the ruin of half the youth of England.'

And then he got up and walked slowly away. I called after him and asked him to stay and have another drink, but he didn't answer.

The waiter, Eduardo, had been sitting at the bar listening to the old man's story; I turned to him then and remarked, 'I spoke too soon. I broke his train of thought.'

Eduardo came over and sat in the old man's chair.

'No, Senhor – you could not understand, but he would not have finished that story in any case. He never does. There was an Englishman I met here once – he had known Senhor Leveret at school, I think – and he told me a thing that made me weep – yes, me, Eduardo, a head waiter, who has heard many tales. For he told me that Senhor Leveret's cousin, the Senhor David you have heard about, he did not enrol in the Intelligence in the war. No, he enrolled in the exército – the English army. He got on a ship – and this ship, it take the men to France – to the war, you understand. Well, this ship had bad weather. It had very bad weather and big waves, and it turned over and sank – it sank in the first week of the war, and the Senhor David, he was drowned. They never find his body.

'And as for the rest – well, Senhor McKean, you and I are men of experience, and have seen many of the things that pass in this world – many, but not all.'

He got up then, and threw his dishcloth over his shoulder; the waiter had returned.

'And now, Senhor – another gin?'

Buffy's Story

THE NEXT meeting of the Sconcing Society did not take place until some six weeks had passed, owing largely to an unexpected run on sterling that kept Sharpe and Penrose in Whitehall on a more or less permanent basis. Sharpe was obliged to postpone his visit to the Porson estate, and many of Buffy's frequent telegrams requesting information on possible dates for the next dinner went unanswered. In time, however, the crisis passed, as crises always do; and a warm evening in mid-May saw Sharpe and Penrose sitting together and smoking on the gallery of Somerset House. The indistinct sounds of the river-borne traffic floated up to the erstwhile Seat of the Admiralty, creating an agreeable air of distant industriousness that soothed overwrought nerves.

'How good it is not to be at work,' said Sharpe, exhaling luxuriously. 'I feel as if I have packed an entire year's worth of hard labour into these past few days.'

'Let's not think of all that now,' said Penrose. 'Indeed I can hardly remember any of it in detail, I'm so confound-edly jaded... I need a holiday, as I've never needed one before. And as the Old Man was good enough to give me a few days extraordinary leave, I mean to take one.'

'I'm owed some leave too. Look, why don't we go and see Buffy? I'm positively crying out for some fresh air, and it would at least put an end to his blasted telegrams...Do you know this fellow Henton?'

'Buffy's pal? I was at school with his brother, Henton Major, and I always thought him rather a bounder, but of course Henton Minor might be different... Do you?'

'No, though I understand he did rather well at Balliol, and I hear that he is well spoken of at the Hurlingham. I suppose a man who scores thrice in one chukka against the Calcutta can't be all bad... Anyway, we'll find out if we go to Buffy's this week – he has him as a guest for a few weeks.'

'Fine,' said Penrose. 'You send the telegram. We'll motor across if it's all the same to you – I want to see how the Lagonda does on that stretch near Newbury; capital country for hard driving.'

If Sharpe's watch is to be trusted, the Lagonda did very well indeed on the aforementioned stretch, beating Penrose's previous record time by a good three minutes. Unfortunately, the same cannot be said for the circuitous and winding road between the White Lion in Marlborough and the Old Sun Inn in Melksham, where the Lagonda acquired a worrying rattle. Penrose diagnosed a blown piston – probably brought about by the furious pace set by him on the preceding reach – and so it was with a suitably lowered speed (and a suitably chastened driver) that the journey to the Porson estate was completed. Buffy noted their unsteady, clanking progress through the Park and was at hand to greet them at the door, together with a bluff, red-headed young man whom they surmised (correctly) to be Henton. Buffy and Henton were already in evening attire.

'What on earth happened to you chaps?' said Buffy. 'We had just about given you up for dead, and were about to go into dinner. Well, better late than never, I suppose, although I was looking forward to polishing off your crèmes brulee for you... Henton, this is Sharpe – and Penrose – good chaps both, as I have been telling you, although rather unreliable.'

'Don't listen to a word he tells you, Henton,' said Penrose as they shook hands. 'Buffy's a good fellow too, but his veracity is not to be relied upon – as will be fulsomely demonstrated by whatever far-fetched yarn he's settled upon for the evening.'

'Well, I couldn't comment on that, of course – duty to one's host, and so on,' said Henton. 'But I must say I'm glad it isn't me for the chop tonight – I'll need to put in some practice before I could get outside a quart of ale in one fell swoop!'

'Well, that's enough jaw,' said Buffy. 'You chaps had better get changed – aperitifs in the Blue Room in a quarter of an hour. Here's Davies' – the butler – 'he'll show you to all the right places.'

Two and a half hours, five courses, three bottles of fine Burgundy, and six cigars later, the four men were to be found reclining in the well-upholstered arm-chairs with which Buffy's great-uncle had so wisely festooned the smoking room. Having seen to it that all the decanters were close at hand, Davies silently withdrew and left at least three members of the Society in a state of pleasurable anticipation – for Davies had also filled with ale a magnificent silver stein (an heirloom of Buffy's great-grandmother, who had been some years at the Schloss in Heidelberg), leaving it in full view on a side-table close to Buffy, who grinned wryly.

'I had rather hoped that Davies would forget that particular instruction,' he said. 'But it falls to us all to face up to our tasks manfully –'

'– and the Society was your idea!'

'– and the Society was, as you say, my idea,' Buffy went on. 'So without further ado, I shall crack on and present to you my tale, entitled (for I feel a title raises the tone somewhat), "The Prince and the Pauper".

'The story begins in the French Alps, although it ends a bit closer to home. As you know, I like to spend a few weeks every year at Chamonix – climbing, principally, but with a fair bit of ski-ing in more recent years. I usually run into a fair number of men I know over there, and this particular year was no exception: within a couple of days of getting to my hotel I came across Durant – you remember Durant, Penrose? – The chap with a passion for geology. He used to gad around with O'Connor, each as crazy as the other. Well, Durant hasn't changed a bit: still as mad as a hatter, and can drink any man I know under the table.

'As a matter of fact it was his enormous capacity for wine that led to my downfall, and to the chain of events that I will narrate in this story. One night we fell to boasting about our climbing exploits, you see, and it was to the accompaniment of a particularly fine Margaux that I told Durant I was damned if any man could climb the eastern side of the Col du Chardonnet faster than me. It was a foolish boast, born of the wine rather than my better judgement, and I suffered for it, you may be sure – for Durant instantly pulled me up on my boast, and wagered he could do the climb more quickly. Rashly, I rose to the challenge; and the next morning saw the two of us setting out for the Col – in my case, rather the worse for wear from the night before.

'Well, to cut a long story short, Durant proved the better man on the ice, and although it was still a close-run thing he ended up besting me by a good ten minutes. As I panted up the final straight and scrambled around the overhang he was already standing there, observing me with an amused look on his face, and barely out of breath, blast him!

'"Porson!" he cried, as I threw myself prostrate on the ground. "I wondered when you would show up. Observing the scenery, were you? Quite a pretty little stroll, I grant you, but hardly warranting your current theatrics… I should watch out, or you'll have an apoplexy…" and many more witty observations of this sort.

'"How did you get up so damned quickly?" I asked, once I had ceased puffing like a grampus. But he wouldn't tell me. I suspect he must have cut sideways across the ridge about two-thirds of the way up – it looked impossible to me, but he must have encompassed it nonetheless.

'Anyhow, whichever way you look at it, there it was – I had lost my wager, and you may be sure Durant was going to make me pay for it.

'"I have been making good use of my long solitude here at the summit," he said, "by drawing up a suitable forfeit for you to carry out – and I believe I have come up with the goods."

'He was right about that – it was pure dynamite. He had just finished reading Buchan's *John Macnab* – it's a shame Buchan couldn't join us this evening, in parenthesis, as my tale is just the kind of thing he'd relish; but he said he'd try to join us next time. But to return to the rub: it was in fact dashed bad luck for me that Durant had happened to read that particular "shilling shocker", as Buchan calls them, for it was the inspiration for the most devilish scheme ever dreamed up by one sportsman for the torment of another. Durant's idea was that I must, in the space of three consecutive days, filch a poacher's snare, a Master of Foxhound's top hat, and a shooting man's flask.

'"…and post said items to me, at my Club, by the end of the month," he concluded.

'Well, I wasn't very happy about this, as you may imagine – pinching a copper's helmet on Boat Race night is one thing, but stealing from fellow countrymen and sportsmen – why, it went against the grain. But, however, Durant was resolute, and all things considered I couldn't very well refuse.

'Nevertheless it was with a heavy and somewhat apprehensive heart that I cut short my stay in Chamonix – for if I was to have said items with Durant by the end of the month I had a stiff job of work ahead – and reserved a compartment on the Paris train. Once back in Grosvenor Square, I marshalled my forces and set about formulating a plan of attack. Durant's rule requiring me to carry out the operations on three consecutive days meant I had to be strategic about choosing my battlegrounds, but of course I wanted to maximise my chances of success too… In the end I settled upon three places I know pretty well, within about two or three hours' drive of each other. That, I thought, should give me sufficient time to do the job, make good my escape, and get settled back into my lodgings – a centrally located inn where I had stayed before – in preparation for the next challenge.

'Well, the poacher's snare was easy enough. There's a little hostelry I know in a hamlet on the road to Guildford, where a mixed crowd gathers most evenings, and where I was fairly sure of a meeting chaps who weren't averse to taking the odd rabbit or two, and perhaps a pheasant on the odd occasion, if nobody was looking. One man in particular caught my eye, once I had forced my way into the packed, smoky bar. He had on a spacious, well-worn sports jacket with some promising bulges in the pockets, and at closing-time (some time after the legal definition of such, I may add) I stuck on his heels like glue – at a safe distance, of course.

'I've a pretty good nose for these things, and it wasn't long before he vindicated my faith in his villainy by ducking down a leafy path and pulling a snare out of his voluminous pockets. When all was set in place he looked warily about him (and the ferocious glint in his eye made me glad I had chosen a safe spot behind a substantial English oak) and set off down the path again, doubtless with other nefarious ends in mind.

'After that it was easy: I undid the snare and stowed it in my pocket. Then, because I felt obscurely guilty, I scribbled a few lines on the back of an envelope and pinned it to a five-pound note.'

'That was good of you, old man – though I doubt the keeper would thank you,' said Sharpe.

'Well, I felt bad enough about stealing from the gentry, but dash it all, your average poacher isn't well endowed with the blessings of the world. And I must confess to a sneaking admiration of the man who gets his partridges from the wrong side of the hedge... It shows a certain spirit, after all. And those of us with interests in politics or commerce know how thin the line is between integrity and hypocrisy... In any case, I felt benevolent towards Mr. Poacher, for, after all, I had been successful in the first part of the challenge; and I motored back to my inn in a mood of some satisfaction.

'I enjoyed the same success when it came to the Master

of Foxhound's top hat on the following day. I decided to play the part of a foot-follower at the ----' – here Buffy named a well-known Buckinghamshire hunt – 'and a foot-follower, moreover, without much in the way of brains.'

'That should have presented no great difficulty,' put in Sharpe.

'Ha! This from the man who once bicycled straight into the Isis – in a dinner jacket, too.'

'At least I was never found face-down in the New College geraniums…' began Sharpe; but Penrose broke in. 'I say, let's not get into a slanging match, you fellows; I think we all of us have some episodes we would rather forget – but can't you get on, Buffy? You were telling us about the foot-follower without much in the top drawer.'

'Yes – so I became a foot-follower for the day – what then? As you know, there's a lot of milling about at the start of every meet – mustering the pack, getting the overweight colonel into his saddle, knocking back a nip of something warming, and so forth. Now, a determined man can accomplish much in this kind of chaos. Accordingly, in my persona as an idiotic follower – mentally I christened him "Jorkins", and set him up as a Maidstone banker out for a jaunt in the countryside – I became excessively familiar, tipping my pork-pie hat to the whipper-in and calling out cheerily to a formidable lady whom I saw seated on a handsome mare. I endured some moments of tension, as you can imagine, especially as I was known by two or three men there; and had I not been hiding behind an expansive set of false moustachios and mutton-chops I would have fairly quivered with embarrassment.

'Worse still was my principal task, which was to approach the Master himself. He was at school with my father and my uncle, and I was certain that he would recognise me as I sidled up to his horse – a well-knit bay with a chest like a barrel – and leaned over his boot to caress the animal's noble flank. Thankfully my worst fears went unrealised: there was no spark of recognition in his eyes as he became aware of my faux-pas, yelled "You, sir! Stand away!", and laid into me with his horsewhip. I cowered away from him, uttering feeble words of apology – but secretly thanking my stars that my ploy had succeeded. I had laid up half the night puzzling out how on earth I was to get away with the top hat, and had eventually come to the realisation that my only chance was to do it without him noticing it, and when nobody else was around.'

'What a genius was lost to crime,' said Penrose, 'when you decided to go straight. Such insight! Such originality!'

'Ha!' said Buffy. 'Wait until you hear what I did, before you sneer in that unattractive manner. As I was saying, I knew I'd never get his hat off unless he was on his own, and I also knew I'd never do it unless he was distracted by something else. When would a Master of Foxhounds be at his most distracted, and when would he be most alone? Well, when you put it like that, the answer is obvious, if your Master is a thruster (as mine was): his hat must be got when he is giving chase.

'Very well: I had settled that. But how was it to be got? I came up with all kinds of schemes – tying ropes across hedges; riding alongside him and reaching across; even casting a line with a fly-rod, hooking the hat, and plucking it wholesale off his head, à la Marryat! But none of these was any good. The rope scheme would never work – how was I to know which hedges they would jump? The riding scheme was out of the question, for the Master is a better horseman than I am, and would simply ride me down and take it back. And as for the fly-rod idea... Well, I can't think of a better definition of lunacy than a chap lurking around hedges trying to catch a top hat – and I would still need to know where he was going to jump.

'It was only when I had almost given up, and was musing on my own hunting experiences, that it came to me. I remembered a time when I was out with the Pytchley, and my boot had come out of the stirrup just before a particularly high hedge. As you can imagine, I very nearly fell off – would have done, in fact, if good old Gleason hadn't caught me under the armpit and thrown me back on. (Gleason is a friend of mine from home, and just about the finest horseman I know.) It happened that I had gone out bare-headed that day, but as I lay there dreaming it struck me suddenly that had I been wearing a hat it would surely have come off.

'Well, the rest was easy. All I had to do was procure a sharp knife – the boot-boy at the inn obliged – and cut half-way through the Master's stirrup leather. This I did while pretending to stroke his horse. Success so far! Now, if I could just keep up with the hunt, and if the Master's stirrup leather broke on a jump, and if his hat fell off... Why, I should have a good chance of picking it up. A long shot, I'll agree – but it was all I had to go on.

'You're a hunting man, Henton, and you other fellows have been out on occasion, I believe, so you will know how impossibly difficult it can be for a foot-follower to keep up, and as it happens I didn't manage it; but as I breasted a hill I saw the Master set his three-year old at a towering great hedge – how I admired his nerve! He cleared it well – such a seat, and such hands – and disappeared over the other side, so I didn't see him land; but coming down from that lofty height must have given that stirrup a mighty jolt, and I had an expectant look on my face as I crept along the hedge and through into the adjoining field. And I'm glad to say that my hopes weren't disappointed – there lay a stirrup, attached to a frayed bit of leather; and beside it a top hat, gleaming in the pale sun and bedecked with droplets of dew from the still-moist grass.'

'That was a dashed poetic line, Buffy,' said Henton. 'You should pack in whatever it is you don't do for a living, and set up as a writer. But I happen to know the Master of that hunt, and I'm surprised that you seem to have had no qualms about robbing him – temper like Nero, a perfect volcano when provoked; and I'm sure he would have been furious to lose his hat – not to mention nearly being pitched off his mount.'

'Never you fear, old chap – I knew a horseman like that wouldn't fall, stirrup or no; and he got his hat back in the end. I'll come to that in a few minutes. But to sum up so far – I had bagged two out of three items I needed to fulfil Durant's damnable Macnab – and in only two days, too, thanks to my Bentley three-litre – how I loved that car! I still rue the day I let young Drogo, my cousin, take the wheel in St Tropez, some months after the events I am relating...He rose like a phoenix from the wreckage, grinning – grinning! – crying out that he was fine, and not to worry – he had scratched his leg, but otherwise he was unscathed. "To hell with your leg," I called out, gazing at the smoking remains of the finest car man ever made. But I digress.

'So – two out of three. So far so good, more or less, with a few hiccoughs along the way. But the third – my word, the third! That is quite a different story.

'You may remember that the third item I had to lay my hands on was a shooter's flask, a hip-flask, you know. By good fortune my uncle, of dear memory, was hosting a party of ten or so at the time at his place in Surrey, to which he had very kindly invited me.'

'You astonish me, Buffy,' said Penrose. 'I had always understood your uncle to be a man of superior taste.'

'That is presumably why he never invited you,' replied Buffy. 'But you make a good point, albeit in your usual offensive manner – my uncle was an important man, in his way, and his guests tended to be so distinguished that I felt rather awkward and out of place.

'For this reason I hadn't been to one of his house parties for an age, and he was delighted to see me – so delighted, that I felt rather uncomfortable, for of course I had come to diddle one of his guests out of his flask. Indeed my finer feelings got the better of me, for once, and I simply had to take him into my confidence. To my surprise he was most enthusiastic – gave out a great peal of laughter and vigorously shook my hand, declaring himself my devoted accomplice. In this role he straightaway urged me out of doors – not a moment to be lost – his friends were out rough-shooting this very minute, after pheasant and woodcock, and if he were in my shoes he would set out at once for the woods on the north-eastern side of the park. There was moreover a particularly genial guest of his, he said – a stout, bearded man with a shabby tweed cap – whom he particularly recommended as a suitable subject for such a caper.

'My uncle's eye twinkled brightly as he said all this, and suddenly I remembered his penchant for high jinks and practical jokes – a penchant which had once led to the German Ambassador being arrested on suspicion of rigging a knobbly knee competition. But (I reassured myself) surely he would never trick his own nephew, his own flesh and blood… Such innocence was quickly disabused. But as the matter was somewhat pressing, I shouldered aside my momentary hesitation, decided to take my uncle at his word, and set out for the aforementioned patch of woodland with a relatively light heart. My schemes had worked out fairly well so far, and there seemed no reason why I shouldn't succeed today as well, and Durant be damned!

'As I came in view of the line of shooting gentlemen, the distant sound of gunfire transformed itself from a pleasant pastoral backdrop into a rather more immediate canvas of action and intent. The bird, chivvied from his leafy hiding-place by the industrious beaters, rises indignantly and soars steeply into the firmament, a dot of black picked out against the pale blue and merino white – the sportsman arches his back (a high bird, this) and mounts his gun – he lines up his sight and tightens on the trigger – a shot rings out between the trees, then another, and the bird traces a parabola before falling to earth. A bloodthirsty spectacle, some may say; but few more appealing to the sporting eye, gentlemen.

'"Well shot, sir!" I cried, walking up towards him. "Well shot, indeed!"'

'He turned to face me as he ejected his cartridges, and thanked me for my congratulations. I noted that he had a beard, and had on a tattered old tweed cap – clearly this was the chap my uncle had suggested as a candidate for my criminal plot.

'Now that I saw him at close quarters, however, I must admit that I began to question my uncle's wisdom; for beneath the cap shone eyes of unusual perspicuity, while the beard seemed to emphasise, rather than conceal, the firm jaw of one accustomed to command. He looked somewhat familiar, too, but I couldn't quite place him. Moreover, there was another sportsman, a youngish chap, within hailing distance, and I would have preferred solitude for my underhand work. I half thought better of pursuing my scheme, but then again I was pretty keen to get it over with… and perhaps I was wrong about this chap. I have been to known to err slightly in that regard, now and again.'

'What – like the time you mistook the Earl of Mortland for the footman, and asked him to bring up a dozen of claret, and be quick about it?' said Sharpe.

'Precisely,' said Buffy. And, in an aside to Henton – 'This was at Fountainhall one year, at the Hunt Ball. But I will just say in my defence that the Mortlands are not a particularly elegant family, and are often taken up by policemen for loitering on the Mall, when they are on their way to see the Prince of Wales.

'But to return to my narrative: for better or worse, I decided to press on with my plan of action. The first stage of my scheme required me to engage the chap in conversation; consequently I did so, babbling about the weather and the birds, and remarking upon the attractiveness of my uncle's parkland. He was a courteous, well-bred fellow enough, and a civil interlocutor, although of course I could tell he was itching to get rid of me and return to his shooting. Nevertheless I drew out the conversation for as long as I decently could, and then began to hint that I would soon be on my way – adding that it was thirsty work tramping around all day. The hint was pretty obvious, and as I had hoped he fished out a hip flask and offered me a dram to speed me on my way. (At this point, I noticed that the other shooter – the young chap – had started walking towards us; presumably he was thirsty too. Confound him! I thought – couldn't he bring his own flask?)

'It was a good single malt, as you would expect – Dalwhinnie, by my guess – and I thanked him for his kindness… But before I returned his flask I pointed to the neighbouring woods and suggested that I had just seen a black grouse, wandering along the edge of the woodland. As he looked eagerly away, I substituted his flask for one I had previously hidden in my waistcoat (with malice aforethought) and pressed my own flask into his hand while his gaze was still directed abroad. When the creature in question failed to appear, I then expressed my apologies – doubtless a trick of the dappled sunlight – and bade him good day.

'Yet I had hardly walked ten yards when I heard raised voices behind me, followed swiftly by a heavy hand falling on my shoulder, and a strong, stern voice entreating me to "Come quietly, sir, if you please – it's best if we has no trouble". Sounds just like a plain-clothes officer, I said to myself – and so he turned out to be.'

'A copper?' said Penrose. 'What on earth was a copper doing wandering around your uncle's estate?'

'I'll come to that in a moment,' said Buffy. 'First I must tell you that he manhandled me most roughly, and extracted the hip flask from the pocket in which I'd placed it. Then he held it up and addressed the man in the tweed cap. "Is this yours, your Majesty?" he asked.'

'Your Majesty?' cried Sharpe.

'Yes indeed – it was the King himself. I was absolutely dumbfounded, as you can imagine, and didn't think to say a word until I found myself locked up in the local constabulary – in Market Colton; you must have driven past it on your way here. They suspected me of attempting to poison the old man, of course, owing to the switched hip flask business, which apparently had been attempted before by a genuine assassin, worse luck.'

'So how did you get out?' prompted Penrose.

'Oh, it was the most gentlemanlike thing – my uncle told HRH about my awkward position, being under an obligation to act like a blackguard, and so on – and the King saw the humour in the thing, damned my eyes, and sent to have me released immediately. Once I was safely returned to the Hall, we had a charming dinner à trois, and of his kindness he gave me his hip flask, with his compliments – said he blamed my uncle for having pointed me in his direction, and that he liked to see a young fellow who values his word. In fact I still have it – I always carry it with me.'

And Buffy passed around a small silver flask that bore the King's arms.

'So you didn't send it to Durant after all?' asked Henton.

'No, I did – of course I did, after all the trouble it had caused me. I sent it and the hat and the poacher's snare to the blighter – but he returned them, like a good fellow, bidding me keep them – he had only meant it as a joke, he said, but was profoundly impressed that I had stuck to my word. I then returned the Master's hat – said I had come across it rambling in the countryside – but kept the snare; at five pounds I considered this an excellent bargain for the poacher. So with the flask and the snare I had at least some recompense for my trouble. And thus my story ends.'

His audience rewarded him with an appreciative round of applause. Soon, however, the men's faces became sombre; and to the accompaniment of frowns, they began to discuss whether or not Buffy should be sconced. Indignantly he swore the truth of his account, and begged to be informed on what grounds he was to be thus punished.

'Why, the black grouse, of course,' said Henton.

'Indeed,' said Sharpe. 'His Majesty is a sporting man of some considerable acumen and renown; he would certainly have known that black grouse have not been seen in your uncle's county since the turn of the century – he would never have fallen for such a ruse de guerre.'

'And moreover,' said Penrose, 'you entitled your story "The Prince and the Pauper". Where is the prince, where is the pauper? We have instead a king and the heir to a great estate. So inexactitude must be added to blatant mendacity...'

'Artistic licence! Poetic licence!' cried Buffy; but to no avail.

'No, no,' said Sharpe. 'It's no good – down the hatch the ale must go, in service of honour, and duty, and the inviolable rules of the Sconcing Society!'

For Valour

I SHOULD have realised that the near-empty car park was a warning of sorts, a red flag from the patron saint of fishermen. (St Peter, I imagine?) On most summer evenings you have to be there early to find a spot – noon the day before might do it – unless of course it's voluntary river-maintenance day, in which case you'd be lucky to find a fisherman within ten miles. They're quite right, too. Last year I foolishly dropped in for an impromptu session on the dry fly without checking the Club schedule, and within ten minutes found myself standing next to a half-naked Yorkshireman, both of us up to the armpits in freezing cold mud and river weed. This year, however, I had cleverly marked all such days in my diary (in order to avoid them like the plague), and I was pretty certain the Club's beats were open tonight. So, as I said, I should have known that something was up.

When the river-fever is on me, however, I seem to lose all capacity for independent thought. The sophisticated concert pianist, the Wigmore Hall regular, the Fellow of the Royal Society of Arts fade and fall away, and I become once more an impatient eight-year-old, possessed of a cheap glass-fibre rod, and slavering with a brutish determination to catch a fish, a fish! My tools have changed – my rods and reels now cost more than my suits – but the inner child has not, and whenever I can snatch half a day away from the piano I rush to the Test with the same delighted abandon as ever. I don't know whether this is a matter for thanksgiving or concern (probably the latter), but – moral musings aside – this aspect of my character undoubtedly played a key part in what followed on this particular occasion. Were it not for my childish enthusiasm, I would scarcely have jumped into my car without so much as a glance at the sky; I would hardly have neglected to listen to the weather forecast on the radio (the Schoenberg on Radio Three was too good to resist); and I would surely have realised that the deserted riverbanks portended something worse than river-maintenance day.

I think it was during my second cast that the wall of hot air reached me. I had walked to the river in my usual state of frenzied deliberation regarding my choice of fly, line and leader, and – bar a vague realisation that the weather was perhaps a touch sultry that evening – had completely failed to notice the ominous darkening of the skies that always presages an almighty downpour. Now I looked up in astonishment as the lowering sky exhaled a long and sulphurous breath, heavy with heat and menace; and as my tangled line hit the water's surface I heard the first threatening rumble of distant thunder.

Belatedly I came to my senses, reeled in, and hurriedly began to pack up my gear. (My river-fever stops just short of a willingness to be fried by a hundred million volts, perfectly conducted through a long, thin wand of carbon-fibre.) The first enormous drops began to fall as I reached the car park, and by the time I was safely installed behind the wheel I was heavier by a good few pints of finest Hampshire rainwater. I remember sitting for some time, drying out (or trying to) with the heater on full blast, and hoping that the storm would pass over before nightfall – a vain hope, as it transpired. Muttering terrible oaths (for this was my first day off in some weeks) I pulled out of the car park and set off on the miserable drive home.

As it happened, however, I didn't get more than five miles from the Clubhouse. I was taking it slowly, on account of the torrents that constantly submerged the windscreen, but even so I damned nearly ran her down. She suddenly appeared at the left-hand side of the road – no more than a wisp of white, half-seen through an unclear glass, but destined to fold under my wheels unless I was quick. I swore, slammed the brakes on, and hoped for the best (she was dangerously close); and thank God it did the trick. I think we both stayed where we were for an instant after the car stopped – me stock-still behind the wheel, and her standing (not stood, as everyone says these days – how I hate that!) like a drooping statue, all doddering shock and ineffectual dismay – though I daresay I probably looked the same to her. Then the moment passed, and I jumped out of the car and ran round to her.

Of course I tried to find out who she was and what an old lady (she must have been at least eighty) was doing out in the storm without so much as a waterproof – she wore only a thin ruffled blouse and skirt, both now thoroughly drenched – but it was hard to get much sense out of her. All she would say was "Thank you, young man – thank you." This showed a grateful spirit but wasn't much use in terms of getting her home (wherever that might be); and naturally she didn't have a wallet or any kind of identification on her. So I bundled her into the passenger seat – my poor upholstery was taking a beating this evening – and set off for the nearest house to see if she was known there.

The nearest house turned out to be Foxley Hall, a country house of Tudor vintage that I'd passed many times on the way to the Club, although I'd never taken the trouble to go in and have a look at it. As I indicated and turned into the drive, I narrowly avoided another collision – this time with a very large horse-box. Several vans were also heading for the main road, and as we reached the house I saw a number of harassed-looking men and women running through the rain to their cars, most carrying bags and boxes of various kinds. The meaning of all this activity was revealed by a now rather forlorn-looking cardboard sign bearing the legend:

'Foxley Hall Wedding Fayre' – why do people insist on using that absurd spelling, I wonder? – and below, 'Ticket's £10, buy in Car Park.' (I will refrain from commenting upon the apostrophe.) Maybe this old woman had come as a guest, with an affianced granddaughter perhaps, and had wondered off in the rain after too much free champagne - or too much free cava, taking the sign and ticket price into account.

In any case, it couldn't hurt to ask if someone had gone missing from the 'Fayre'. With this in mind, I drew up to the main entrance, jumped out, and, realising that someone was closing the door, stuck my foot in it. After a moment's hesitation, the door swung open again, and a mottled and very elderly face, preceded by a large and bibulous nose, peered around its edge.

'Can I help you, sir?' enquired the face, which, I now realised, belonged to some kind of butler.

'Well, I hope so,' I replied. 'I found this old lady' – pointing to my car – 'wandering around on the road, and I thought perhaps...'

I got no further than this, however, for as soon as he saw who was in the car he grunted, elbowed me out of the way, and hobbled quickly to the passenger door. This he opened, and, extending a solicitous hand to my new acquaintance, muttered something that sounded like 'My Lady'. She stared at him for a long moment before responding, but eventually she said something to him – I couldn't make it out over the noise of the storm – and took the proffered hand. I grabbed one of the umbrellas that rested in an elephant-foot stand and shielded them from the worst of the rain as they made their way to the house.

Once inside, the butler shuffled off to fetch a towel, which he draped around the old lady before leading her down a side passage to a cosy little parlour – his own, I suspected. He sat her by the fire and gave her a stiff nip of whisky, talking to her all the while in a soothing undertone that I found unexpectedly moving from such a source. She didn't respond to his remarks, but seemed vaguely comforted. I hung around in the background while this was going on, feeling I ought to do something but not sure precisely what. Could this really be the lady of Foxley Hall – I half remembered hearing the name Lady Anston, or something like that, in a conversation at the Club – and if so, was this antediluvian servant really the only person she had to look after her? Nevertheless, I thought of edging towards the door in preparation for taking my leave – I had still to get back to town, the traffic would be hellish in this weather, and I had a full day's rehearsal planned for tomorrow...

I had almost resolved to slip out and get back on the road, when to my surprise I found myself tapping the old butler on the shoulder – his name, I later found out, was George Sinclair, but clearly he should have been called Carruthers – and suggesting that he get a doctor to look at the old lady.

'Her name, sir, is Lady Helen Anstey,' he replied, somewhat haughtily – a touch of his youthful pride, perhaps. But then he seemed to subside a little, and conceded the point. He directed me to an address-book that lay on the desk beside an old telephone – one of the types that have a real bell, and which require you to turn the dial all the way round for each number – and asked me to call Doctor Barclay. The good doctor agreed to leave his supper and come out to see Lady Helen, and requested that in the meantime she be put into a hot bath and given another whisky, preferably in the form of a hot toddy. (I approved of Doctor Barclay already.) The butler took care of these things, of course, but before going upstairs he asked me to wait in the drawing room next to the front door, in order to welcome the doctor upon his arrival.

The room in question was cold and unlit, and smelled rather musty, like a drawer that hasn't been opened for months. I switched on the lights, gathered my still-damp coat around my shoulders, and tried to light a fire in the grate. I soon found out that the wood was as damp as everything else in the room, so I gave up on that, and passed the time by examining the various photographs with which the tables were liberally strewn.

Evidently the Anstey family had once been both numerous and prosperous, and there were many black-and-white photos showing joyful faces on long-ago excursions and forgotten holidays. I recognised scenes from Venice, Paris, and Monaco; there were also sailing trips at Cowes, salmon-fishing expeditions in Scotland, and tennis-parties in London; and many hunting scenes from the 40s and 50s, most of which featured a dapper, monocled, and top-hatted horseman that I guessed might be the (presumably now deceased) Lord Anstey, and a younger, more thickset man, that I imagined must be a son. Yet the photographs seemed to more or less stop around the 1970s, and bar a few colour photos of a recognisably younger Lady Helen with the butler and some housemaids, there were none more recent than the 1980s. And indeed the room was furnished as if for a 1950s period drama, all chintz curtains and pincushions. It all seemed a little neglected, and somehow rather sad.

I am sensitive to atmosphere, and had begun to feel a little depressed sitting in that time-capsule of a room; so I was glad when the doctor arrived and asked where Lady Helen was to be found. I could tell that he was curious as to my rôle in proceedings, and as we walked upstairs I told him how I had met the old lady. He thanked me for my kindness, which I didn't think necessary, and told me in turn how he had repeatedly urged Lady Helen to employ a full-time, live-in nurse.

'She's eighty-three next year, you know, Mr…?'

'Arno – Christian Arno.'

'Well, Mr Arno, eighty-three is a great age, but you have to take account of it – you have to act accordingly. There's no shame in having somebody at hand, to help out when required. But she won't have it. Anyway, it's lucky you saw her, and not somebody else – so many idiots on the road these days…'

I was about to express my wholehearted agreement with this sentiment – only last month I had had to replace my wing-mirror after a close shave with a drunk driver – when we saw Sinclair, the butler, limping across the corridor with an empty glass in his hand. The doctor just had time to whisper to me – 'And he's no better; should be in a home himself' – before we came upon him and asked how Lady Helen fared.

'Ah, Doctor,' he said. 'And Mr – well, I didn't quite catch your name, sir.' And after I had told him, he went on: 'Well, Mr Arno, we're very grateful to you for your assistance. If you hadn't found her... But anyway, she's much better now, Doctor. She's had her bath, and a hot toddy, as you said, and she's in bed now and ready to see you.'

Whilst the doctor was in with her, the butler shook my hand and thanked me again for my assistance. He then went on to ask me to stay the night. Well, that is more or less what he did, although he puffed himself up and phrased it as if they were offering me a viceroyalty:

'Her Ladyship would be delighted to offer you her hospitality, and to accommodate you at the Hall to-night' – I felt certain that he would have put the hyphen there – 'in order to lessen any inconvenience you may have suffered as a result of your kindness.'

To be honest, I wasn't quite sure what to say by way of response. From what I had seen while walking upstairs, most of the house was in the same state of suspended animation as the drawing room, and I suspected that the bed-linen (about which I am inordinately fussy) would be as damp as my sodden overcoat. But on the other hand I could drive up to town tomorrow morning and avoid this storm... And of course there was the old lady. I couldn't tell for sure, but I thought there may have been a faint entreaty hidden within the butler's pompous words – as if he felt he might not be quite up to the job of looking after his mistress, but couldn't bear to say so. Again I had half decided to go, and again I found myself doing something quite different; I found myself agreeing, that is, to spend the night at Foxley Hall.

Well, it wasn't much of a night. As I had guessed, the bed-linen in my room, or rather suite of rooms – called the Garden Suite, the butler said, owing to its views of the formal garden – was thoroughly damp. After enduring a couple of hours of tossing and turning, I gave it up as a bad job and tried to get some sleep in a chair by the fire – Sinclair had at least got a fire going, and more to the point had left a decanter of good single malt on a table close by, so I wasn't too badly off.

Nevertheless I was glad to see the first glimmerings of dawn appearing over the treetops, and when eight o'clock arrived I made my way downstairs to cast about for the butler and for breakfast.

Rather to my surprise, Sinclair was already up and doing. Following the enticing scent of eggs and bacon, I found my way to an enormous octagonal kitchen, pierced through with great oaken beams and replete with the heavy ironmongery of a bygone age. Sinclair had laid the table for two.

When I entered he turned round to greet me, looking somewhat incongruous in a floral apron.

'Ah, good morning, sir! I trust you slept well? I hope you don't mind sharing the table with me this morning. The dining room has been hired out to – to someone or other; a business from Basingstoke, I think.'

'And Lady Helen?' I asked as I sat down. 'Have you seen her this morning – will she want any breakfast?'

'Oh, I've already been up to see her,' said the butler. 'She rises very early. She's – she's more in her right mind this morning, if you'll pardon me saying so, Mr Arno, and would be glad to see you this morning before you go.'

Well, I didn't particularly want to be held up by a long conversation with an old lady, and in fact I hadn't thought she would have recovered by now; but on the other hand I couldn't deny the fact that I was mildly curious about her. What had happened in her life, that she should be so alone in her old age? And I supposed the piano could wait half an hour; after all, the recital wasn't until next month. So I agreed to go up and see her after breakfast.

Eggs and bacon duly despatched, to say nothing of good beef sausages, two pots of coffee, and a ridiculous amount of toast, I wended my way upstairs for what I hoped would be the last time. My fingers were already itching to get onto the concerto's third movement – the scherzo was ludicrously difficult, and I knew I wouldn't rest until I'd mastered it. My mind drifted away into the score (as my mind tends to do), and by the time I knocked on Lady Helen's door I had almost forgotten where I was.

'Enter,' she called; with a start I pulled myself together and went in. She was sitting up in a chair by the window, bathed in the clean, washed light that so often follows a storm. I noticed the sound of birdsong floating through an open pane. She turned her face towards me, and I saw confirmed that which the drawing room photographs had suggested (but which the storm had hidden from me): she had once been a strikingly handsome woman. Her eyes were deepest blue, and of a clarity almost shocking in one so old. The doddery old woman of yesterday evening had been replaced by a very different creature – frail, yes, but with a strength and determination that I had failed to perceive amidst the downpour. She smiled, and indicated a nearby chair with her hand.

'Come in and sit down,' she said in a low and surprisingly musical voice. 'Mr Arno, is it not? Now, where might I have heard that name before? I know it is familiar.'

'Well, I'm a concert pianist,' I said, sitting down. 'You may have heard my name in that connection – I've done a few things on the radio, and I was in the Proms last year.'

'Of course, of course,' she said, her face lighting up with joy. 'Christian Arno. I remember now. I have seen your name on the Wigmore Hall music lists. I am one of their patrons, and they send me the lists several times a year. I can't go up to town anymore – I am too old, as no doubt you have noticed – but I like to read the lists and imagine that I am there. Now what was it you played earlier this year – one of the Coffee Concerts, I believe – yes – the Romantics! Chopin and Liszt, and some Schubert – am I correct?'

'Swap Schubert for Schumann and you are there,' I said. I was impressed by her memory, especially as I frequently forget what I have played in my own recitals.

'How I wish I could have heard you play,' she went on. 'Such concerts we attended, when Henry was alive – my husband, that is – the last Lord Anstey. We heard Claudio Arrau at the Albert Hall, Walter Gieseking at the Paris Conservatoire, Kathleen Ferrier at Covent Garden...'

'Wonderful,' I said, and meant it.

'Yes,' she said softly; and her eyes looked beyond me,

deep into the past. Then she sighed, and seemed to collect herself.

'But I must not delay you by going on about what is dead and gone,' she said. 'Sinclair has told me you are eager to leave us.' I made polite noises to the contrary, but she waved her hand as if to silence me. 'Oh, I don't blame you – you must have many more interesting things to do than sit around a crumbling old house, listening to an old fool like me. But before you leave I wanted to thank you for your kindness last night. I am deeply indebted to you for looking after me so well, and for getting me home in one piece. I hope you didn't have to drive around for too long, before you chanced upon the Hall?'

'Not at all,' I said. 'In fact this was the first place I tried. A stroke of good luck.'

'It was – for me,' she said. 'But I'm afraid you must have found it most inconvenient, and I will delay you no longer. Sinclair is waiting to show you to your car, and I will accompany you out myself – if you will be so good as to pass me my stick? Thank you – and if you would just help me up – thank you – we may go downstairs now.'

As we walked down the sweeping staircase, heavy with Persian carpets and thick mahogany balustrades, I took in once more the general air of decay and neglect, and was uncharitably reminded of Miss Haversham and the house from Great Expectations. Was there no Estrella here? I was still curious as to why nobody remained to look after Lady Helen except the (admittedly devoted) butler. The lack of recent photographs in the drawing room seemed to suggest a family scandal at the very least, but of course I couldn't just ask her straight out… In any case I think I'd just about resigned myself to leaving the place with my lukewarm curiosity unsatisfied when Sinclair came out of a room I hadn't yet entered, and whose open door revealed a familiar sight: daylight reflected on the open lid of a grand piano.

Now, I can't walk past a piano without inspecting it any more than I can pass a river or stream without looking for trout, and in no time at all I had steered the old lady (whose arm was in mine) to the door and was asking for permission to reconnoitre further.

'By all means,' she said. 'It is a Bechstein, and it was my wedding gift from Henry. I'm afraid, however, that you will find its appearance sadly altered since then.'

And indeed the beautiful rosewood casing bore the unmistakeable marks of misuse – white rings where cups or glasses had been set down, and a sticky brown mess on the upper part of the keyboard that looked rather like spilled beer. In response to my mute appeal, she went on: 'They did this yesterday, at the wedding fair. Some people ignored the 'private' signs and came up into this part of the house, and I'm afraid they brought their drinks with them. I have never understood why there needs to be a bar open at these things… Isn't the prospect of getting married excitement enough? But anyway, there it is.'

She walked up to the piano and played a few chords; I thought I recognised the beginning of Rusalka's *Song to the Moon*.

'It isn't just the piano, of course,' she went on. 'It's the people who come to these things – I see them slouching about in their jeans and their running shoes. Why can't anybody dress properly anymore? And half of them overweight, and guzzling the free cake and wine, and giving their dreadful children free rein to run about, shouting and screaming. One has to put up with these things, of course, to pay the bills… But when I realised they were in here, singing – I heard them from my bedroom, and I can assure you it was can belto rather than bel canto – and when I saw what they had done to Henry's piano, it was – well, it was intolerable. I think I must have lost my head and rushed out into the rain. How silly you must think me, to do a thing like that!'

'Not at all,' I said. 'To spoil such a beautiful piano – to spill *beer* over it…' I stood shaking my head in silent condemnation of such sacrilege. Then I played a few chords myself, and said to the old lady: 'But what a beautiful tone it has, nevertheless. Listen – let me clean this mess off for you, and call a French polisher to come and look at the stains. I've seen them work wonders with this kind of thing.'

'Oh, please don't — you have done enough, far more than enough.' She sat down on the stool with a sudden air of resignation. 'And it doesn't really matter, anyway — it will all go to the Moorlands, or the National Trust. Let them put it right, if they can be bothered.'

'The Moorlands?' I asked.

'Rupert Moorland, and his brood,' she replied. 'Descendants of my maternal cousin, Richard Moorland, the writer — and they have inherited all his weaknesses and none of his redeeming brilliance... Now that Henry and Alistair — my son — are dead, I am the last of the line; once I go, the estate will pass to the Moorlands, unless I bequeath it to the National Trust.'

'I'm sorry that your son — I'm sorry to hear that he is gone,' I said. Now I understood the lack of recent photographs in the drawing-room.

'Oh, it was long ago... He became addicted to drugs at university. Then he went to Australia and died from an overdose in a bar in Melbourne. I don't think about that — I try to remember him as he was here, before he went away — such a jolly, kind-hearted boy, with a tousled head of hair and never a care in the world. But he's gone, and that's that — so to the Moorlands, or the Trust, the house will go, lock, stock and barrel; and soon, when my time is spent, other people will walk in these rooms, and strangers — or perhaps worse, the Moorlands — will sit at my table. Dear old George will be bereft. The Anstey crest will just be a quaint decoration on the wall, and all this' — she swept her hand around the room — 'will simply be a good day out for families whose names are quite unknown to me.'

'The Moorlands are coming to see me again on Wednesday — no doubt they will try once more to persuade me to give it them. How I dread their visits... And the National Trust is no better. The man who came to see me said the public has a right to share the house,' she went on. 'Why, I asked him, did they build it?' She gave a quick snort of laughter, but then she fell silent. She got up and walked sadly

– I had never before realised how sadly a person can walk – to a window overlooking the park.

'No, Mr Arno,' she said softly. 'They did not build it.' And as she gazed out I saw a single magpie fly mournfully across her view – one for sorrow, of course; and though I willed another to appear, for joy, there was none to be seen.

I looked at the piano, and made my decision.

'Look,' I said. 'Let me at least get your piano cleaned up for you, as I said. And listen – I could stay for a few days, if you like – to help out around the place – to help put things in order.' I left unsaid my offer of moral support, for I knew she would reject it.

She turned to look at me. 'But what about your recitals – your rehearsals?'

'Well, this Bechstein is better than my own piano,' I said. 'I could easily practise here. Of course, the noise might irritate you – I'm learning a modern concerto at the moment, so it's not desperately tuneful…'

'Oh, never mind about that – I have heard plenty of Berg and Webern in my time!' she said, plainly overjoyed at my offer. But then she asked: 'But don't you have somebody waiting for you in London – a handsome young chap like you surely has a sweetheart!'

I smiled at the old-fashioned term, and in response told her that my fiancée, Alex, had gone away on a trip with a number of her colleagues. 'All barristers,' I went on. 'God help anyone who gets on the wrong side of them.'

'Well, in that case we – I – would be delighted if you could stay. And George – Sinclair, I mean – said that you had been fishing before you picked me up. There are plenty of tench in the lake, if that would interest you – and there is some good walked-up shooting in the park.'

'I would love to fish your lake – but I'm afraid I don't shoot.' As a twelve-year-old I had been unfortunate enough to read that Dr John Henry Walsh, a childhood hero and author of The Pursuit of Wild Animals for Sport, had lost several fingers owing to an exploding barrel. The very thought of losing even one of the digits with which I earn a living was enough to bring me out in goose bumps; and ever since that day I had, reluctantly, foresworn the delights of the grouse-moor and the rough-shoot.

I denied myself, therefore, the pleasure of taking a crack at Foxley Hall's grey-leg partridges and wild pheasants, although I almost had second thoughts when Sinclair showed me the gun-room. I have been the guest at several country houses, some of them wildly opulent; but never before have I looked upon such a pair of guns as that day at Foxley. Mere words cannot do justice to the perfect balance of two fault-lessly paired best English guns, the shimmering lustre of their walnut stocks, and the sheer virtuosity of the engraving (in particular a left-and-right brace of snipe, and an evoca-tive wild-fowling scene); all summed up and crowned by the immortal name 'Purdey.' If ever I was to become a shooting man, I remarked to Sinclair, these would be the guns for me. Reluctantly I replaced them in their case – itself an incompa-rable work of art – and left behind the ever-tempting perfume of gun-oil and scented wood.

However, while I renounced this particular pleasure, I did not stint myself in other regards during my too-short stay at Foxley. Once I had cleaned the beer off the Bechstein's keyboard, I made good progress with the concerto; and two days later, when the French polishers came in to have a look at the piano's rosewood case, I decided to get some fresh air. Sinclair produced an old split-cane rod and centrepin reel that had been given to him in his youth by Lord Anstey, and with Sinclair's help and advice (for I had done little coarse fishing at that time) I hauled a good number of fat, glistening tench out of the shallow and heavily-silted pond that masqueraded as 'The Lake'. Afterwards I sat with Sinclair in a couple of old deck-chairs outside the potting-shed, while he smoked his pipe and told me about the good old days, when the Hall boasted a staff of twenty-three domestic servants plus two full-time keepers, and when the Duke of Kent had come to stay in 1953, to shoot the grey partridges.

His reminiscences were cut short, however, by the sound of a car on the drive.

'The Moorlands,' he groaned. 'Right on time, same as last month. You'd almost think they did it on purpose. Excuse me, sir, won't you,' – and he beetled off to the house, presumably to prepare afternoon tea for our importunate guests, and to let his poor mistress know that the dreaded moment had arrived. I followed in his wake, and asked Lady Helen if she would prefer me to make myself scarce during the visit.

'Not at all,' she said firmly. 'You are my guest, and if you would like some afternoon tea, then you shall have it.' – This was not quite what I had said, but I admired her subtlety; and of course I was happy to give her some moral support against the barbarians.

The barbarians themselves, when confined to the Damask Drawing Room (so-called because of the now-fading wallpaper), seemed less fearsome than I had expected. From Lady Helen's remarks, I had built up a mental image of them as Machiavellian schemers of a rather aristocratic kind – all fine features, dark hair, and flashing eyes, with an eye fixed firmly on the big prize. In comparison with this Byronic scenario, the real Moorlands were rather disappointing. The father, Rupert, was particularly dull – he was some kind of minor bank manager, I was given to understand, and he looked just like it; he even had a little moustache – but his air of mediocre drabness also hung like a pall over his wife and their gaggle of children. I was heartily bored before ever they opened their mouths, which is a depressing way to spend afternoon tea.

The only real entertainment offered by the meal was the Moorlands' palpable discomfort and indeed resentment at my presence in Foxley Hall. Who was this upstart newcomer, their bristling faces silently whispered, and what mischief was he up to? Was he from the National Trust – or was he perhaps some long-lost relation, come to do them out of their rightful inheritance? I took to counting the number of malevolent glances the mother and father shot in my direction – twenty-two and thirty-eight, respectively – and wondered at the clumsiness of their efforts to hide their naked acquisitiveness.

The whole scenario would have been quite amusing if it had not been for the distress it caused Lady Helen – visible to me, but not, I suspect, to her last surviving relations – and if it had not been for a slight but definite sense of unease that gained upon me as the afternoon progressed. Presumably my disquiet was simply the product of an overactive imagination working on my boredom and my dislike of the Moorlands – but I could almost have sworn that the house itself was troubled. At times a faint rumble reached the edge of my hearing, as if the bricks themselves were grating and shifting upon one another; and at one point I thought I saw a thin drizzle of dust falling from the ceiling – although I found nothing when I inspected the carpet later. Nevertheless I had a strong feeling that it wouldn't do the Moorlands any good to inherit the house, for it had taken against them; and for my part I applauded its good taste, and shared the relief it doubtless felt when the Moorlands finally took their leave, having failed to secure any definite commitments from Lady Helen.

Lady Helen seemed disinclined to talk of them (I could hardly blame her), and proposed instead a guided tour of the estate. As the polishers were still at work on the Bechstein, I readily agreed. Sinclair served as chauffeur as we rattled around in an antiquated Land Rover that (like its driver) had seen better days; and as we drove she pointed out various places where this and that had happened, where Henry or Alistair or her friend Rose had said this or done that. It was full of meaning to her, and full of life, in a sense; but the lives that had filled this estate and given it meaning had run their course; and none that came after her would remember – nobody would know that Alistair had fallen out of this wall, or that Rose had sat on that old tree-stump when she twisted her ankle. As we drove back to the house, Lady Helen fell silent again; and I knew that she was seeing those figures, those dear loved ones, running again over the empty grass, or perhaps sitting, in summer dress, under a favourite tree for a picnic, long ago.

I returned after dinner to the (now pristine) Bechstein, but found that I could not launch straight into the modern concerto. I was still too charged, too full of the sorrow I had seen in Lady Helen's eyes, and I chose instead to play Liszt's

Cantique d'Amour. As I played, the setting sun kindled a glow that seemed, in its very beauty, to echo and amplify Liszt's outpouring of romantic loss; and again I felt the immense and perfectly tangible symmetry between art and life that impresses itself upon me at times of need, and which sustains me through the endless hours of arid practice. As the cadences rang from the walls, gloriously rich and unashamedly tragic, I felt that Liszt, by some prophetic magic, had somehow captured and distilled Lady Helen and the long decline of Foxley Hall; and to this day I cannot play the *Cantique* without bringing that golden, sad evening to mind, and feeling once more the bitter-sweetness of change and the ending of things.

Beside the Liszt, there was one more piece of music that I remember from that evening so full of music and memory. I went to get myself a whisky after I had finished playing, and as I replaced the decanter I heard the sound of stringed instruments coming from one of the sitting-rooms. When I knocked on the door and went in, I saw Lady Helen gazing into the fire; the *Larghetto* from Elgar's *Serenade* was playing on an old-fashioned gramophone. I could tell that she had heard me come in, but she didn't turn to look at me; I knew then that she was deeply moved, and as I reached her I was unsurprised to see a tear run down her cheek. After a long moment she smiled briefly at me, and began to talk:

'You know, my father died in the War – the First World War, although for me it will always simply be 'the War', the war that changed everything. I was only two years old when he died; and I remember my mother listening to this music all through my childhood – she said it reminded her of him. They gave him the Victoria Cross, you know; I keep it in a case over there, above the fire. Mother used to look at it as she listened.'

As I got up to look at the little scrap of metal and cloth that meant so much, she went on: 'Henry sat as a magistrate for twenty years from 1951, and I remember once he had to discipline some boys who had been caught defacing a war memorial. It seemed to affect him very deeply. He said he wished those boys could have seen what he saw in the second

War – what he did so that they could have their freedom – the freedom they abused so terribly. He said he wished he could exchange the current generation for our fathers' generation – for all the young men who died in the War, all those whose nobility and brilliance and selflessness went down to die in the Somme. I scolded him at the time for being an old stick-in-the-mud, and told him that boys would always do silly, thoughtless things; but as I get older I sometimes wonder if perhaps he was right all along...'

'Look at the Moorlands,' she went on. 'They are dreadful, but dreadful as they are, we must admit that people like them are the better sort, these days. They don't go around drinking and shouting and falling over in the streets, or committing these horrible crimes that people commit nowadays...'

'Surely people don't grow more evil over time?' I said. 'Surely the same crimes were committed in 1900 as in 2000?'

In response she simply looked at me; and while I adhered nevertheless to my essentially Whiggish views, I silently conceded the attractiveness of her old England – an England that perhaps had never existed (or at least hadn't existed for everyone), but in which an overarching morality at least received lip-service, and in which the sense of duty was stronger than the sense of right; an England in which a majority of the population still understood and valued the pastoral roots which had nurtured the country and its people for hundreds, even thousands of years; an England that, like Foxley Hall and indeed Lady Helen herself, was fading away – an England that, perhaps, had already disappeared.

'I will admit,' I said carefully, 'that I have sometimes thought it would be better to live somewhere a little – a little quieter; somewhere with fewer people, and perhaps a slower pace of life.'

She looked directly at me then, and said: 'Would you not count that as running away, Mr Arno? As – as a form of cowardice?'

'Say bravery, rather,' I said. I was slightly stung by her words, not realising their true meaning until considerably later; and I talked up the quality of life in places such as my ancestral Norway, or the eastern seaboard of America. 'I lived in Oslo for a while,' I ended by saying, 'and when you see how clean the streets are, and how,' – I searched for the mot juste – 'how *well-behaved* everyone is... We suffer by comparison, to be honest.'

'Oh, if I went away, I think I'd go somewhere quite different,' she said, shaking her head. 'I have always wanted to go to Prince Edward Island – where Lucy Maud Montgomery set her books – *Anne of Green Gables*, among others. How I loved to read her work, when I was younger! And ever since then I have wondered if that island could possibly be as magical as it sounds... How I hope so! There is less and less magic in the world these days, you know, Mr Arno... They started with God, now they're getting rid of Lords and Ladies; soon there will be no Kings or Queens left in England. But, you know, people don't write fairy tales about trade unionists or politicians!'

⬤

Three days later I found I had missed a call from my agent. Foxley Hall was like a bad hotel in one sense – it had no reception. However, I had discovered that my mobile would receive calls and texts if I left it perched on a vase in an alcove in my room, although if I picked it up it would instantly go out of contact. As a result I had become accustomed to listening to my messages from Alex with my head tilted over to one side and my back bent double; and it was in this undignified position that I heard my agent excitedly squawking about the biggest opportunity of my professional career. Matthias Goldberg had had to cancel his Carnegie Hall series – a broken wrist, or some such – and they had contacted my agent to see if I would consider stepping in. It was a big commitment at such short notice – eleven concerts in five weeks, including Beethoven's *Emperor* concerto, and with the first scheduled for next Tuesday – but, my agent anxiously added, I could chose my own programmes apart from the Beethoven, it would be madness to turn it down, and could I please call him back as soon as I could?

Needless to say, I called him back (from Lady Helen's telephone), and agreed to do it – of course I did – my agent was quite right: it was the biggest opportunity of my career. But as I packed my things into the back of my car, wrung Sinclair's hand, and shook hands more decorously with Lady Helen, I began to feel rather shamefaced. Their faces betrayed no hint of reproach, of course, but as they disappeared from sight in my rear-view mirror I couldn't help thinking that I had in some small way betrayed their trust – that I was abandoning them on the eve of battle.

In order to assuage my creeping sense of guilt, I telephoned them during my weeks in New York – regularly at first, but as the burden of giving so many recitals at short notice began to take its toll, I called less frequently; and by the time I gave my last recital I hadn't spoken to them for almost a week. On a whim I had included Liszt's *Cantique d'Amour* in the programme, and as I played it the memories of Foxley Hall came flooding back with renewed poignancy. I imagined I could see Lady Helen in the front row, sitting next to her beloved Henry as she had done so many times before; or perhaps next to an unusually dapper George Sinclair, looking uncomfortable in white tie, but bearing up heroically. Impelled by this curious vision, I made a point of telephoning Foxley Hall as soon as my usual post-recital euphoria had worn away. Rather than hearing Sinclair's familiar and lugubrious tones, however, I heard only a recorded message telling me that the line had been disconnected. Of course I knew that the Foxley Hall balance sheet was somewhat fragile – why else would Lady Helen have opened up the house to spillers of beer and spoilers of pianos? – but I had no idea that things were this bad. I resolved to take another trip to the Hall upon my return, to see what little I could do to help.

When I got back to my London flat, however, I found two items of post waiting for me that rather altered things. To be precise, I found one small letter and a Post Office note asking me to pick up a parcel from the local depot. Sighing deeply, for it had been a tiresome journey from America, I decided to go and pick it up straightaway, and get it over with. Stuffing the letter into my pocket, I set off for the depot. When I got there, the parcel was so large and heavy that I almost had to ask for help to get it into the car; and when I unwrapped it at home, I was astonished to see a Purdey gun-case emerging from the layers of paper and bubble-wrap, and the familiar, coveted pair of best guns nestling within. A small piece of paper was folded into one of the recesses, and when I opened it I read simply: 'In case you change your mind. Sinclair.'

I still couldn't reach them on the phone, and of course I wanted to thank them for this princely gift, so I decided to drive down at once, jetlag or no jetlag. As I drove I listened to a comedy programme on Radio Four, and so arrived at the familiar gates in excellent spirits. My smile lessened and died away, however, when I saw the blue-and-white plastic tape across the entrance, and read 'Police' on a number of official-looking signs scattered liberally about the gateposts. Beyond the gates I could see plumes of smoke still rising tiredly from the burnt-out wreckage of the house, and my shock was so great that I could hardly make sense of the fact that Foxley Hall was gone, and doubtless Lady Helen and Sinclair with it. Had the butler left a candle burning by a curtain – or had the parlour fire flung a piece of coal from the grate? Had Sinclair dropped his pipe, or left a frying-pan on the stove? I remember sitting motionless in my car, the engine still running, while fevered speculation ran riot in my mind.

Sooner or later I remembered the letter I had thrust into my pocket at the flat. I hadn't recognised the handwriting, but now, as I inspected it again, it seemed to have an old-fashioned look to it that made me wonder if perhaps it could be... The postmark was from Prince Edward Island, Canada, and when I opened it I read:

Dearest Mr Arno,

By now you will have returned from your concert series at the Carnegie Hall; we so loved hearing from you in New York, and were delighted that you were enjoying yourself and doing so well. You will have received the Purdeys – dear George is hoping that they will bring you round at last; and he swears by the safety of the barrels! The Bechstein is currently being kept for you at the Bechstein show-room in London, and will be yours forever – a little sign of appreciation for all the wonderful music you brought to the house during your stay.

Dear old Foxley! It is gone now, and lives on only in our memories; but I simply couldn't bear to see any more strangers there; still less could I bear the thought of it going to the Moorlands. If you hadn't come, I should never have had the courage to say good-bye to it; but in tribute to the bravery you inspired in me, I have enclosed the Cross that my father won in the War. He would be glad to know that it was in your keeping.

Helen Anstey

P.S. Prince Edward Island is everything I had imagined; there is still magic to be found in the world, if you are prepared to look hard enough! If ever you give a piano recital in Canada, do come and stay with us; and play for us, to your heart's desire.

I tipped up the envelope, and out fell the familiar wine-red ribbon and the cross pattée; and the cross bore the inscription, 'For Valour.'

I turned to look again at the ruins of Foxley Hall, which Lady Helen had destroyed rather than give into the hands of the unworthy. Criminal vandalism, some would say – but I couldn't help thinking that the daughter's valour was worthy of her father's. In my eyes, at least, she had earned the little Cross all over again.

Penrose's Story

'NO, THE BURGUNDY – I distinctly remember ordering a dozen of Burgundy – and a Gewürztraminer to follow, to accompany the cheese – and Barlowe, you did remember to lay in enough Roquefort this time? The dinner I put on for the Cabinet last month was shockingly under-provisioned...'

Sharpe's voice, uncharacteristically shrill with irritation and indeed indignation (for the butler's obstructiveness had reached new heights of late), echoed through the august chambers of the R----- Club, adding an additional and somewhat wearing layer to the usual hum of rustling newspapers and pre-prandial conversation. A tallish man with a patrician air raised an eyebrow and lowered his copy of *The Times*.

'Why Sharpe persists in staying on here – why he doesn't join us over at B------ ' – here he named another London Club – 'I cannot imagine,' he said.

'Oh, come now, Buchan,' said Buffy. 'You know how stubborn he is, and how devoted to family tradition; it would be gall and wormwood to him to leave his father's Club.'

'Not to mention their chef – Auguste Charles de Chantal – the finest chap in the cooking line since Careme himself,' said Henton.

'That's right,' said Buffy. 'Though on the other hand their cellar leaves something to be desired – I had a bottle of

Pétrus last year that was certainly corked – and their décor is positively antediluvian.'

'That's just what I mean to say,' said Buchan. 'I think –'. But what Buchan thought on the topic was destined to be lost to posterity, for at that moment a disgruntled Sharpe came bustling into the Drawing Room, with the air of one who has suffered much – Prometheus, Aeneas, Boethius.

'Ah, there you are, Buchan,' he said. 'Glad you could join us. Good to see you again, Henton – and you other chaps, of course. I believe we will be called through shortly – I have opted for the Reynolds Room this time, owing to our greater numbers. Yes – there is the footman now. Come on – follow me!'

The Reynolds Room was a charming sight, with an array of Club silver glittering in the candlelight and serried rows of portraits receding into the darkness. The company seated itself amidst a fine rattle of conversation, and soon the servants were hurrying around the table with the hors d'oeuvres. In due course, the dinner party wended its merry way to the accompaniment of repartee from Buffy, sprightly political commentary from Buchan, and an intriguing discussion of contemporary Alexandrian literature on the part of Henton and Penrose, who had befriended Cavafy, the writer, on a recent trip to the Mediterranean. The combination of good food, good wine, and good company worked its customary magic, and Sharpe could be seen visibly unbending as he put away glass after glass of a truly excellent Burgundy. (Buffy's apprehension regarding the cellar, on this occasion at least, was misplaced.)

Yet as the courses came and went and the wine changed and changed again, Penrose could not deny that a certain tension was beginning to take hold within. He told himself that this was ridiculous – that he had nothing to fear, and that he did not get nervous when advancing a proposal to the Attorney General – but his feelings proved stubbornly resistant to manipulation, and it was with a definite sensation of apprehension that Penrose beheld the circulation of the port and madeira. The name of Penrose was not renowned for nothing, however – his ancestors had not won their spurs at Ramillies and Oudenarde for lack of bottom – and he had a firm, set look on his face as he picked up a silver spoon and tapped his port glass three times.

'It's time, is it?' asked Buchan, as an expectant silence fell on the company. 'I must say I'm looking forward to this, Penrose – Sharpe has filled me in on the proceedings of your previous meetings, and it sounds like you have rather a splendid time amusing each other with your far-fetched tales. As a matter of fact I'm rather hoping to get some material for my next book!'

'Well, you're absolutely right about Buffy and Sharpe,' replied Penrose. 'Their stories were entirely unbelievable, and it was only just and right that they suffered the consequences. But if you're looking for wild yarns, you've come to the wrong shop this evening, I'm afraid, for my tale sticks to the truth as luck sticks to the Irish.'

'Ha!' said Buffy. 'We'll see about that. Why don't you get started, anyhow, instead of slandering two good men? The tankard awaits…'

'There will be no need for that, I assure you,' replied Penrose. 'Indeed I might remind you that those who seek to bring about a sconcing on illegitimate grounds are liable to be sconced themselves, so – beware!'

'But you're right, it is time for me to begin,' he went on. 'My story – my truthful, trustworthy story – took place about a year ago. I was between postings at the time, and my Chief told me to take a holiday and get away from town for a few weeks. I didn't argue with him, for I had been closely involved with the Home Office wrangling – the Witcham-Murdoch affair, if you recall – and had hardly laid head to pillow for a month or more. By a stroke of good luck I had recently received a handsome invitation from Armytage to come up and shoot some of his deer on Jura. We were at school together but had only been in touch sporadically since then, so I suspected the invitation had come at the bidding of his new bride, who used to be called Lady Chetwynd but is now called Lady Armytage, of course – Geraldine Chetwynd; perhaps you knew her from your days in Kensington, Sharpe?

'Well, in any case I hadn't seen the delightful creature for years, so I had another reason for accepting the invitation with alacrity – as if Jura's deer weren't enough! I don't know if you chaps have ever been there, but there must be at least twenty times as many deer as inhabitants. Fine beasts; and they do a fine job of keeping the place free of woodland. In turn it's the stalker's duty to prevent them from overrunning the place altogether, not least as Armytage is raising a fine plantation of palm trees – astonishing that they survive in that climate, but there it is, they do. Armytage's desmesne, I should explain, is on the south-facing side of the island, towards Islay, and so has the best of the weather. The northern side is a different story – but I'll come to that in a bit.

'Well, I had a delightful journey there: the express from London, a fine Glasgow hotel, three local trains to the coast and then a succession of ramshackle ferries – I had my heart in my mouth half the time, gentlemen, I assure you; a most invigorating experience – before finally landing at the little town of Port Askraig on Jura. Armytage met me on his palomino, leading a fine bay for my own use, and together we hacked along the single-track route to the house.

'This was my first time on Jura, and like all visitors I was struck by the sparseness of the landscape. As I mentioned earlier the deer have stripped the island of most of its primitive vegetation (although Armytage tells me the Danes knew it as the Island of Yews). As a consequence you can see for a great distance across the moorland, and I could easily make out the three Paps – Beinn an Òir, or the mountain of gold; Beinn Shiantaidh, the holy mountain; and Beinn a' Chaolais, the mountain of the kyle. I got their names from a little guidebook I bought in Glasgow, but no guidebook can do justice to the bleak nobility of the landscape as I first saw it on that blustery day in June.

'The clouds scudded overhead like great ships of the line, their bluff lines mirrored in the sea – such a blue you never saw in your life – and all the time the seagulls calling, calling in those great empty spaces… It struck me then, and haunts me still, as perhaps the most perfect corner on God's earth. And Armytage's house, built by some forgotten genius on just about the most blessed spot on the Isle, was a good candidate for a second Garden of Eden.

'Armytage's hospitality was all that you would expect, and it was wonderful to see Geraldine again. But it's tedious to hear about other people's friends, and as nobody here knows them well I won't expatiate at any length. It is probably sufficient for the purposes of my tale to know that I had a dashed good time both in the house and without. The stalking was magnificent – I shot a twelve-point beast, and could have had a sixteen-pointer, only the wind was in the wrong corner – and the fishing was both plentiful and varied. We had some excellent days exploring the unnamed lochs on the west of the Isle – I particularly remember a brace of wild brown trout, taken on the rise one breathless evening as the sun dipped into the sea – and some splendid sport on the River Corran, with goats' milk cheese, oat farls and sweet, nutty ale to regale us between spells. We also took Armytage's dory out into the Small Isle Bay in front of Craighouse, and returned with baskets of mackerel and saithe that we cooked ourselves on the shore. It was Arcadia, I tell you, and I mean to go back as soon as ever I can.

'To return to my tale: one evening Armytage was busy with his tenants, and Geraldine had ridden over to Jura House to see Ayla Campbell – you know her, surely, Buffy? – so I was pretty much left to my own devices for the time being. As you know I have something of a taste for unusual company, and as I had nothing particular to do I thought I would hack over to Craighouse and see whatever there was to be seen at the hotel. It was a fine evening – such a fine evening, indeed, that I hardly had the heart to abandon the fragrant coastal path in favour of a stuffy little bar, such as most hotels boast in those parts. As I rode northwards, however, I caught wind of the earthy tang of malt that is your one sure sign of a distillery nearby – the Isle of Jura distillery, of course – and as it is a principle of mine never to leave a local brew untasted, I hastened on to the hotel with renewed enthusiasm.

'When I arrived I found I had been quite mistaken about the stuffy little hotel bar. It was, in fact, a perfectly delightful hostelry, with an altogether charming (and furiously scrubbed) little saloon furnished with relics of the past age – curling pictures of three-masted ships, ancient telescopes, and fishing nets – you know the sort of place I mean. They had an excellent selection of malts, too, though of course I plumped for Isle of Jura. It was still quite early and I found a table without any trouble. I sat down, lit my pipe, and sipped my whisky, awaiting the advent of such company as might appear.

'This method of entertainment rarely fails; it enlivened many a slow evening during my postings overseas, and to this day I count an Uzbekistani sheep-herder and a Somalian prince as among the most interesting fellows I have ever met. Neither was I to be disappointed on this occasion, for within half an hour a group of locals burst in, smelling strongly of fish, and demanded beer and whisky. ('Not much call for anything else around here,' the landlord told me later, although he was clearly an optimistic man – I noticed a crate of claret under the counter, and I would swear I saw an ancient bottle of good port behind a keg of ale.)

'They were a pretty diverse lot. There was an ancient man of the sea, with a face that should have been painted by Sargent; another chap, clearly his son, about twice his size and with a great beard to match; and a couple of stunted young lads with faces prematurely aged by wind and spume. Another man there was too, a sprightly fellow of about middle-age, with a puckish ginger beard and shining eyes. As it happened this was the fellow who provided my entertainment (and indeed the impulse for this story), for as soon as he had downed his first pint – a thirsty lot, these islanders, and it went down in the twinkling of an eye – as soon as he had downed it, his eyes darted around the little snug and fixed upon me.

Clearly I was a stranger and somewhat out of place, with my smart new tweeds and pale, Sassenach face; but this bothered him not a jot – not this lad! Straightaway he headed over to my table, and without so much as a by-your-leave he sat himself down at my side.

'"Darroch's the name," said he, with a great grin splitting his face. "What's yours?"

'"Penrose, as a matter of fact," I replied. "Will you join me in a drink?" He said he would, so I signalled to the barman and he brought the drinks across. He quaffed deeply and sat back in his chair, scrutinising me carefully with his bright emerald eyes.

'"And what would an Englishman be doing on the Isle of Jura?" he asked. The words were perhaps somewhat pointed, but I could take no offence from this chap — he was a born sportsman, that was as clear as day. So I replied civilly enough, mentioning a visit to some friends and a spot of sporting endeavour along the way. In response to a further enquiry, I alluded to my luck with the stag and the trout, and with the sea-fish. He seemed quite happy with my answers to his questions, and indeed chuckled away to himself quite happily for such a long time that I began to wonder if he might be quite right in the head.

'When he looked up again his eyes were perfectly sane, however, and he began to tell me a very interesting story about the whirlpool of Corrievreckan. Have any of you heard tell of it? Well, nor had I — but I made up for my ignorance by the end of my stay, I can tell you.

'It's a great whirlpool that sulks and growls up at the north end of the island, in the middle of the gulf between Jura and Scarba. Armytage tells me the Gulf descends to a fearsome depth in what the natives call the Gateway to Hell, and that out of the Dantesque gloom a great underwater stone pinnacle rises to within a few fathoms of the surface. As the tide runs northwards it sucks the Clyde Estuary dry and races at a tremendous speed into the narrow strait between Jura and its neighbour; then the water gets sucked down, and thrust up again, and undergoes all kinds of convulsions — your circus contortionist would scarcely get a look-in — with the result that a great and hideous whirlpool is formed. Such a vortex, such a maelstrom, you can hardly conceive! And soon I would be sucked into its ghastly maw — but I mustn't anticipate.

'Darroch's tale, which you rotten lot would probably sconce if you heard it, related to sightings of a strange creature in the whirlpool over the past few weeks. "A funny wee look it had, ma cousin tell't me," he said. – Well, perhaps I will leave the Scottish dialect to Buchan from now on, if it gives Buffy such amusement, and continue as if Darroch spoke in the King's English. "An odd look it had, my cousin told me," he said. "Like a great fush – er, fish – swimming around on the surface of the Pool." His cousin had never seen anything like it, was staggered by its size, was struck by its resemblance to his Great-Aunt Abigail, and so forth. Darroch went on to note that no islander had yet been able to land the strange fish, before suggesting that no doubt a sportsman like myself would like to have a crack.

'Clearly Darroch was making game of me, but as I was enjoying the entertainment I decided to call his bluff and play along. I asked him where exactly the Pool was, at what times the creature was usually sighted, and so forth. He was very forthcoming, as you might expect, as were his companions (who had come over to join the fun as soon as they heard the name of Corrievreckan), and when I left the hotel some hours later it was to a veritable deluge of suggestions, directions, and wishes of good luck.

'Armytage was rather sceptical upon my return, as you might reasonably expect – he mentioned that he had heard these kind of stories before, and that I would do well to ignore them. But I was determined to set out and give it a shot. I was rather taken with Darroch and his tall tales, and wanted to show the fellow that I wasn't afraid of any little whirlpool, or of any yarn he could dream up. And in case I was pretty curious by now about the Pool, which sounded like a fairly interesting place.

'Armytage is a good fellow and didn't put up too much of a fight; indeed, the next morning he helped me to launch the dory and get the Seagull outboard motor going. He gave me a couple of charts in a waterproof packet, some stern advice about not venturing too close to the Pool, and a leather satchel with some provisions that Geraldine had put up, and set me on my way. I love a fellow who doesn't fuss!

'The sea can be pretty rough in those parts and I had on my oilskins, but as it happened it was a pretty smooth journey up the Isle's eastern coast and into the Sound of Jura. After a while I found the warmth of the sun and the sound of the engine's steady toiling rather soporific, and was obliged to take off my skins and splash my face with sea-water to stay awake. As I motored along the coastline, bleak, low-lying, and rather beautiful, I remembered what Geraldine had told me about the myths of the Pool over breakfast that morning.

'The 'old people', as she called them, held that Cailleach Bheur, a hag-witch of winter, uses the strait between Jura and Scarba as a wash-pot for her plaid for a period of three days, thus impelling the turn of the seasons. When she is finished with her laundry and her plaid is pure white again, its whiteness becomes the snow that falls upon the country, and covers it from peak to peak, and fills all the depressions in the land. As I say, it was a cheerful day, with warm, benevolent weather; but as I steered I meditated on the desolate ages in which such legends had been formed, by sages whispering in the darkness by smouldering embers; and I shivered, in spite of the warmth.

'Geraldine also mentioned another legend that surrounds the Pool, according to which a Norse prince, Brecon, drowned while engaged in a test of endurance undertaken for the hand of his beloved. He had fallen in love with a daughter of the Isle, you see. Her father promised him her hand in wedlock if he could but survive three nights on the Pool in an open boat; he lasted for two nights, but on the third his rope parted and he perished, amidst the whirlpool's primeval chaos. It later occurred to me that this was a timely reminder of what would happen to me, should I fail to pay due care and attention to what I was doing – but at the time I was too full of anticipation and excitement to pay much heed to it.

'Towards late afternoon – Jura is upwards of thirty miles long – I began to approach the Pool. I could tell because of the noise – you feel a low rumbling in your chest, as if an enormous engine were labouring somewhere nearby – they tell me you can hear it in Ireland when the wind is in the right corner; and then as you come nearer you hear more distinctly the swish and tumble of the tumult as it races around the narrow confines of the Gulf. You can also see the great swelling of the water as it strikes the base of the underwater pinnacle and surges upwards until it reaches the surface, appearing sometimes as a curious set of twitchings and boilings, and sometimes as a smooth, undisturbed expanse of water that reflects the sky in its burnished surface. The inexperienced boatman (in which category I count myself) is apt to be somewhat surprised by the strange, almost wilful effects of the currents, eddies, and whorls on the motion of surface vessels: no sooner did I point my prow towards Jura than I found it was pointing at Scarba, and vice versa.

'I found the complexity of currents somewhat overwhelming, even at a distance, and decided to put into shore for a little while, to survey the lay of the land (or rather sea) and to see if I could see any sign of Darroch's mysterious sea creature. I forgot to say that I had of course brought some fishing tackle – my trout rod, and also my saltwater gear, and some nets of varying size – and some equipment with which to construct a bivouac for an overnight stay, so I was well-equipped should anything unusual appear (and assuming that there was any truth in Darroch's words, of course).

'It was with some relief that I beached the dory on the Jura side of the Gulf, and immediately proceeded to refresh myself with some of Geraldine's excellent provisions. Bodily needs attended to, I began to pay more attention to my surroundings. There was a kind of promontory within walking distance, and I made use of this to reconnoitre the layout of the Gulf and the noisome Pool it contains. I say noisome, for even on that warm, lovely evening there was a palpable menace about the place, as if the vortex was seeking to draw in all light and goodness, and smother it in its lifeless depths.

'In order to dispel such morbid thoughts – brought on, no doubt, by an excessive indulgence in the excellent cheese Geraldine had supplied – I took out my binoculars and began to survey the waters for any sign of Darroch's mythical monster.

I stood there for some time without any luck (although it was fascinating to watch the play of the innumerable currents in the Pool), and was about to give it up as a bad job and retire for the night when I seemed to catch a gleam of something on the far side of the Gulf – near a little sandy inlet on Scarba. I refocused the binoculars and stared intently in the dying light. Yes – yes, there was something there – I caught a glimpse of a long, grey flank low in the water, and an odd sort of projection pointing up in the air – but then it submerged and was lost to sight.

'Instantly I ran down to the dory and got the Seagull going – a tricky, dangerous job in a hurry, as any of you will know, if you follow the sea – but somehow I managed it with both hands intact. That took ten minutes or so, and all the time I was cursing myself for a fool for having doubted Darroch's word. "What an excellent fellow!" I told myself as I launched the dory. Here was my chance for sporting fame, I thought – an unknown sea-creature, mine for the taking. I'm afraid that my steady stream of sporting success on Jura had quite dulled any sense of prudence or of the need to tread delicately and propitiate the gods, as Buchan put it so nicely in one of his recent yarns.'

'Thanks, old man,' said Buchan, raising his glass.

'Not at all,' said Penrose, raising his. 'To return to my tale: I now had the boat in the water and was heading out towards the spot where I had last seen the creature. This course took me pretty close to the centre of the Pool – too close, in fact, and in a terrifying moment of clarity I realised that I had strayed into the grip of its swirling currents… The boat rocked violently from side to side, the prow swung crazily around (I must have boxed the compass three times at least), and with the acuity that so often accompanies a crisis I distinctly noticed that the water level was several feet higher on one side of the Pool than on the other. That was pretty much the last thing I had time to notice in the boat, for after a particularly violent heave I found myself pitched head-first into the whirlpool.

'My first thought was to avoid the Seagull's threshing propeller, which can do terrible things to a man in the water;

but then I realised that the boat had been sucked down entire into the abyss, rods and tackle and all. I experienced a moment of piercing regret for my fly-rod, which had been a gift from my father; and then I was sucked under myself. A chaotic sensation of being tossed around like so much flotsam and jetsam, a desperate and futile striking out for the surface, and a dim perception of a great pillar of stone rising from the deep like some prehistoric monster, dark and malign; and then, just before I passed out, a thin grey shape emerging from the deep...

'When I came to I was lying on the shore where I had beached the dory earlier. A familiar face was leaning over me – it was Lockwood, a Christ Church man with whom I'd played rugger for the Varsity. "Lockwood!" I spluttered. "It is Lockwood, isn't it? I thought – where did you come from – what was that thing?" and so on.

'"Just lie back for now, there's a good chap," said Lockwood. "You've had a bit of an upset, and I'm afraid your dinghy has bought it. Dashed lucky you didn't go the same way. Here – drink this," and so saying he applied the best medicine known to man – a mouthful of finest Armagnac. After a while I recovered my senses and began to look around me. A wonderful contraption lay next to me on the beach – this was Darroch's sea creature, without a doubt, only it had a white ensign painted on one flank and the legend 'Royal Navy Experimental Unit' on the other.

'"It's a submersible canoe, old thing," said Lockwood, laughing. "Top secret, you know, and I suppose I should really turn you in – for the good of the Kingdom, and the protection of the Realm."

'"Oh, don't talk rot, Lockwood," I replied. "I'm sure that half the island knows all about your blasted canoe... Is there a friend of yours called Darroch, by any chance? He's been leading me a merry dance."

'Lockwood laughed. "Yes, that sounds like him... He's an adviser to the Navy. Knows these waters like the back of his hands. He must have thought you looked like you could take care of yourself, or he wouldn't have made such game of you… He paid you a compliment, if you like."

"'Well, it's a damned funny kind of compliment," I said, "but I suppose it's better than the alternative… But look here, Lockwood, I'm terribly grateful for the rescue effort, and all that. Now just put me on the back of that thing and let's get back to Armytage's place – he's got a wonderful Chablis to which I'd like to introduce you, and I'm shivering like an aspen…"

'And with that my story is more or less complete,' Penrose went on. 'Lockwood and I did not in fact go all the way to Armytage's on the back of his special canoe – it was battery-powered and had a useful range of about five sea-miles – but he got on to a little radio concealed in the canoe, and before long a little minesweeper hove into view – it must have been anchored to the north of the Isle. Soon we were steaming down the coast at a fair rate of knots – how the Navy navigates those straits in pitch darkness I really cannot tell - and before long we arrived at Armytage's for a welcome change of attire and a hot meal. He and Lockwood got on very well, of course, and indeed it wasn't long before Lockwood got the hotel on the telephone and invited the villain of the piece, Darroch himself, to come and have a nightcap. We all ended up the best of friends, or at least to as great an extent as possible with a chap who almost sent you to a watery grave!'

'Bravo! Bravo!' cried the company, clapping and stamping their feet in appreciation. 'Jolly good, Penrose,' said Sharpe; 'Dashed good yarn,' said Buchan; 'Most edifying,' said Buffy. 'But it's no good, you know, Penrose old chap,' he went on. 'Your story was highly entertaining, but a fabrication is a fabrication.'

'Are you thinking of the scene in the hotel bar?' asked Buchan.

'Yes, indeed,' replied Buffy. 'You say that you bought a drink for this fellow Darroch – yet none of us has ever seen you buy a drink for anyone, at any time, let alone a chap you had never seen before.'

'Completely incredible,' added Henton.

'Oh, I say,' cried Penrose. 'That's a bit steep – I must

135

have stood you gallons of champagne, over the years! I swear it's all true…'

But it was no good. The certain knowledge that he had done precisely the same thing to Buffy and Sharpe, and indeed that unjust sconcing had become a kind of de facto rule in the Society, overruled any further objections, and he gave in with good grace. He took the silver tankard in both hands, said 'Gentlemen, I give you the Sconcing Society!', and drank every drop of the ale within.

On the Wing

'COME ON, Nimrod, come on! It's time to get up, old boy. Ssshh! There's no need to bark – d'you want to wake up old Mrs Headlam? She might not give us our breakfast when we get back, and that would never do, would it? Come on, now.'

It was still dark when I tiptoed down the stairs (which creaked loudly despite all my efforts) and opened the rickety door to the gun-room. Nimrod, by now wide awake and wagging his tail in enthusiastic anticipation of the morning's sport, dashed in ahead of me and began to worry at my cartridge-bag; this immediately fell to the floor with a muffled crash, followed by a noise like falling hailstones as a good three dozen cartridges scattered themselves across the flagstones. Surveying the chaos he had wrought with a satisfied air, my villain of a dog turned to look up at me with blameless eyes and his usual fatuous, idiotically good-natured smile; and for perhaps the hundredth time I wished I had gone for a proper gun-dog instead of a mongrel terrier that had been only three months old when his then-owner Mr Walsh, the veterinarian who lived two houses along from me in Hampstead, had passed away.

At times like this I tried to remind myself of Nimrod's undoubted virtues: his wonderfully soft mouth (never a mark yet on pheasant, rabbit, or duck), his sensational nose, and his namesake's zeal for game; there was, too, his unfailing sweetness of temper – the most biddable of creatures too, when in the right mood – and sufficient vigour to last him a long day in the field or on the foreshore. He delighted in humiliating those of his canine counterparts who boasted more illustrious lineages than himself, and I had once seen him instantly track down a winged snipe of which a friend's (fairly distinguished) setter had long despaired. Not long afterwards, and even more to my relish, I had enjoyed the supreme spectacle of Nimrod flushing a brace of pheasants out of a covert where Lord Stanley's Sussex Spaniels had drawn a blank. All the same, I doubted whether Lord Stanley's spaniels had ever been obliged to be rescued, whimpering, from a rowan-tree into which they had somehow leapt whilst in pursuit of a cat; neither did I believe that my uncle's setter had ever knocked down four bookcases in his master's study. I can still remember the curious sight of the four tall cases, complete with glass frontages and yards of books, toppling into one another like a giant set of dominos; and there was Nimrod, panting furiously behind the first domino and thumping his tail on the floor, the happiest scoundrel in Christendom. I may have obtained him free of charge, but he has been making up the balance ever since.

'You'll have to earn your keep all over again today, you rascal,' I whispered to him as I gathered up the cartridges. 'Now be quiet and sit still, while I get my gun out of the case.'

The gun in question was a lovely little specimen – I say little, but in fact it was a middle-weight twelve-bore whose only claim to diminutive size came about in comparison with the enormous (and to my mind impossibly unwieldy) six- and eight-bore shoulder duck guns that were still in vogue at that time, relics of Queen Victoria's reign and the days of truly enormous bags. For my part I prefer to take one or two fowl on the wing, eagerly awaited and cleanly shot, than a multitude on the ground; and as I also prefer a gun that I can carry across marsh and stream without pulling my arms out of their sockets, the twelve-bore made perfect sense.

I had signally failed, however, to convey this point of view to Mr Headlam, the proprietor of the Hanham Arms (the little inn on the Norfolk coast where I was currently lodging), or any of the seasoned fowlers who used the place as a watering-hole after the evening flight. These chaps seemed to take inordinate pleasure in disparaging innovations of any kind and in pretending it was 1812 rather than 1912. 'The old ways are the best ways,' they would say through their enormous whiskers, 'and there ain't nobody can say different.' Word had also got about that I hadn't followed the usual practice of engaging a local man to show me the best spots on the foreshore – a sin that doubtless compounded the offence of my diminutive fowling-piece. Consequently an air of general disapproval seemed to follow me about the village and its surrounds, so that I could hardly go to the post office to buy a newspaper without someone or other pursing their lips and shaking their head at my passing.

But then I have always been a solitary kind of fellow, preferring my own company (and that of Nimrod) to that of some hired man I don't know from Adam, and who feels obliged to be nice to me in order to earn my shilling. Worse still are those gloomy customers who like to mutter dismissive remarks about one's dress, deportment, gun, or (heaven forbid) marksmanship; and worst of all are the chaps who never shut up from dawn to dusk, issuing an endless stream of unwanted advice and quite spoiling the sense of immersion in nature which is surely the whole point of the exercise in the first place. Things are a little different in New Zealand, where I spent my youth and earned my money; and while I'm generally quite a pragmatic sort of chap who doesn't hanker after places where he isn't, I do miss the fact that in Hawke's Bay or Marlborough a gentleman can get up and go fishing or shooting without a lot of ghillies and loaders and whatnot dancing in attendance.

And so it was in solitary but contented state that I set off with Nimrod to the foreshore, he scampering around and running lightly through the grass and me stepping warily in my gumboots, feeling for the exiguous pathway that wandered across the short yards from Hunstanton to the sea. The sea! It had played heavily in my consciousness from the day when, as a boy, I set off across the wide, trackless ocean to Christchurch, there to be raised by my late father's cousins. Ever since those long weeks on the steamer from Southampton the sea has drawn me back, redolent of sadness but also somehow comforting in its bleak vastness. It had consoled me then for the loss of my parents, and as a grown man it seemed always to absorb and diminish the petty troubles of civilisation. Now, as I approached the beginnings of the foreshore, I could smell the salt hanging heavily in the air, and in the darkness I felt the sea looming; soon I could hear the noise of its sighing as it washed upon the strand, and my accustomed eyes perceived the shifting greys of its distant and heaving surface. As I neared the shoreline I felt the old tranquillity return, mingled today (as on all fowling days) with a scarcely suppressed sense of excited anticipation; for I knew what the dawn would bring.

Nimrod had by now run far ahead of me, as was his wont, but I knew he would be waiting for me by a familiar tussock of coarse grass that served as my lodestone for navigating across the sands. From here I turned to the east to strike out across a damp, marshy piece of land inhabited by creeping willow and hundreds of rabbits; this tract led to my favoured spot just on the edge of the beach – a spot blessed with a ridge of sand, matted together with couch-grass and of a perfect height to render superfluous the unpleasant task of digging of a grave in the mud. In this natural alcove I checked and prepared my gun and fed Nimrod a morsel or two to keep him quiet – a perpetual concern in this silent cathedral of a darkened world – before taking up position to await the coming of the light.

I didn't have long to wait. Already a cold gleam had appeared above the eastern seas, and soon I heard the sounds of rushing wings as the waders flew overhead, unseen and untouched – my business was not with them. Gradually a colourless glow spread across the sky and revealed the vague contours of the desolate landscape that surrounded me; somehow the greyish light ironed out the imperfections visible by day, and rendered the foreshore a place of dim but luminous beauty. The world seemed to tremble on the verge of something both immensely significant and wholly ineffable, and as always I strained as if to understand what was being said; and as always the whispering voice fell just outside the bounds of my senses. Soon a dull violet streak crept into the sky and shed its radiance on the earth; day was come, and the spell broken.

But no sooner had the bonds of this enchantment fallen away than another, less mysterious perhaps but no less wonderful, came to entrance me: the distant calls of wildfowl. A few skeins of duck came first – some widgeon and teal, and a few pochards – but I had promised myself a brace of goose for the table, and so left them alone. Nimrod barked noisily as they flew overhead, and then turned to look at me with reproachful eyes.

'Be patient, old man,' I said soothingly as I fed him another titbit. 'And for heavens' sake stop making such a racket!'

On that particular morning, however, Nimrod showed more wisdom than I did; for there was practically no wind to speak of, and the geese – mostly pink-foot but with some white-front and brent – flew so high overhead that there was little chance of a clean shot; and I never shoot unless I can guarantee a clean shot. I did try for one gander that had dropped out of position, but went well behind; and after that I put my gun down (much to Nimrod's disgust) and simply watched the geese as they flew over in wave after perfectly-organised wave. I marvelled at the animal intelligence that enabled them to coordinate such immaculately shaped formations, as they had done for many thousands of years, and doubtless would continue to do after man's dominion is over and our species is forgotten.

As time passed the number of waves passing over diminished and the soft gabbling sounds died away; I stirred myself and woke up Nimrod, who had gone disconsolately and pointedly to sleep. It was just as I was stretching my stiff limbs and preparing to stand up that I saw the lone pink-foot flying low and fast across the mudflats. Quickly I took up my gun: here was a golden opportunity to make all good at the last minute, and to return in triumph to the Hanham

Arms – for although I care less about the opinion of my fellow man than some, I did not relish the thought of the smug and self-righteous expressions of the faces I would meet should I return empty-handed. I lined up on the pink-foot, and with my right leg pushed Nimrod away – he had suddenly started yapping and jumping on my leg, something he does whenever he wishes to attract my attention (which is far too often).

I followed the bird as he swung to the left – I pushed ahead of his outstretched beak and tightened on the trigger – and then I suddenly dropped the muzzle with an explosive oath, for I had seen an unexpected shape out of the corner of my eye. When I looked round to behold a startled-looking man in trench-coat and gum-boots, I realised I had narrowly avoided shooting another human being, and was momentarily relieved (despite the rapidly disappearing pink-foot).

Unfortunately (but perhaps understandably in the circumstances), my relief soon turned to anger.

'What the devil do you think you're doing?' I cried. 'You bloody fool, creeping up on me like that – you might very well have been killed.'

'My dear sir,' he replied, striding forward with a look of concern on his face. 'I can't apologise enough. As you can see' – here he gestured to a pair of binoculars around his neck – 'I have been watching the birds. I amuse myself with ornithology whenever I manage to get away from work – you know how it is. But on this occasion I have clearly allowed my enthusiasm to get the better of me – my sincere apologies, sir, for having made you miss your goose, your pink-footed goose.'

It would have taken a more churlish man than me to refuse such an apology; in fact, it's a quirk of mine instantly to regret any loss of my temper; and so I shook his outstretched hand with a feeling of some mortification, though I should admit that this feeling was mixed with a lingering regret for the solitary goose and annoyance that this bungling birdwatcher's antics should have caused me to lose him. Probably this complicated (and doubtless unappealing) combination of emotions appeared on my face, for he seemed at a loss for what to say next.

'Frenchay,' he said, finding inspiration at last. 'Maurice Frenchay.'

'Hugh McParland,' I answered. 'And this is Nimrod. Are you staying nearby?'

'In a way,' he said. 'I'm staying on a wherry – the *Hathor*. She's moored on the Norfolk rivers – well, Horsey Mere, to be precise. I left my crew and motored over from the East Coast this morning, in order to see the geese. You?'

'Oh, just over at the Hanham Arms – a little inn about a mile that way,' and as I pointed I remembered with an inward groan that I would now have to return empty-handed after all.

'Ah yes,' said Frenchay, in a tone that left me in no doubt as to his opinion of my humble lodgings. I've never been particularly fussy about where I lay my head, and have slept in the field and the barn time without number; but clearly my interlocutor was of a different stamp. Indeed, now that I had had the time to survey him in a little more detail, I could see that his coat was of an excellent cut, and that his binoculars were of an expensive Swiss make. His punctilious, carefully-modulated voice pointed towards a costly education, and his manners and finely-drawn features were such as to guarantee effortless membership of society's higher echelons. I knew, too, that hiring a pleasure wherry and crew didn't come cheap; I am not what could be considered a poor man, but I suspected that my purse would baulk at such an extravagance.

'If you are not otherwise engaged this morning, McParland, can I invite you – and your dog, of course! – to motor back and breakfast with me aboard *Hathor*?' he said. Bestowing a charming smile on me, he added: 'It is the least I can do, to make amends for disturbing your sport. And I doubt if the Hanham Arms can boast a bottle of '95 Laurent-Perrier!'

I conceded that this was almost undoubtedly the case – the finest tipple available at the inn was probably the raw brandy kept in a stone jug under the counter – and decided to make the most of the morning's disappointment by taking advantage of this unexpected offer. I am a forgiving type on the whole, and prepared to let bygones be bygones – especially if the supplicant keeps a decent cellar. I packed up my things and the three of us set of together for Frenchay's motor-car – Nimrod shooting off ahead as usual, and having to be called back numerous times from treacherous bogs and marshes.

As we drove over to the East Coast I found out that Frenchay was a specialist in international law, with chambers in town. I told him a little of my past – how I had moved back to the old country after spending most of my youth in New Zealand, and how I dabbled in Dominion politics when I had a mind, and occupied myself with shooting when I didn't. Then Frenchay told me that he was holidaying in Norfolk on the advice of his medical advisor in Harley Street. The medico had recommended some weeks of fresh air to strengthen Frenchay's constitution, which had been weakened by an extended period of extremely hard graft; the doctor had moreover averred (with perfect veracity) that few places promised more in the way of fresh air than the Norfolk coast in the depths of winter.

Frenchay had dutifully followed the advice and had cast around aimlessly for a while – I got the impression that he had become mightily bored – before he somehow discovered that *Hathor* was laid up for the winter at Martham, the owners being abroad until spring. Well, anyhow, he was struck by the wherry's name – it turned out later that he was an Egyptologist – and he took it into his head to take her for a cruise.

He persuaded the agent to let him take her for a couple of months, complete with her regular crew – probably they were glad of the work. Since then they had been making their way around the Norfolk and Suffolk rivers – down to Yarmouth and Lowestoft, and then back up to Hickling and Horsey on the Thurne, where they had been staying for a fortnight while Frenchay took walking and motoring trips to various points on the coast, and back again.

He spoke well of the crew, but I guessed he had found that the long evening hours hung heavily on his hands, and that he was glad of some educated company. In any case, whether it was because of boredom, or because (*contra* the Harley Street man) the fresh air had disagreed with him somehow, I could tell he was far from being a healthy man. There was a yellowish tinge to his skin, which seemed to be drawn tightly over his cheekbones; and as we parked the motor-car and walked to the dyke where he had moored *Hathor*'s tender he smoked an immoderate number of Gauloises, lighting each one from the end of its predecessor. However, he jumped into the little dinghy adroitly enough, and pulled us out to the wherry with the strong, regular stroke of an experienced oarsman; and when we reached *Hathor* he climbed over the gunwale with a lithe celerity that I found difficult to match. I wondered then if he could be suffering from his nerves rather than exhaustion.

The breakfast he laid on for me did little to dispel this impression, despite its opulence – the promised champagne made its appearance, of course, but there were also fresh eggs, bacon, sausages, caviar, and even some kippers the crew had bought that morning. It was wonderful – but he hardly touched a scrap, and after a few minutes' toying with his plate he sat back and lit another cigarette. I don't much like being watched while I eat, but he merely shook his head and smiled when I tried to offer him food from his own table. On my urging, he gave the remnants from his own plate to an eagerly expectant Nimrod, who consumed the leftovers with an enthusiasm that verged on indecency.

Frenchay mightn't have eaten much, but he did at least keep company with me on the champagne; and when I had finished eating we took another bottle outside and made our way carefully to the vessel's bows. As soon as we were safely established on a little bench facing aft, Frenchay asked me if I should like to go for a sail; as it happens I am rather fond of sailing, and so I agreed with some gusto. He then nodded to a member of the crew, who promptly roused his fellow sailors from their slumbers on the cabin roof. Moving with accustomed ease and surety, the three of them then removed the sail covers and stowed them below, before attaching the blocks and winching the gaff up so the crutches could be taken down. Then they lowered the gaff again, took off the sail ties, and attached the blocks in a different way. Then two of them

set about raising the mud-weight that had anchored *Hathor* –
quite a job, judging from the sounds of exertion – while the
third got to work on the winch again, and began to raise the
gaff and the truly enormous sail to which it was attached. Soon
one of the others ran to help him, with the third controlling
the rising sail with a gaff line. The sail raised and the halyard
made fast, two of them laboured to fit the bonnet – necessary
in these light breezes, Frenchay murmured – while the third,
now at the helm, gazed up at the long, red vane and adjusted
his course accordingly. *Hathor* came alive and gained way, and
soon we heard one of the most delightful sounds I know: the
trickle of water along the side of a clinker-built boat.

Nimrod was entranced, of course, and stuck his head
over the strake to gaze at the steadily passing whorls. In
due course he became mesmerised by the water, as I knew
he would, and he was soon in danger of falling asleep and
pitching wholesale over the side. I reached out and grabbed
him by the scruff of the neck, placing him by my feet where
he could come to no mischief. Frenchay smiled, and said:

'It must be pleasant to have such a companion.'

I laughed at this. 'Well, I suppose it is. He causes a lot of
trouble, mind you. You're seeing him at his best behaviour, but
when he's at home he's a handful, aren't you, boy?' Nimrod
ignored this last statement; he was capable of an impressive
hauteur when he felt his honour was being impugned.

'You never had a dog?' I asked as we left Horsey Mere
and made our stately way down Meadow Dyke.

'Yes – when I was young,' he replied. 'He was rather
like your Nimrod, in fact. But that was long ago... Perhaps
you are right, though; perhaps I should get one. My line of
work is somewhat – lonely.' Frenchay had a disconcerting habit
of speaking to one's thought rather than one's word, although
in this instance I had been thinking of the man himself rather
than his work, and I couldn't quite see why a lawyer's work
should be especially solitary unless he was having trouble being
briefed. I could hardly ask him if this was the case, however.

In order to forestall an awkward silence, I asked him
about the wherry's name, which I hadn't come across before –

was it German, I asked?

He started. 'German?' he said. 'Why would you say that?'

'I don't know,' I replied, surprised at his reaction. 'It just sounds German. Heart-or. Like Goethe, or Werther – you know.'

'Well, it isn't,' he said, sounding almost offended. 'It's Egyptian. *Hathor* was the goddess of love and joy. She – '

At this juncture he was interrupted by Nimrod, who had spied a cormorant sitting on top of one of the large wooden posts that mark the channel. As usual it was all I could do to restrain him from jumping overboard and investigating more closely, and in the fuss and general merriment we lost the thread of our conversation. I thought I had heard the last of Egypt and the ancient Egyptians, but he brought them up again that evening, at dinner. (I should explain that in the meantime he had asked me to stay with him for a couple of days, and as I was rather intrigued by my new friend and had in any case already fallen quite in love with *Hathor*, I willingly agreed. He sent one of his crew to fetch my things from the inn in Hunstanton – happily there was to be no return, empty-handed, to the Hanham Arms!)

We dined in the saloon on good Norfolk beef that one of the sailors cooked in the wherry's little galley. Frenchay gave me a capital bottle of claret to go with it, and a startlingly good cognac to follow. I had been fairly famished after the day's sailing – somehow I always am in Norfolk, and usually go back to town heavier by a stone – and had set to without thinking much about my surroundings. The same had been true at breakfast, and of course I had also been distracted then by my speculations about Frenchay's nerves. But now, as I sat back with one of his excellent cigars and with Nimrod's head resting sleepily on my knee, I began to inspect the curious shapes and designs that adorned the saloon walls.

'What unusual marquetry,' I remarked, pointing with my cigar.

'Yes – themes from ancient Egypt, you see,' he said, his sallow face lighting up. 'There you have frogs, and lotus flowers, and crocodiles – and behind you there are hares, all of teak and dyed sycamore. The lamp above us has serpents' heads worked into the design, and there, on those doors, you may have noticed some hieroglyphics.'

'How interesting,' I said politely. 'I take it the owners have a passion for Egypt, then?'

'In a way... It's rather a sad story, as a matter of fact. The owners are the Colman family, who, I understand, made their fortune in mustard. The agent told me that one of the Colmans – the old man's son, Alan – fell ill with consumption fifteen or twenty years ago. His medics prescribed a trip somewhere hot and dry, so the whole family set out for Egypt and took a cruise on the Nile. Unfortunately, the change of climate did nothing to fight the illness, and the poor man perished at Luxor. The family returned home with broken hearts.

'When they got back, however, they decided to build a wherry in memory of the son; and they named her *Hathor*, after the boat that had carried them on the Nile. There was an architect in the family, the agent said, who was responsible for the décor. And what an excellent job he did, too. Look at that set of hieroglyphs – I don't suppose you can read them?'

'I'm afraid not,' I said. 'Never went in for it.'

'Well, I can tell you what it says: it lists some of the titles of the goddess *Hathor*.' And then he declaimed: 'Thou art the Mistress of Jubilation, the Queen of the Dance, the Mistress of Music, the Queen of the Harp Playing, the Lady of the Choral Dance, the Queen of Wreath Weaving, the Mistress of Inebriety Without End.'

He pronounced the titles with indescribable relish, and added a couple of his own that the architect must have missed; I remember 'The One who Fills the Sanctuary with Joy.' Not exactly my cup of tea, but I suppose if one was to go in for that kind of thing, at least the goddess in question seemed a reasonably cheerful one. I said as much to Frenchay, though not in as many words; I think I said something facetious about inebriety without end. He smiled, and again spoke to my thought rather than my words.

'Perhaps you think I am an enthusiast, or a – how do you say – a crackpot,' he said. 'But you see, I made a study of philology in my leisure hours when I was at university, and acquired then what you might call a professional interest in the Pharaohs and their ancient dynasties. I was penniless then, of course, but now that I have means of my own I am able to indulge myself, from time to time, in little items or souvenirs, thus expanding my knowledge of that great people through the very artifacts they once owned. My proudest possession is a papyrus roll listing spells from the Book of the Dead – spells designed to guide the deceased through the Underworld, and thus guarantee life eternal. This I leave always in a secure place – I bought it for a trifling sum from a man who did not know its worth, but its value is incalculable.

'But let me show you something that I do carry about with me – something of less value, but fascinating nonetheless – a commemorative scarab from the reign of Amenhotep III. I have it here in the locker.'

And he got up from the table and reached over to a large cabinet above the saloon table. As he opened it, a quantity of charts and maps fell out – an unexpected quantity, indeed, for a gentle cruise on the Norfolk rivers, especially as I could see that many of them charted the coast rather than inland waterways. I didn't pass any remarks, but he seemed aware of my surprise, for he turned over his shoulder as he tidied them away, and mentioned that he had a keen interest in something he called 'orienteering' – a Scandinavian pursuit, he said, that involved navigating between points on foot using a hand-compass. It struck me that he had a goodish number of arcane pastimes, but again I refrained from comment. And in any case he had now found that which he sought – a small jade box, covered in esoteric carvings – which he lost no time in thrusting into my hands.

'Open it,' he said. 'But carefully!'

Dutifully I opened the little box with considerable care, and beheld within an item perhaps four inches across and six long, made of a dull blue material, and bearing numerous hieroglyphics. In all honesty I didn't think a great deal of it, but when I looked at Frenchay his eyes were sparkling.

'It is a Lion Hunt scarab,' he breathed. 'It records the bravery of Amenhotep III, who killed more than a hundred lions during the first ten years of his reign. Many copies were made of the original scarab, and circulated in Egypt to proclaim the Pharaoh's bravery; this is one such. Listen to what the hieroglyphs say – ' and he began to translate them for my ignorant ears. He then went on to list the other kinds of commemorative scarabs issued by the Pharaoh, and recounted many of the doings of the long-dead king. I could feel little interest in these; but Frenchay himself made a powerful and curious impression on me as he hunched over his precious scrap of history.

I noted that the punctiliousness of his speech, already marked, became ever more so as he recited Amenhotep's dynastic provenance; and as he discoursed on the greatness of ancient Egypt – which, he assured me, would rise again in the fullness of time – I also noted that the ordering of his words had subtly altered and changed, until one could almost think he was a foreigner. It seemed rather odd to me; but then I remembered that he was an international lawyer. One has to make allowances for the effect that all that Pufendorf and Grotius must have on a fellow.

I think he sensed my lack of genuine interest after a while, and quietly put the scarab away; I admired him for that, as your genuine enthusiast can be rather a bore. He turned the conversation round to me after that. I think he had noticed my love of sailing, for he asked me about what kind of yacht I preferred, and where I had sailed. I told him about the six-ton sloop owned by my friend Carstairs, and our occasional jaunts along the south coast. He seemed to approve of this, for he nodded his head and said:

'It is good for Englishmen to stay in touch with the sea. The sea is the lifeblood of an island nation – for trade, for transport, and most of all for defence. What would England be without the Royal Navy? Where would she be without her mighty battleships and cruisers, or her fleets of destroyers and frigates? They keep the seas free for England, and encircle the globe in steel; but you – we – must not forget the little waters nearer to home. It is all too easy to dream of great empires and dominions, and forget the need to maintain a watch in home waters. There must be Sons of Martha, as well as Sons of Mary, to keep England safe.'

He gave me an earnest look then, his eyes glinting in the gentle light cast by the oil lamp, and I almost wondered if he was trying to warn me about something. I knew the Kipling poem to which he had alluded, and had always been struck by the lines:

It is their care in all the ages to take the buffet and cushion the shock.
It is their care that the gear engages; it is their care that the switches lock.

With hindsight, of course, it was easy to see what he was getting at, but at the time I was somewhat perplexed by my companion and his strange conversation. I wondered if the cognac, or perhaps the very rich sauce served with the beef, had disagreed with him – sensitive chaps like him are often susceptible to indigestion, I have found.

The peculiarity of his behaviour became even more marked on the morrow, although the day began innocuously enough. I had had an excellent night's sleep in a cosy little two-berth cabin, in which, I was amused to note, the owners had placed books by Apollonius of Rhodes alongside two volumes of excerpts from the Napoleonic *Description de l'Égypte* – dry as dust, of course, but full marks for effort.

Once again I breakfasted well, and once again the ever-hungry Nimrod benefited from our host's lack of appetite. Afterwards Frenchay suggested we shoot some coot or grebe, but as I've never found much fun in that kind of sport I proposed we be put ashore at Hickling and try for some duck among the reeds, with Nimrod serving as beater and retriever. To this proposal Frenchay readily agreed, and we spent a pleasant few hours' shooting around Catfield Dyke.

I bagged a fine mallard and a brace of snipe, while Frenchay, who proved himself a very pretty shot with a twenty-bore borrowed from a locker in *Hathor*, accounted for three pochards. It really is the most tremendous country for river-work, despite being somewhat marshy and boggy in parts; and Nimrod thoroughly enjoyed himself both in the water and on land.

We ate luncheon at a little pub near Catfield Staithe, and as we sat smoking afterwards we discussed what to do in the afternoon. He proposed fishing, but I was keen to sail again, and perhaps to take the helm this time. He assented with good grace, and after the crew picked us up in the tender I went below to change my things in preparation for a sail on Hickling; Frenchay stayed on deck to talk to the crew. As I was changing I happened to look out of the porthole, and noticed a smart-looking motor launch bustling past and throwing up a fine bow-wave. The chap at the helm sported a blue-and-white boating blazer that I rather admired, and I saw him waving as he passed. When I came on deck, Frenchay was standing by the skipper's cuddy, watching the launch recede into the distance. I remarked on her looks and speed, but when Frenchay turned to me I realised he was looking rather unwell – positively green around the gills.

'Are you feeling all right?' I said. 'Look here, we don't have to sail if you are under the weather. Why don't you lie down in your cabin for a spell? I'll be quite happy here on deck, with my pipe and a book.'

'No, it isn't that,' he replied quickly. But then he paused, before continuing: 'Well, perhaps you're right – maybe I will lie down. But we'll move off Hickling, if you don't mind – perhaps it's the motion,' – for the wind had got up since the morning, and Hickling is no kind of a haven when there's a blow coming. I agreed, of course, though privately cursing my luck, for I love nothing more than sailing in a really good breeze; and before he went below he got the crew to quant us off the broad in search of quiet moorings. Wrapped in my warmest clothing, I sat in solitary state on the little white bench in the bows and watched the man drop the long quant into the broad before putting it to his shoulder and walking the length of the deck. He then plucked it out and walked back to the bow before repeating the process; thus we moved slowly across

Hickling towards Heigham Sound and the Upper Thurne, while Frenchay rested below.

Apart from a soft tapping noise that came from below – presumably one of the sailors repairing something – there was only the noise of the wind and the water, and an occasional squawk from a coot or a moorhen, to trouble my senses. As time passed I became philosophical about the lost opportunity to sail *Hathor* on Hickling, and resigned myself to observing my surroundings. I waved to the few boats that passed us – a Norfolk punt, and an eelman's boat; also a steam-launch with a party of cold-looking fishermen, and lastly a converted ship's lifeboat, painted black all over and flying the skull and cross-bones; *Death and Glory* was her name. She bore a crew of four – a mother and father, clearly, with a girl at the helm and a small boy sitting on the forrard end of the cabin.

Our skipper seemed to know them, and he shouted over to ask if the mooring by the cow-field was free. Yes, they said, but we had better hurry, for they had seen *Olive* coming up-river, and that was one of her favourite spots. *Olive*, I later gathered, was a wherry yacht, whose captain our own skipper cordially disliked. He thanked the *Death and Glory*, and muttered a word to the sailor wielding the quant, who redoubled his efforts – anything to beat the *Olive* seemed the order of the day.

It was, therefore, with a surprising velocity that we arrived at our chosen spot, which I found charming – so delightful, indeed, that I could quite understand why it was so sought after by the skipper. There was plenty of room even for the widest-beamed wherry, and also a long and firm bank into which to place the rond-anchors that would secure us overnight. The bank formed the edge of a water-meadow, dotted here and there with grazing cows and clumps of reeds. The trees were rather more numerous here, and the wind was somewhat lessened; with the willows sighing over the water and the sailors casting a line for roach, it really became quite a charming pastoral scene.

After a while Frenchay reappeared, looking wan, and frailer than ever, but he also had a set jaw and a curiously resolute look on his face. He replied positively when I asked him if he felt better after his rest, and at his suggestion we whiled away the afternoon by joining the crew in a spot of fishing. (Thirteen roach and six rudd for me; Frenchay had an even bigger bag, although of course we put all but three back, since most coarse fish taste rather like cotton wool stuffed with needles. The three we kept were consumed by the undiscerning Nimrod.) Frenchay seemed to relax as the afternoon wore on, and by the time we thought of packing up he was looking rather better.

Oddly enough, it was the launch that set him off again – the motor launch that I had seen on Hickling. She came around the corner as we wound in our lines for the last time, her powerful engine rumbling heavily in the twilight amidst Nimrod's loud barking; and in the garish glow cast by her searchlight I saw Frenchay's face turning pale. I was about to ask him what on earth was the matter when I realised the launch had throttled back and was coasting towards us. She had an expert at the helm, for her polished side touched our gunwale with the gentlest of kisses. Then her helmsman switched off and stood up, and I saw that it was the chap with the smart blazer, now sporting a pair of binoculars around his neck.

On closer inspection he wasn't quite the pleasure-seeking dilettante I had expected, although his pencil moustache was as dapper as anything you'd see in Piccadilly; rather, he had a boxer's shoulders and an air of cautious belligerence about him, if the contradiction can be forgiven – a sense of tremendous strength and extreme acuity concealed under an elegant exterior. He smiled across at us.

'I say, you fellows,' he said, in an Etonian drawl. 'I wonder if you can help me – I'm looking for some very rare birds.'

'What kind of birds?' said Frenchay quietly. I noticed that a muscle had begun to twitch in his cheek.

'Oh, you know – the rare kind,' replied the blazer pleasantly. He seemed rather amused about something. 'The kind that scuttles around in the undergrowth, rooting around for morsels. They trust to their disguises, but sometimes they are painfully obvious to their predators. They can be dangerous when cornered, but if watched with care they can't do much harm.'

'Yet sometimes they can surprise even the most knowledgeable of observers,' said Frenchay. Much to my astonishment, they went on in this bizarrely opaque manner for some minutes. Clearly they knew each other, but Frenchay didn't trouble to introduce me, and although the other chap looked at me a few times (mostly with a faint tinge of puzzlement crossing his features), he didn't ask for my name. It was all very odd at the time, although (as with many things) painfully obvious with hindsight.

After several more exchanges of the kind related above, the blazer restarted his engine, and with one final (and, it seemed to me, rather significant) look at Frenchay, roared off into the deepening gloom. Frenchay then descended into a brown study, and despite my efforts to rouse him he didn't speak to me much at dinner, nor over our cigars and cognac afterwards. All he would say was, 'I am still not quite myself.' And when I asked him about the blazer, he wouldn't speak; he just waved his hand as if to dismiss the matter from thought.

He did speak to me just before we retired, however. I was pretty fed up with his behaviour by then, and had resolved to leave *Hathor* and return to the Hanham Arms on the next day (shame or no shame). He must have realised this, for as I wished him good night and got up to go, he grasped my arm.

'You're a good fellow, McParland,' he said. 'A damned good fellow. I'm sorry about how I've behaved this evening – it's no use explaining it now. Only – I hope you can forgive me, some day, when I am free to tell you... Perhaps you will understand later, if not now.'

I must confess that this strange confidence didn't change my mind about the Hanham Arms – his words were just as obscure as his exchanges with the blazer. But I could see he was in earnest, all the same, and I think I muttered some platitude and gave him a cursory smile as I headed to my cabin. If I had known that that would be the last time I would see him… But of course I didn't. So I merely lay down on the little bunk bed, scratched Nimrod on the ear (his favourite spot), lit a final cigarette as I read some pages from Apollonius, and went to sleep.

It wasn't long before I was woken, however, although I thought at the time that I was dreaming – I seemed to hear muffled voices, soft thumps and splashes, and a distant tapping, tapping, tapping… At one point I think I must have got up to look out of the porthole, for I have a distant memory of stars glimpsed through fog, and of the quant moving gracefully past my eyes, propelled by a sailor walking silently along the deck. I think Nimrod gave a sleepy bark or two. But I must have gone back to sleep afterwards, and I didn't wake until the wherry bumped up against a quayside. It was still dark, so I switched on the light and looked at my watch: a quarter past seven. I felt the wherry shift slightly as the crew made her fast to the bollards, and wondered what on earth was going on. Had Frenchay decided to shift his mooring in the night for some reason?

It was as I lay on my berth that I heard a familiar rumble in the distance: the launch's engine, surely. Judging by the noise, it was coming closer – and at a rate of knots. Suddenly I heard hasty footsteps on the wherry's deck, followed by a gap, and then the sound of a man running very fast on gravel. I jumped up and looked out of the window, and saw a figure disappearing into the fog: Frenchay, I'd swear to it.

I told myself that I had to get to the bottom of this; Nimrod apparently agreed, for he was barking as if a whole squadron of duck had landed on the wherry roof. I got up and threw a coat over my pyjamas before dashing out of my cabin and through the saloon door to the deck; from there I rushed past the astonished crew, clambered over the gunwale and jumped onto the quayside, and was about to head off in pursuit of Frenchay with Nimrod at my heels when I heard the launch roaring into the dyke. Its searchlight was as glaringly bright as ever, and I remember noticing a sign on the staithe bearing the legend 'The Pleasure Boat', and realising that we had come back to Hickling. I paused and turned as I heard more running footsteps; then the blazer appeared, looking grimly determined as he made to follow Frenchay. Suddenly I felt angry, on Frenchay's behalf, with this excessively competent and aggressive individual, who seemed able to inspire the poor fellow with such fear.

'Not so fast, old man,' I said, stepping into his path. But then I stepped back in shock, for the blazer had reached into his jacket pocket with a determined look on his face. Surely he wasn't going to shoot me? Nimrod evidently thought this a possibility, and set about barking furiously at the blazer, and nipping at his legs.

It wasn't a revolver that he withdrew from his pocket, however, but some kind of wallet with identification papers inside.

'Stay here, you fool,' he rasped, showing me the papers while simultaneously fending off Nimrod. 'I'm with the Secret Service – and that man is a bloody spy!' And having said this he set off in pursuit of Frenchay. I think I stood there for some time as I digested this latest piece of information. All the odd things about my erstwhile companion suddenly fell into place – his punctilious English, his odd word order, his sudden change of behaviour when he realised the Secret Service was onto him – and the tapping noise I heard, which of course could only have come from a battery-powered wireless transmitter. I cursed him then for having lied to me and taken me in, but at the same time I feared for his safety at the hands of the Service…

Anyway, this was no time for standing about thinking – I had to get after them and see what had happened. I try to keep myself fairly fit, but I remember that journey from the wherry to the sea as one of the most nightmarish in my experience: whirling fog, hardly any light to see by, tussocks of rough grass everywhere, and of course Nimrod running back and forward and barking, and getting under my feet… By the time I neared the sea I was pretty near done in, and the perspiration ran unchecked down my forehead and into my eyes. There was more light now, of course, but still plenty of fog, and nothing to be seen to left or right. I waited for

Nimrod to show me where they had gone, but even he was perplexed at first. He cast around for a while without any luck, but soon his nose told him where to go, and he disappeared into the fog to the east.

I waited a minute or two, to get my breath back, and then set off after him. As I began to run I heard a gunshot, muffled but unmistakeable despite the fog; and then another, and another. Suddenly fearful, I redoubled my efforts. It fairly turned my stomach to think of a man like Frenchay being pursued like an animal, spy or no; but what I would do if I came upon them, I had no idea – thank God it didn't come to that. In any case, I had a feeling that Frenchay and his pursuer had curved around to the right, so I decided to cut across in that direction – a fateful decision, as it happened, for I took a tumble in a marshy bit of land, and went over on my ankle. After that I could barely hobble, and when Nimrod came back to find me a few minutes later I had hardly moved a hundred yards. I moved down to the beach and found a bit of driftwood to serve as a crutch; after that I got along a bit more quickly, and with Nimrod's encouragement managed to keep going on Frenchay's trail.

As I shuffled along the fog began to clear, and after a few minutes I thought I could make something out on the beach ahead – a dark shape on the ground. I feared the worst; but when I finally reached it I realised it was the blazer, and that he had merely been knocked out cold. A revolver lay beside him, along with some expended cartridges. I dragged him down to the water's edge and splashed his face; he muttered something and moved his arm, but didn't come round – Frenchay must have given him a fair blow.

As I tended to the blazer – whose conveniently anonymous name, it turned out, was Smith – I seemed to hear the distant pulse of an engine, out to sea. I looked out across the waves, and while I wouldn't swear to it, I thought I saw the outline of a trawler, with a man standing in the bows. Whether it was just my imagination, I can't say – but I like to think I saw him raise his hand, as if in farewell. And whether I saw him or not, I'm half glad he got away – he was a good fellow, after all, even if (as I later found out) Smith had been watching him on suspicion of charting and surveying our coastal waters and, specifically, their defences. I couldn't deny this – witness the profusion of charts I had seen fall from the locker – but neither could I forget that he had asked me to stay with him, had welcomed my company as a diversion from his lonely and perilous occupation, had even warned me to look to our coastal defences, should war come.

When War did come, I joined the Navy and worked on the very defences he had warned me to prepare. I never saw Frenchay again; but whenever I took Nimrod wild-fowling after the war I thought of the lone pink-foot goose, and of our strange host on *Hathor*, who loved wildfowling and the sea, and who sailed away from our shores in a trawler. He may have been a spy, but he was also a patriot in his own way, and a gentleman, and a sportsman; and I know of no higher accolade than that.

Henton's Story

WHEN NOT being shot at by Members, the woodpigeons resident in the trees dotted around the grounds of the Hurlingham Club were frequently privileged to witness some of the finest sporting spectacles in the land. It was commonplace to see the national lawn tennis champion playing on the courts, for example, or the Club XI contending with an MCC team on the spacious cricket pitch; and as a result the birds had become somewhat blasé in sporting matters.

They tended to affect nonchalance during the visits of such luminaries as Eric Liddell and Jack Hobbs, and just last week they had been observed flying past Lord Black, the finest shot in England and a perpetual threat to feathered life, with a noticeable air of boredom. Even the amazing sight of Major Coker defeating the Very Reverend (ret'd) Archibald Fraser at croquet after nearly a decade of humiliation had failed to rouse them to a state of genuine enthusiasm.

Nevertheless, it could not be denied that the woodpigeons still maintained a certain interest in equestrian pursuits. The younger and more vigorous birds would occasionally fly to Ascot to see the races, or perhaps make a weekend of it in some quiet spot in the country with point-to-points on offer; but the majority preferred to spectate in a less strenuous fashion, by watching polo on the Club fields. The Hurlingham at that time was the most venerable polo club in the country, and the very oldest birds could dimly remember the great year of 1908, when the Summer Olympics polo matches had been held there. Ever since those halcyon days, an enduring love of the game had often been all that stood between the woodpigeons and that fate worse than death – a life devoid of sporting interest – with the result that a significant majority of matches were played out to the accompaniment of much hooting and cooing.

The polo match with which this narrative begins – a friendly Club affair, between a Hurlingham team and a four from one of the smarter regiments – was no exception. In fact, the chorus of appreciative noise that met the quartets as they lined up on the field was such as to occasion some surprise amongst the visiting team.

'Bit of a racket, what?' said their Number Two.

'I'll say,' said Number One. 'I thought they were famous for their shooting, but on this evidence...'

'Well, as long as their horsemanship is as poor as their marksmanship, I shall be happy enough,' declared Number Two.

'I wouldn't be too sure about that, old boy,' said Number Three. 'We're a goal down in the handicap, so we've got our work cut out. Their Number Three is fairly stalwart, I've heard, and that chap Henton is pretty well-known as a sharp-shooter. Make sure you keep an eye on him, Greenwood!' – This to his Number Four. And indeed Henton kept Greenwood very busy during the first chukka, and also the second, third, fourth, fifth, and sixth. The teams were fairly evenly matched, but Henton's fearless riding-off and daring offensive play – the spectators had gasped, woodpigeons and men alike, at his neck- and tail-shots – had proved decisive, and the home team carried the day by fifteen to twelve.

Henton had noticed a familiar figure pressing the divots during the treading-in, and was unsurprised to see Sharpe approaching as he jumped out of the saddle after the final chukka.

'Well played, Henton – well played, indeed!' said Sharpe, shaking his hand. 'It's been years since I saw such a display – such neat riding and mallet-work. Listen, how about a drink? Come and join me in the Bar when you've changed, and I'll stand you a gin. There's something I want to discuss with you.'

Henton had a fairly good idea of what it was that Sharpe wanted to discuss, and his face took on a resigned air as he walked into the Bar. As Sharpe turned to greet him, Henton held up his hand.

'Don't say it,' he said. 'I know why you're here. You're here to tell me there's another meeting of the Sconcing Society coming up, and that it's my turn to take guard.'

'Quite right, old chap,' beamed Sharpe, who, having been through the wringer himself, found it surprisingly enjoyable to put others on the spot. 'It's been far too long since we last met, and now that Parliament has gone into recess for the summer Penrose and I have plenty of time on our hands. So – how about it? Are you game?'

Henton took a deep breath.

'Yes,' he said. 'I'm game. But I want the meeting here at the Club, on my own turf – fair enough?'

'Fair enough,' said Sharpe. 'The last request of the condemned man, and all that…I'll leave it to you to make the arrangements, and let us know the date. And never fear – I'll bring the sconcing vessel myself!'

'I thought you might,' said Henton. 'But you might as well save yourself the trouble – you won't need it!'

'We'll be the judge of that,' said Sharpe, and called for another gin.

——◦◦——

Some days later the Hurlingham Club chef received notice of a private dinner-party to be held the following week, for four gentlemen – Sharpe, Penrose, Buffy, and Henton, of course – and an extra place to be prepared in case a fifth gentleman was able to attend. The gentleman in question was the elusive Trevithick, a close associate of Penrose and well-known to Buffy also. He was much sought-after for his unparalleled stock of risqué anecdotes, and although Sharpe privately thought that his tales of derring-do were sometimes a trifle near, he freely admitted that Trevithick's particular brand of frankly incredible conversation was just what they were looking for in the Sconcing Society. Apart from anything else, no member would ever find reasons for sconcing him hard to come by; and in this selfless and collegial spirit Penrose and Buffy had recently descended upon his rooms in Mayfair in a concerted attempt to twist the Trevithick arm.

'Come on, Harry,' Penrose had said. 'You're so confoundedly hard to pin down – just promise us you'll be there, and I give you my word you won't regret it. Buchan can't join us this time, worst luck, and Brudenell and Hickson are still overseas, but you know Sharpe already, and Henton – the chap who'll be telling the tale – is an absolute brick. He's a polo fanatic, like you, and Sharpe said he never saw a finer horseman.'

In response, the monocled Harry Trevithick had waved an airy cigarette and sipped a careless flute of champagne. 'If I can be there, I will, old boy,' he said. 'But you know how it is – so many demands upon my time... I believe I have already told the Marquis of Salisbury I'll go to his rout that evening.'

'Oh, bother the Marquis of Salisbury,' said Buffy – or words to that effect. 'I've been to his parties before – nothing but a lot of loud music and silly talk – made me sick.'

'There's something in what you say, of course,' mused Trevithick. 'Well, I'll make you no promises, but set a place for me at your table, and perhaps I'll be there.' And with that they had to be content.

⏤ ∘ ⏤

The day of the meeting having duly arrived, and Henton having furtively augmented his courage by means of a triple whisky in the Polo Bar, the Sconcing Society reconvened in a private room at the Hurlingham Club.

'This is rather nice,' murmured Sharpe as they entered the room.

'You do yourselves very well here, Henton,' agreed Penrose. 'I'm almost tempted to join myself.'

'Hmm,' said Buffy. 'I think they would probably black-ball you, Penrose, in light of your mendacious story-telling.'

'That's rich, coming from you,' began Penrose, but Henton frowned and said: 'Let's not harp on too much about mendacity in story-telling,' he said. 'It sets an ominous precedent for the remainder of the evening. Now look here – is this fellow Trevithick coming or not? The butler will want to know.'

Sharpe opened his mouth to answer, but was forestalled by a cheerful voice that declared: 'Tally-ho!' The voice belonged, of course, to Trevithick, who had just entered the room clad in the startling attire of top hat, pink coat, jodhpurs, and mud-spattered top boots. The other four stared at him in amazement.

Henton broke the silence. 'How on earth did you get in here looking like that?' (The Hurlingham was known for the rigour of its dress code.)

'Oh, I know the doorman,' said Trevithick, tossing his top hat onto an easy chair. Sensing that more was required in the way of explanation, he added: 'We were in clink together a couple of years ago. I got mixed up in a disagreement with a gentleman of the turf, and Sam – the doorman – stepped in on my side, thus earning himself a free night's accommodation, courtesy of His Majesty's Constabulary. A perfect gentleman. But I say, you must be Henton, of polo-playing fame? I'm Harry Trevithick.'

Henton, somewhat staggered, shook his hand; then his sense of humour won over his sense of loyalty to the Club rules, and he laughed aloud. 'Well, I'm jiggered,' he said. 'If the President could see you in togs like that... But I applaud you for it.'

'Nothing to applaud, old boy,' said Trevithick. 'I was hunting earlier, as you can see, and simply decided to drive across afterwards for your meeting, and to hell with Salisbury... Now, what's the plan of action here? Foodbag first, then the tale – or is it a pre-prandial affair?'

'No, no,' said Penrose, clearly shocked. 'You don't think we dare to tell our tales on an empty stomach, or without a bottle or two of fortifying wine!'

'Well, I'm glad to hear that,' said Trevithick. 'I could eat a horse, though I wouldn't like old Cassius – my hunter – to hear me say it. Let us proceed!'

On this point the company agreed, and they took their seats at table (assisted by a footman who spent much of the following hour or two directing pointed looks at Trevithick's entirely unsuitable attire). Henton had slipped the chef a guinea in order to make the menu as alcoholic as possible, on the grounds that the more pop-eyed the Society, the less likely he was to be sconced. There was little the chef could do with the fish, but he did prepare a spectacular potato soup with lashings of Russian vodka and a saddle of mutton drowned in Burgundy, and also a sumptuous chocolate dessert laced with Jamaican rum. There was also the wine: a different bottle with every course, and the strongest of dessert wines to follow. In short, Henton had done everything to ensure an audience composed of semi-conscious inebriates.

However, Henton had reckoned without two factors: first, the cunning of Sharpe, Penrose, and Buffy, who, having attempted the same thing without much success, were conspicuously (and unusually) temperate in their imbibing; and second, Trevithick's iron-cast constitution, which allowed him to put away surprising amounts of alcohol without showing any ill-effects whatsoever. It was with an air of disappointment that Henton finally gave up the attempt, and tapped his glass with a fork.

'Well, gentlemen, I think it is time for port and cigars. Given the weather, I propose we move outside – I have asked for a table to be set up under the oak by the polo fields, where we can sit and watch the light fade in perfect comfort.'

To this they all agreed, and the Society was soon seated under the shapely boughs of the great tree. The decanter was passed around with enthusiasm (although Henton sighed at the moderate glasses they poured themselves) and the party soon threatened to disappear in the voluminous clouds of cigar smoke they produced. The generous Club grounds exuded an air of tranquil relaxation under the soft colours of the setting sun, and – bar the singing of birds – there was hardly a noise to be heard. The birds were in particularly good voice that evening: in the nature of things it is difficult for woodpigeons to crow, but they were doing their best to gloat about the Club's success on the polo fields, and had Henton looked up as he began his story, he would have seen a number of birds regarding him with benevolence, as the architect of the Hurlingham victory.

'We have developed a tradition of giving our stories titles,' he explained to Trevithick, 'and I have decided to call mine 'Ex Libris', for it came out of a book – in a fairly literal manner.'

'Very mysterious,' grinned Trevithick. 'Are you always this enigmatic?'

'Not on the polo field, with a mallet in my hand,' responded Henton. 'But in fact my story is pretty straightforward in one sense, although it concerns not just me but also another member of the Society.'

'That isn't much clearer than your first remark,' said Penrose.

'Yes, do try to speak in plain English, Henton old chap, Brackenbury Scholarship notwithstanding,' said Sharpe (for Henton had read Classics at Balliol). 'Hear, hear,' said Buffy. Henton sighed again, and said: 'Alright, then, I'll start at the beginning – and in this case the beginning begins a long time ago.'

'For heaven's sake...' muttered Sharpe; but Buffy shook his head, and whispered, 'Just let him do it in his own way. I've a feeling this will be a good one.'

'As I was saying,' said Henton, giving Sharpe a look – 'As I was saying, the beginning begins a long time ago – when I was about seven or eight, in fact. My story is about memory and reality, and the strange links between the two; about the way in which the past can jump in upon the present, and change them both in the process. Have you ever seen a house with an old advertisement for something on the gable-end, which has been painted over? You'll know, then, that it's nearly impossible to conceal completely the lettering that lies underneath; that in certain conditions – say, bright sunshine – you can still see what was written there, and that the gable-end looks quite different as a result.

'Well, that's just what I'm getting at with my tale: the thing lying underneath, the memory, is still there; and in certain conditions the memory comes to the surface, and everything is transformed.'

He paused to re-light his cigar, the tip glowing in the falling darkness.

'In this case the memory concerns my childhood summers spent in Ireland – County Down, to be precise – with relatives on my mother's side. I had cousins in Warrenpoint and sometimes spent a week or two with them; but mostly I stayed with my mother's sister, Mary, and her husband Felix in their house at Tamnaharry, while my parents were overseas. Mary and Felix both died of the 'flu when I was eleven, and I was heartbroken, of course; I couldn't bring myself to go back after that, and begged my parents to let me travel out to their diplomatic residences between school terms.

'They wouldn't have it, however – said Cairo and Khartoum were no places for a boy, and I daresay they were right – but as that meant I had to spend my summers with the frightful Mitchells (some distant relations of my father, but the worst kind of arrivistes) I bitterly resented their decision. By comparison with the Mitchells' suburban villa, my late lamented aunt's ancient farmhouse at Tamnaharry seemed the very image of perfection: clear skies, green fields, a noble view of Carlingford Lough, and the strong shoulders of the Mourne Mountains as they roll down to the sea.

'There was something about the place – something magical – something that even then, as a boy (or perhaps especially as a boy) I recognised as utterly different from the manicured lawns and hallowed towers of England. I felt the call of the hills, of the sea – the call of loneliness itself – and once you've heard it, you can't forget it. You chaps will know what I'm talking about, for it's in the heart of every sportsman to get away, to be alone in the hidden depths of the hills.'

'Oh, is that what it is?' said Buffy. 'For my part, I like

being alone so that no-one can see how bad a shot I am!'

The company laughed, and Henton conceded the point with good grace.

'There's that, too,' he said. 'Perhaps I exaggerate, but I'm sure you'll know what I mean, when I say that perfect happiness consists of a warm sun on your back, a fly-rod in your hand, and an unknown stream in front of you, that no-one else has ever fished.' Buffy waved his cigar in assent, and Henton carried on with his tale.

'I think my uncle realised I had a feeling for the country, for he made a point of taking me around the mountains on walking expeditions – often with a gun or rod apiece, for he was a born sportsman and knew all the best spots thereabouts. Many times we returned with bird or fish for the table, to my aunt's delight; but there were also times when we did not shoot or cast a line. My uncle was a keen historian, and was pretty near obsessed with the ancient relics that lie scattered about the Mournes. He showed me the menhir at Tamnaharry, and the Cloughmore Stone on Slieve Martin above Rostrevor; I can still remember the look of wild enthusiasm on his face as he told me the old legend regarding the Stone, that it had been thrown by the giant Fionn mac Cumhaill from the other side of Carlingford Lough. That would have been quite a throw, by the way – the Stone must weigh thirty or forty tons.

'But of all the jaunts we took, one in particular stuck in my memory. It was a beautiful summer day of a kind so rare in Ireland, where it seems to rain six days in a week and eleven months in the year. We set off early on our bicycles, for we had a long cycle ahead of us; and we took our fly-rods and creels, for my uncle knew of a remote lake where (it was said) Arctic Char were to be had. Lough Shannagh was the water's name – the lake of the foxes, my uncle explained as we cycled up the Newry Road to Hilltown. As we passed through Hilltown and set off southwards past the River Bann, he told me how his father had once taken him up to Lough Shannagh as a boy, but as they had come without tackle they had left without wetting a line. My uncle told me his father had always said it was the most beautiful lough in Ireland, and that he, my uncle, had always planned to walk up and have a look at it, but had put it off endlessly (as one does); he was glad, he said, to have someone else to show the lough, for nothing else would have made him get on and do it.

'Anyway, once we got south of Stang we looked around for somewhere to leave our bicycles and set out on foot. Soon we found a little track heading north-east of the road, and followed that up to the foot of Sliabh an Chairn. It was a glorious day, as I said, and I remember my reaction as we rounded the southern edge of the hill and saw Lough Shannagh for the first time, shining in the noonday sun. I was struck by the air of unearthly peace which hung over its waters – placid now, save for an occasional breeze which ruffled its surface; but I knew even then that the weather in the Mournes is fickle indeed, and I imagined the same lough in the depths of winter, with a lowering bank of rain-clouds threatening the massed peaks and beating down upon the lake's surface with relentless blast of air and water.

'This thought frightened my childish mind, but in some way this menacing undertone also seemed to underpin the lough's appeal that day, in the sweet radiance of the summer's warmth. The summer beauty and the winter wildness were two sides of the same coin, and they combined now to cast a spell of ancient power – a spell whose words had long been forgotten, or whose forming had come perhaps from a time before language; but a spell that spoke nevertheless, talking of the silence that inhabits the mountain and rests upon the waters.'

As if to honour the tranquillity of which he spoke, Henton paused awhile, and silence fell upon the Society as they sat smoking in the twilight. After a few minutes Penrose roused himself – Henton's words had (appropriately enough) cast a kind of enchantment upon him, he reflected – and stubbed out the remains of his cigar.

'I say, you chaps,' he said. 'How about moving inside? It's beginning to get distinctly chilly, and speaking for myself I'd rather avoid the falling damps.'

'No, no,' said Buffy. 'It's the rising damps you want to worry about, old man.'

'Poppycock,' put in Sharpe. 'Penrose is right and you are wrong. It was the falling damps that did for my great-uncle Hamish, and before he expired he gave my father a lurid warning regarding the dangers of said damps. He said...' And Sharpe proceeded to relate the warning given to Sharpe's father by his great uncle, to the accompaniment of which enthralling anecdote the party gathered up their things and moved indoors.

Once the Society had re-established themselves in the private room in which they had dined, Henton rang the bell and called for whisky – Irish whiskey, if there was any in the House – 'to put us in the mood.' (Clearly he was still trying to win his audience over through alcoholic means.) Once every man had a glass in his hand, he began again.

'Now, where was I? Oh yes – Lough Shannagh, and its sublime peacefulness. You may be surprised to learn that my uncle and I, on that far-off day, were so enchanted that we hadn't the heart to cast a line. Perhaps it is hard to believe that any two sportsmen could travel so far, on bicycle and foot, with a lot of heavy tackle, without troubling the waters – but if you could have just seen the place, you would have understood.

'Instead of organising our tackle, we sat down on the slopes of Sliabh an Chairn and ate the simple lunch we had brought with us. After that we walked around the edge of the water towards a little grey fishing lodge perched on the Lough's north-eastern lip, drinking in the blessed quietness as we walked. My uncle told me he had a vague recollection of the man who lived in the lodge, whom his father had talked to on their visit some years before. They don't trouble about formalities in Ireland, you know, and he just marched up to the door and knocked on it once before pushing it open and calling out, 'Anyone at home?' A voice answered, and was soon given bodily accompaniment in the form of a man whom I judged to be in his late forties, dressed (to use the expression rather loosely) in a very old and tattered suit, and smoking a rough clay pipe. I remember little of what he said to my uncle, or vice versa – but I do vaguely recall shaking his hand when I was introduced, and answering in the negative when he asked if I knew 'another English fella' who occasionally came up to visit the lough. We passed a pleasant hour or two in his company, and after an additional walk to bag the peak of Sliabh an Chairn we set off home. And that was the end of that – I never visited the lough with my uncle again, although I have always treasured the memory of the visit.'

Henton paused here to refill his glass, and the others exchanged glances.

'Henton, old chap,' said Trevithick. 'That isn't the end of the story, is it? Only I've been led to believe that the Society was set up for the purpose of telling tall tales – and I'm afraid that your story hasn't stretched my credulity one little bit!'

Henton laughed. 'No, don't worry – I haven't finished yet; and the bit you might find hard to swallow is still to come! Here, let me top you up' – plying the decanter – 'and you, Penrose. Come on, Buffy and Sharpe – drink up! That's right – here's some more. Now we can settle down for the second half of my story – the best half, if I'm any judge.

'It may have struck the more astute of you that I have a remarkable memory for geography – for the roads, mountains, rivers, and so forth, involved in this particular expedition. Well, you'd be wrong. I didn't remember any of that whatsoever – what boy remembers that kind of thing? No, the reason I know is that I recently visited the lake again – and entirely by accident.'

'By accident? How can you visit a lake by accident?' said Buffy.

'With the greatest of ease, given the right conditions,' said Henton. 'This is how it came about:

'I happened to be in Belfast a month or so ago to carry out some work for my firm; it was a tricky business at first, though I managed to get it sorted out in the end, and three weeks saw the job finished. Well, I had planned to be in Ireland for a fortnight longer than that, and when I cabled HQ to let them know they very kindly told me to take a holiday.'

'Gosh, that's a bit of luck,' breathed Penrose.

'It certainly was, and I meant to make the most of it,

you may be sure. I began by spending a day or two shooting grey partridges in County Antrim, and after that I took the train to Downpatrick. I had a notion to visit the Mourne Mountains, you see, and to see again my aunt's old house at Tamnaharry. Like a fool I had come without my fishing tackle, and so I tracked down a little tackle shop in Downpatrick and bought a few essentials there. It was an attractive little place, all crooked beams and smoke-stained walls, and I spent some time admiring the proprietor's extensive collection of horse-brasses. As I was about to settle up, I noticed a little bookcase by the door, containing a dog-eared miscellany of sporting books – novels by Surtees, fishing texts by Greendrake, and Captain Chapman's hunting reminiscences – all for sale at a bob apiece. It so happens that I have a particular passion for the adventures of Jorrocks, so I picked up a copy of 'Handley Hall' and added it to my bill.

'The next day I set out for the Mournes. My plan was first to visit the house at Tamnaharry, as I said, and then to wander the mountains in search of sport. I did of course remember Lough Shannagh – or, rather, I remembered that my uncle had taken me to a lake that we found too beautiful to fish; I could no more have pinpointed it on a map than flown to the moon. I entertained few hopes of coming across it by accident, but during the next week or so I tramped across a fair amount of countryside with just that aim in mind. By day I fished in little streams and loughs too small to name, and stayed at country inns by night. Occasionally I happened across bridges, or houses, or prehistoric monuments that I had visited with my uncle; and of course I was able to find the house at Tamnaharry without any difficulty. It had been let out after my aunt and uncle died, but the tenants themselves had since died, and the house had been allowed to fall into disrepair. The roof had fallen in over one of the wings, and many of the doors and windows were sagging open. I decided – probably against my better judgement – that I would go in and have a look around.

'Well, there are few things more depressing than poking round a derelict house where once lights burned brightly and friendly voices rang in laughter. Even now, some weeks later, I can still feel the desolation I felt then; it was like losing my aunt and uncle all over again. But I won't linger on this miserable topic; I mention all this merely to set the scene for what happened next.

'As I went down to dinner at the little inn where I was staying that night, I felt pretty low in my spirits, and decided to cheer myself up by reading Surtees' 'Handley Hall' between courses.'

'I say,' put in Buffy. 'Can a fellow be sconced for brute bad manners?'

'Oh, don't play the fool, Buffy,' said Sharpe. 'My father used to visit that part of the world, too, and he always said he loved the lack of ceremony. Nobody would blink an eyelid at a fellow reading a book at table – am I right, Henton?'

'Yes, indeed,' said Henton. 'In fact, a chap in Ireland would be more likely to attract censure for reading at table on the grounds that he wasn't being lively enough! But to return to my tale: it was while committing this most egregious of social faults that I made an interesting discovery. I happened to drop the book on the floor when the waiter brought my beefsteak, and it fell open at the back page. It was then I realised that a previous owner had written copious notes on the back of the book and (flicking through the later chapters) on many other pages also.

'I clicked my tongue in irritation, for I detest annotations of any kind. They distract one's eye from the text, and they rarely, if anything, add anything to what the author has already said... Oh, I know you will cite Dr Johnson, and Milton, and so forth,' – this to Buffy, who had opened his mouth to speak – 'but how often does a Johnson, a Milton, lay pen to paper? Not once in an age.'

'Actually, old bean,' said Buffy, 'I was just going to say that I always liked doing those drawings on the corners of my Latin books. You know, a chap runs up and bowls, the ball flies down the wicket, and the batsman hits a smashing straight drive for six! Passed many happy hours when I should have been studying the old hic, haec, hoc.'

The others laughed, but Henton closed his eyes and drew in a deep breath.

'Thank you for that erudite contribution, Buffy,' he said. 'But you make a good point, in your idiotic way – some annotations can be entertaining and interesting. And in any case, I defy anyone who opens an annotated text not to read what has been written; there is always the chance that it was a Johnson or a Milton!

'In this case, however, I realised that the 'annotations' were in fact not annotations at all, but, rather, excerpts from a game book.'

'A game book? How do you mean?' said Penrose.

'Just what I said,' replied Henton. 'A game book. You know, entries of hunting, shooting, and fishing expeditions, weather, species bagged, company, location – all the usual things. Clearly this chap had forgotten his own game book and had made do with the back of a novel instead.'

'Dashed ingenious, I call it,' said Trevithick.

'He'd done pretty well, too,' said Henton. 'He'd fished all around the Mournes, and had also done some good work in the adjoining counties. It was fascinating stuff, and over the next few days I began to follow in his footsteps, to see if I could emulate his success. I was in luck, for he'd obviously been on a walking-tour like mine, so I had at least a sporting chance of covering the same ground. He'd been a stickler for geography, and had put in little sketch maps detailing how he'd got to the loughs and streams he'd fished.

'Neverthless I was pretty hard-pressed, for he clearly knew his stuff – and while as far as I could make out he had pretty much always gone home with a fish or two, I blanked several times. It became quite a game with me, and instilled a note of urgency into my supposedly relaxing holiday. I pushed myself to walk farther and faster, to cover more ground and get to more waters. Each day I got the book out at dawn and read a new entry, and then set about getting to the water in question.

'It was about a week later that I came to the most interesting entry of all. By that time I was up near Hilltown, and had stayed the night before in the little town of Stang. You may remember that I mentioned this place previously, when I told you the route I took with my uncle when I visited Lough Shannagh with him. I knew that the lough was somewhere in the Mournes, but I had no idea of how close I was to it.

'So when I read the next entry it simply didn't occur to me that it could be Lough Shannagh. The entry omitted the name of the water, which was odd, as all the other entries had been scrupulous on that point. And moreover the entry said nothing about fishing at all – no details of flies, or the bag he'd gone home with. It was odd, as I say; but I thought nothing more of it, guessing that perhaps the chap had got home too late to write up his notes. I think I even gave in to the optimism that haunts fishermen, allowing myself to believe that perhaps he had got home late because he had caught so many fish!

'Then I set off from Stang just after dawn. It was spring, of course, but I had been unlucky with the weather and the past week had had its fair share of icy winds and torrential downpours; and unfortunately that morning was no exception. It was to the accompaniment of a howling gale and horizontal rain that I struck off the Slievenaman Road and set out across the hills, occasionally turning my back against the weather to inspect the miniature sketch-map that was my only navigational aid.

'After about two hours of scrambling across the difficult countryside I saw a couple of low peaks emerge out of the squalls on the horizon, and perhaps half an hour after that I came upon a smallish lough. By this time I had pretty nearly had enough of the cold and the wet, and when I saw a little house with smoke pouring out of its chimney I made for it like a bee makes for nectar. I rapped on the door and pushed inside when it was opened in front of me.

'Once inside I turned to my host to apologise for my rudeness, but when I saw the man's face I was rendered mute, for it was the very same man I had visited with my uncle all those years ago. I dashed back to the door and wrenched it open to look on the lough, and it seemed as if the landscape, recently so hostile and menacing, had suddenly become familiar and more than familiar, a thing known and loved of old. I now recognised the shape of the lough and remembered the names of the mountains – how had I not done so before? – and when I turned to face the old man again I found I could picture my uncle talking to him, as he had done on that far-off day. It was as if the sun had come out and shone upon one of those gable-end advertisements I mentioned at the start, and brought all the lettering through bright and clear. I wrung the old man by the hand, and explained who I was and why I had come. He nodded when I mentioned my uncle, and told me he had been a good man, the best of men.

'He gave me tea and wheaten bread with thick-cut marmalade, and the warmth of his fire was heavenly after my long exposure to the bleak weather outside. We talked of the area and of my uncle; he even said that he remembered my visit as a boy, though I suspect he was being kind. We got to talking about my walking-trip, and of course I produced my Surtees novel and showed him the improvised game book sketched on its pages.

'He seemed to get excited about this, and turned the book over and over in his hands while looking up at the ceiling; I got the impression he was trying to bring a memory to the surface. Was there a name in the book, he asked, and flicked through the title pages. Just an initialling, I said – J.S. – and a year, 1911. He sat for a while then, staring into the fire and running his hand over his forehead, presumably as if he could physically coax the stubborn strands of memory into carrying out their duty.

'Suddenly he slapped his leg. "Sharpe!" he cried out.'

'Sharpe?' cried Penrose, staring at the Sharpe in their midst.

'Sharpe,' said Henton. 'He went on: "Julian Sharpe. That's the feller. Finest fisherman I ever saw this side of Lough Neagh."'

'Julian Sharpe was my father,' said Sharpe, wonderingly.

'I know,' said Henton. 'He was "J.S.", and the author of the game book, and a damned good sportsman to boot. I

177

think you should have this,' and he took the Surtees novel out of his pocket and handed it to Sharpe.

'This is his handwriting,' said Sharpe, opening the book. 'And he used to go to Ireland for the fishing once a year, until he got his beat on the Tay... I often accompanied him, but there were a couple of summers I spent in France and Italy instead – that must have been when he went to the Mournes. But how did you know that Julian Sharpe was my father?'

'Well, I didn't know, of course,' said Henton. 'Call it intuition, or perhaps an educated guess – you fish, so perhaps your father fished... Once I got back to London I made sure of it, though – I looked up your father in an old *Who's Who*, and wrote to his Club, and they confirmed that the description of him I'd got from the old chap – whose name is McKeown, by the way – was unquestionably your father. I say, Sharpe, what a sportsman your father was! He beat me hands down on pretty much every water.'

'Well, I'm jiggered,' said Sharpe. He looked again at the pages filled with his father's handwriting, and went on: 'I suppose he must have copied out his notes into a proper game book when he got back to Downpatrick, and left the novel behind when he left. I'm sure he would have been delighted to know that it found its way to me. Thanks, old chap,' and, visibly moved, he leaned over to shake Henton by the hand.

'My pleasure, old boy,' said Henton. 'And just one last thing I thought you might like to know – McKeown said that your father came back to visit him again before he left to return to England, and that on neither visit had your father got his rod out to fish the lough. Apparently he told McKeown it was too beautiful to fish, and that all he wanted to do was to smoke his pipe and look at it – rather like my uncle, in fact. I suppose the finest things in sport are sometimes the things we *don't* do.'

'That's a noble end to the story,' cried Trevithick, and the Society applauded heartily by way of agreement.

'Moreover, there doesn't seem much doubt that your story is true,' went on Trevithick.

'Absolutely,' said Henton. 'There is the novel to prove it.'

'So I imagine there will be no sconcing, after all,' said Trevithick with a disappointed air.

Henton had just heaved a sigh of relief when Penrose began knocking softly on the table. 'Hold hard a moment,' he said. 'There's no doubt the story is true, but what about your title – "Ex Libris", wasn't it?'

'Yes,' said a puzzled Henton. 'What's that got to do with anything?'

'I think I can see what Penrose is getting at,' said Sharpe. '"Libris" is the plural, thus implying a translation of "library" rather than "book" singular... And as your story refers to a singular book rather than a library, surely you should have called it "Ex Libro"...'

'Oh, you can't be serious,' began Henton; but he looked around the table and saw frowns, shaking heads, and looks of grave concern; and he knew the game was up. Resignedly he rang a little bell that the waiter had left on the table, and soon the Society beheld a familiar sight: Sharpe's sconcing vessel, full to the brim with English ale. The waiter brought the tankard to Henton, who with a wry smile grasped it firmly, and drank its contents down to the sound of cheering.

He set it down, wiped his lips, and looked squarely at Trevithick.

'You're next,' he said.

But Trevithick merely grinned, raised his glass, and proposed a toast to the Society.

'In vino veritas!' he cried.

'In vino veritas!' they replied, and emptied their glasses, to a man.

Pink Coats and Coronets

TO MOST ordinary Britons, the châtelaine's lot appears an enviable one. Surrounded by tranquil parkland rather than tumultuous streets, and ensconced in ivy-clad battlements as opposed to smoke-stained brick, she is mistress of all that she surveys. A legion of liveried lackeys at her beck and call, her merest whim is holy writ; and heaven forfend that anything as vulgar as a balance-sheet should intrude upon her management of internal affairs. The hoi polloi may struggle to keep their heads above water, but she sails serenely onwards, buoyed up by a thousand years of inherited wealth, privilege, and misshaped noses. Man is born to misery, as the sparks fly upwards – this she may concede; but as for women, and especially this woman, well! She will simply raise a handsomely-shaped eyebrow, draw in her breath and shrink you down to size with a withering look. Far from suffering the slings and arrows of outrageous fortune, she dauntlessly opposes (and ends) a sea of troubles, frequently before breakfast, and certainly well before luncheon.

Or so it might appear to the greengrocer or haber-dasher who, on a warm summer afternoon, surrenders a coin or two in exchange for the chance to walk around a few rooms with roped-off paintings and little signs explaining the provenance of this or that priceless objet d'art. Catching a distant glimpse of the Lady of the House, they draw in their breath, and cast jealous looks in her direction. What luck, they mutter to themselves, to live in such surroundings – to dispose of such opulence and splendour.

As with many first impressions, however, the truth of the matter is rather more vexed than appearances – in this case, the gleaming silver and sumptuous tapestries – might suggest. Take, for instance, Lady Fiona Spence, comptroller-general of Hailsham Castle, Shropshire, a striking example of late mediaeval style and the centrepiece of a large and beautiful estate. Lady Fiona may have had a staff of forty-six at her command, two Holbeins in the Library, and part of a skull supposed to have belonged to Saint Edward the Confessor in the Chapel, but at the moment when this narrative begins she was to be found sitting at her bureau with furrowed brow and wearied countenance, elegant face buried in elegant hands, and muttering to herself like a religious fanatic.

'The writers next to the Wylies – no, of course, must have alternating sexes... There is still the Viscount and his fiancée – not to mention Oakeshott and his ... And where to put Brother Cedd and Miss Osmond? Oh, bother it all!' And she so far forgot herself as to thump on the bureau in a most unladylike fashion, making Castor and Pollux (her corgis) start in surprise, and knocking over her cup of Earl Grey. 'Damn and blast...' she cried, jumping to her feet and snatching a (now rather waterlogged) sheet of paper from the desk.

'Having trouble, sister dear?' enquired an amused voice.

'Oh, Ian,' said Lady Fiona, spinning round to face her brother. 'You gave me such a shock! Look at this – this mess – my favourite cardigan, ruined. And as for this seating plan... I will never finish it! Be quiet, Castor! Hush, Pollux!'

The Fifth Earl of Hailsham, dressed in a hacking jacket and top-boots, stepped forward and took the drooping paper from her hand. 'It is rather a muddle, old girl,' he said, having inspected the provisional seating arrangements for supper that evening. 'Why, you've put me next to the Viscount Northam, and another man on his left – that will never do. Look, why don't you tell me who our guests are this week, and I will create order from chaos. Come on, sit down in that chair, and I'll get a fresh sheet of paper. Now, let's see – bureau sopping wet – apply handkerchief. Handkerchief ruined, surface dried. Corgis removed to another room, and pencil sharpened – right, fire away!'

'Thank you, Ian,' said Lady Fiona. 'This is just what I need... someone else to blame when things go wrong tonight! Well, let's see' – consulting a notebook – 'first of all we have two itinerant writers – Axel Andersson, a Swedish novelist, and Tania Espinoza, an Argentinean scholar. I met them in Paris when I stayed with Countess d'Agoult on the Rue de Montholon last summer. Such erudition; you would scarcely credit it. Then there are the Wylie girls – Patricia and Sarah; perhaps you remember them from last season – they made rather a stir at Henley. Charming girls, altogether – Patricia is a philanthropist, and Sarah an actress, and they are relations of Peter Wylie, the famous South American explorer. There is Miss Charlotte Osmond, the celebrated showjumper and veterinarian, who has promised to help me with my riding. Next on my list – let's see – ah yes, Brother Cedd Mannion, a monk and a scholar, who was invited by Aunt Felicity to advise on the restoration of the Chapel. Then we have the Viscount Northam, whom you know, of course – and his fiancée, Claire Kennedy.'

'I haven't met Miss Kennedy – I suppose she is an indoors type of girl, rather like Northam?'

'I'm not sure Northam would be pleased to be described as a girl of any description,' replied Lady Fiona, 'and in any case Miss Kennedy is not at all indoorsy. She is some kind of a luminary at the Royal Geographical, I understand, and much given to adventuring overseas. We also have Francis Oakeshott – one of the Hertfordshire Oakeshotts, I believe – and a Miss Heather Andrew, Oakeshott's fiancée.'

'Two engaged couples!' said the Earl of Hailsham. 'I didn't realise it would be such a romantic weekend. I have met

Oakeshott before, and heard that he had got engaged – very recently, I believe – but again I am unacquainted with the lady. Miss Andrew, you say?'

'Yes – she is a very artistic girl, and I hear from Lady Carlisle in Belgravia that she has done great things in the pre-Raphaelite line; but Oakeshott I do not know at all. I understand from Lady Carlisle, however, that he is a kindred spirit in the artistic sense; although I had always heard that the Oakeshotts were great enthusiasts for hunting and shooting.

'And there is also you and me, and Aunt Felicity; and that is all,' concluded Lady Fiona.

'That is all, you say!' said a stunned-looking Lord Hailsham. 'I see now why you had some trouble with the arrangements... Well, let us see what intelligence and application can accomplish.'

'Oh, is someone else joining us?' enquired Lady Fiona artlessly.

'You may sneer,' replied her brother, somewhat haughtily. 'But I have rather a knack for this kind of thing, and I promise you that tonight will be a roaring success.'

And while pride of any kind is apt to be followed by a fall, Lord Hailsham was delighted to observe that the evening's repast was indeed consumed to the accompaniment of enthusiastic conversation, with all the newly-arrived guests showing genuine pleasure and interest in their dining companions. Brother Cedd and the Wylies, who were seated one on each side, became embroiled in a fierce (but good-hearted) debate regarding the virtues of various theatrical and musical productions currently showing in London, while Charlotte Osmond and the peripatetic authors, Andersson and Espinoza, entertained themselves with a lengthy discussion concerning the different riding styles employed in their respective homelands. Lady Fiona, Lord Hailsham, and Lady Felicity, for their part, spent an enjoyable hour or two swapping the latest London society gossip.

But the Earl of Hailsham's masterstroke was to seat the affianced couples together. As the courses came and went, the quartet found they had much in common with each other.

When Lord Northam discovered that Miss Heather Andrew had been raised in Cumbria, he waxed lyrical about Ruskin and Wordsworth, and declared that a visit to Dove Cottage had been the highlight of a recent trip to the North – though, he added hurriedly (and somewhat to Heather's surprise), it had been nothing to compare with the fishing to be had thereabouts. To this, Oakeshott cried 'Shame!' and asserted his view that while sporting pursuits had their place, and while he knew for a fact that Northam was absolutely right concerning the excellence of Cumbria's fishing, there was surely nothing in the piscatorial world that could compare to a single page of Coleridge or Keats. Heather nodded approvingly, but in response Claire Kennedy enquired if Mr Oakeshott had ever seen the Great Rift Valley in Kenya, especially north of Nairobi, where the rift is at its most dramatic; Oakeshott replied in the negative, at which point Claire described the appearance of the Valley at sunrise, as she had seen it just the year before.

'That may give your poets a run for their money, I suggest,' she concluded.

'I say,' said Oakeshott, eyes aglow. 'That sounds worth seeing, by Jove! Nothing finer than a new land to explore, and new game to pursue – er – nothing finer, that is, except the artist's commemoration of such beauty in fitting works of inspiration,' he added, looking at Heather, who pursed her lips and smiled in (somewhat grudging) approbation. His remarks seemed to find more favour with Northam, who nodded enthusiastically, and asked if any of the company had seen the paintings of Dutton, an intrepid artist who had travelled the length of Africa in order to paint new subjects, and who had exhibited the resulting works in a small but exclusive gallery in Chelsea.

His words of praise struck a chord with Heather, who happened greatly to admire Dutton's work; and so the conversation went back and forth all evening, and indeed continued the next day, when the two couples foregathered in front of Hailsham Castle early in the morning, in advance of a fishing expedition to the nearby River Tern. The rest of the house party were still happily asleep; Oakeshott had insisted on a pre-dawn start, having heard that the fishing on the Tern was usually best in the early morning – and, of course, he added, the peace and tranquillity of the sunrise hour was always a source of artistic renewal. Heather, who rarely rose before noon, nevertheless found it difficult to argue with this, and so found herself woken by her maid at an unspeakable hour; Northam, too, was yawning as he made his way reluctantly downstairs, only to find Claire and Oakeshott, ridiculously animated for the time of day, deep in a discussion of the Buddhist monasteries of Tibet.

'I say, you two,' said Northam. 'Better not chatter too loudly, or you'll wake up all the others. Where's Miss Andrew?'

'Here,' said a sleepy voice. 'Here I am – though it's a pretty poor show, to drag us out of bed this early in the morning, all for the sake of a few fish!'

'Oh, Hetty,' said Oakeshott. 'Surely it is romantic, and rather fun, to rise before the sun, and breakfast at daybreak, and set off on horseback to who knows where? Or, in our case, to the River Tern, by motor-car,' he added, rather spoiling the effect; but Claire nodded vigorously nonetheless.

'I couldn't agree more,' she said. 'If we must live in such a dull, tame country as England, surely we must do something out of the ordinary run of things, or go melancholy mad with boredom – I know I should, anyhow. Don't you agree, darling?' – this to Northam, who simpered his agreement, but in a somewhat half-hearted fashion.

'Shall we go, then?' enquired Heather, rather in the manner of a condemned prisoner eager to get the execution over with. To this the others agreed, and as quietly as possible they left the castle and tiptoed round to the stables to pick up the cars. The groom had already packed the cars with their tackle, and in a matter of minutes Claire, who loved driving, and Oakeshott, were behind their respective steering-wheels, driving their future spouses northwards to the Tern – Northam in a state of some terror (for Claire rarely spared the horses), and Heather in a state of unconsciousness, having submitted to fatigue and the (admittedly soporific) sound of Oakeshott discoursing on the wet-fly tactics he planned to use that day. In half an hour or so the party arrived at the chosen beat, and Northam and Oakeshott cast their first lines just as the sun was dawning.

'Beautiful,' said a revived Heather, whipping out a sketchpad and setting down the beginnings of a new interpretation of *The Lady of Shalott*. 'Hear a song that echoes cheerly/ From the river winding clearly,/down to towered Camelot,' she murmured as she drew.

'Yes, very nice,' said Claire briskly. 'I say, Julian,' she called to Northam, 'I think I saw some fish darting about over there, on the far side – why don't you wade in a little, and see if you can cast over them? Your gum-boots will keep you perfectly dry. Go on – just a little deeper – oh, Julian!' she cried, for the Viscount Northam, venturing too quickly and too deep, had stepped on an algae-clad rock, and, losing his footing, fell headlong into the river.

'Oof – up you come!' said Oakeshott, who had dashed into the water to rescue the hapless nobleman. Soon a dripping Northam lay panting on the bank, his tackle all awry, and missing a shoe.

'Are you alright, Julian?' enquired Claire. Northam answered in the affirmative, although with a touch of asperity – he had not forgotten on whose bidding he had waded into the river. His irritation was heightened rather than diminished when Claire, realising that Northam had lost one of his shoes, saw the funny side of proceedings, and began to giggle infectiously. At least, Oakeshott found her amusement to be catching, and was soon hooting with laughter, much to Northam's annoyance; but his temper was soothed by Heather's air of slight impatience with Claire and Oakeshott, and by the sympathetic way in which she removed three strands of weed and a frog from his waistcoat.

Northam was also gratified when Heather asked him if he would be willing to serve as the model for Lancelot in her Lady of Shalott.

'Why, of course,' he said. 'I'd be honoured.'

'Are you *blushing*, Northam?' cried Claire. 'I shouldn't

have asked him, if I were you, Heather – he's as big-headed as an elephant, and vain as a peacock. Now, can't you forget about art for a little while – present company excepted, Heather, of course – and do some fishing?'

But art came up again later that day, when a tired but satisfied fishing party – nine brown trout and a grayling to Oakeshott, four trout to a still-damp Northam – wandered into the garden-house for a late tea. There they found the Wylie sisters, Charlotte Osmond, and Lord Hailsham, sitting in comfortable chairs and sipping cups of tea while watching a young artist, suitably attired in smock and beret, putting the finishing touches to the last in a series of neo-classical frescoes.

'The true buon fresco!' cried Northam, rushing up to the paintings for a closer look. 'This is something you rarely see. And my congratulations, sir, if I may say so' – this to the artist, who nodded politely – 'I have rarely seen such a fine Roman capriccio.' Having said this, he realised that Claire was looking at him rather strangely, and so felt obliged to add: 'Not that I know anything of such matters, of course!'

'Isn't Roman architecture one of your special interests, Francis?' asked Heather, encouragingly.

'Ah – yes – indeed,' stammered Oakeshott. 'I agree with everything Northam here says – the finest Parthenon I ever saw. Or, rather, the finest Colosseum. Or is it the Pantheon? Well, dash it all, it's very good, anyway,' he finished, blushing in his turn.

'Are you coming out tomorrow?' said Claire to Lord Hailsham, shelving the subject altogether.

'For the meet?' he said. 'Oh, certainly – wouldn't miss it – though I believe that Lady Fiona will sit this one out, as she has a bad knee at present; an old hockey injury playing up. She tells me that she has fixed you up with her Mephisto? A wonderful jumper – Miss Osmond was putting her through her paces in the park today, and had nothing but good words to say about her.'

'I think you will do very well on her,' said Charlotte. 'She is the neatest little thing – and full of nerve. There isn't a fence in the park she couldn't skip over!'

'You will ride side-saddle, I presume, dearest?' enquired Northam, who had never hunted with his fiancée before.

'Nothing of the sort,' said Claire. 'Never have, and never will. They don't ride side-saddle in Kenya, you know – and that's where I learned to ride! Don't worry, darling – I won't have any trouble, you'll see. Are you joining us, Heather?'

'No fear,' said the artist. 'I'm going to sleep in very late indeed, and then do some more sketches for the Lady of Shalott. But I hope you will look after Northam in the field – I want my Lancelot in one piece at the end of the day!'

'What about your Oakeshott?' said the possessor of that name. 'Don't I deserve any of your concern?'

'Oh – yes, of course, darling,' said Heather. 'Of course you do. I just didn't think you'd be going out. I thought – well, I thought perhaps you would find hunting too sanguinary a pastime.'

'Oh, no,' said Oakeshott. 'Try to stop me going out with the North Shropshire! The finest pack in the county… and such a rustic scene,' he added quickly. 'Just the thing for a spot of artistic contemplation, on the nature of country traditions, and all that.'

'Quite,' said Heather, looking slightly discontented. 'Well, I hope you all enjoy yourselves. I shan't come and see you off – I need to catch up on my beauty-sleep, after our fiendishly early start this morning. In fact, I hope you won't mind if I don't appear for supper this evening – I'm going for a bath and then straight to work. When I need to paint, I can do nothing else. I may walk out and meet you coming back tomorrow. Until then - toodle pip!' And with that she swept from the room and was gone.

Heather was true to her word, and although lights could be seen shining from her rooms until the early hours of the morning, her curtains remained firmly drawn when the horses and hounds of the North Shropshire began to gather outside Hailsham Castle next morning. Even the usual cacophony of barking, calling, and blowing of horns failed to wake her; but they did alert Northam, Oakeshott, and

Claire, who had lingered over a tremendous breakfast, that some despatch was required lest the hunt depart without them. They ran down the staircase together, Northam throwing on his pink coat and adjusting his stock as he ran and Claire struggling to secure her hairnet without dropping her whip. She wore jodhpurs, of course, and drew admiring glances from several of the huntsmen as she leapt into the saddle.

'Let's be off, then,' she cried; and having drained a stirrup cup, she gave Mephisto a rousing kick and trotted after the departing pack. Northam and Oakeshott exchanged a look and set off in her wake.

Thus began what, for Oakeshott, was one of the most exhilarating rides of his life and, for Northam, one of the most petrifying. Claire never rode without setting herself at the steepest and most vertiginous obstacles for miles around, and both men made a valiant attempt to keep up – Northam from duty, and Oakeshott from delight. When Claire set herself at a hedge in defiance of height or a ditch in defiance of width, Oakeshott also threw himself over with gusto; but poor Northam, a cautious rider at best, approached each barrier with turned head and eyes half shut, which as every rider knows is a recipe for disaster.

Sure enough, it was not long before the Viscount lost his balance completely on an especially precipitous jump, and pitched over his mount's flank. Upon reaching earth, he bowled across the grass like a circus tumbler before finally coming to rest against a tree-stump of unarguably solid dimensions. His horse, seemingly disoriented, galloped on after the pack.

Looking back and seeing the Viscount's downfall, Claire swore vehemently, then circled back from the vanguard and galloped towards where he lay. Having reached him, she jumped down from Mephisto and ran to his side. Oakeshott, having just cleared a difficult stretch of hawthorn, caught sight of the scene, and also made his way across.

'Darling,' said Claire urgently. 'Darling, are you alright? Talk to me!'

The words swam through Northam's befuddled mind and summoned him to full consciousness. Slowly opening his eyes, he made out Claire's features against the sky.

'You came back for me,' he said, smiling weakly and sitting up carefully. 'I say, darling, I don't think...' But when Claire saw that the Viscount was capable of speech and movement, and was therefore unlikely to be seriously injured, she called out, 'Right – back to it! See you at the castle,' and jumped back into the saddle. Oakeshott, who had not dismounted at all, grinned at Northam and touched his whip to the brim of his hat; then the two riders set off at a furious gallop, to make up the lost time.

When they were lost to sight, Northam lay back against the tree-stump and, sighing deeply, lit a thoughtful cigarette. His recent engagement to Miss Kennedy had taken place in rather a whirlwind, with the aforementioned lady sweeping Northam off his feet at a reception held at St James's. Had Shakespeare been present at that rather ponderous function, and had declaimed his famous line 'Her beauty makes/This vault a feasting presence full of light,' Northam would have patted him on the back and given him a cigar, in recognition of the Bard having hit the nail squarely on the head. Northam had no quarrel with her beauty; but her temperament had of late seemed rather more dynamic than he had at first thought – more Henry V, perhaps, than Juliet of the House of Capulet.

And while Northam applauded Claire's ambition to be the first woman to travel from Cape Town to Cairo by motor-car, increasingly he wondered if he would be required to accompany her on such trips – and if so, where would he find time to work on his magnus opus? – For in this nobleman beat a decidedly literary heart, and it had long been Northam's dearest ambition to publish a little volume of poetry (provisionally entitled *Roses of Melancholy, Bluebells of Solitude*). For these and other reasons, Northam had begun to question whether Claire was indeed the soul-mate he sought. He lay back, and smoked, and thought; and as he did so, he began to murmur some lines from his collection of verse:

'When I went out, the sun was hot/It shone upon my flower pot/And there I saw a spike of green/That no-one else had ever seen...'

'I say,' said a gentle voice. 'That's rather striking – where did you hear it?'

Northam started up to discover that the voice belonged to Heather, who, having finally woken from her slumbers, had decided to take a walk in the fields.

'Oh, Miss Andrew!' said Northam.

'Do call me Heather,' she replied.

'Heather, then,' he said. 'And as for the poetry – well, I don't usually tell people about my work – but in fact I was reciting one of my own poems.'

'My goodness,' said Heather. 'I didn't realise you were a poet! I wish Oakeshott could write a line like that…'

'Well, I try to hide it – I mean, Claire has been encouraging me to develop my more active side.'

'Hmm,' said Heather. 'I sometimes wonder if… But no. Come on – let's go back to the castle. I can start sketching you for Lancelot. Goodness,' she said, as Northam got up to reveal the unmistakeable signs of having suffered equestrian misfortune, 'did you fall? And where is your horse?' Northam explained what had happened, and to the gratifying sounds of feminine sympathy they walked back to the castle, where Northam, once bathed and fortified by a strong brandy, spent some enjoyable hours posing as Lancelot in Heather's temporary studio. Indeed, the pair enjoyed themselves so much that Lady Fiona, passing Heather's room and hearing the sounds of merriment within, paused and smiled. 'I wouldn't be surprised if the next few days have some surprises in store,' she said to herself. 'Anything can happen, in Shropshire!'

The wisdom of her words was demonstrated later in the week, when the Earl of Hailsham played host to the annual Masked Ball, the pride of the county and the highlight of the social season for many miles around. For two days beforehand, the castle was entirely taken over by decorators, who clothed the ancient stone from top to bottom with luxurious Venetian fabrics and displays of every kind, from a temporary crystal fountain in the courtyard to a genuine gondola filled with bottles of champagne and strewn with rare blossoms from the hothouse.

On the evening of the Ball, the inhabitants of the castle, inspired by the unusual extravagance of their surroundings, likewise bedecked themselves in borrowed finery in preparation for the evening's festivities. Lord Hailsham had promised them gallons of nectar and acres of provender, with entertainments ranging from dancing troupes to a full-blown Masque; and none of his house-guests was disappointed. Brother Cedd described the Ball as the finest in his experience (and he was a long habitué of La Serenissima), while Charlotte Osmond and the Wylie girls pronounced themselves in very heaven. The writers, Andersson and Espinoza, were very taken with the Ball as the inspiration for (respectively) a novel exploring the fate of different characters in attendance and a philosophical tract investigating the symbolism (both sacred and profane) employed by the Venetian Carnival, while Lady Fiona experienced the relief felt by every responsible hostess when a social event has gone according to plan. (Her aunt, Lady Felicity, was allergic to parties, and had retired to bed the day before, leaving instructions not to disturb her until the following Sunday.)

Yet the guests who were in later days most appreciative of the evening's festivities were the two affianced couples. During the course of the evening they became separated in the mêlée, and in the profusion of other guests, all cloaked and masked in more or less identical fashion, it became quite difficult to find each other again. At one point Northam found a stately female figure surveying proceedings from a gallery, and (thinking that there was perhaps some slight resemblance to his fiancée's appearance) enquired if she was Miss Claire Kennedy.

'Why should I be Miss Claire Kennedy?' enquired the woman, with a hint of amusement in her voice. 'Do I resemble the lady in question?'

'Well, dash it, it's hard to say, isn't it,' replied Northam. 'You all look the same this evening, if you'll pardon me for saying so.'

'It is perhaps the only occasion on which such a remark would be pardoned,' said the lady with a smile. 'Is Miss

Kennedy your sweetheart, then?'

'My fiancée, in fact,' said Northam. He seemed to stop himself from adding a remark; but then, his inhibitions overcome by the anonymity of the masks, a twinkle in the eye of his interlocutor, and a pint or two of champagne, he went on: 'I don't mind telling you that I've been wondering how much longer it can go on for. I must say I didn't realise how much I'd have to pretend to be this daring, reckless, adventurer type – not my strong suit at all, really, and I'm beginning to think I might prefer someone a little more thoughtful, more artistic...' But his voice trailed away in horror, for the lady next to him had removed her mask, revealing the surprised face of Heather Andrew. Then she smiled tentatively at him; and Northam felt his heart turn somersaults. He reached out and took her hand.

Just around the corner, meanwhile, Oakeshott had also fallen into conversation with a masked lady, who was walking along the corridor that led towards the gallery. Having ascertained that she was not his fiancée, he then fell into praising the merits of sportsmanlike, dashing, and handsome young women, who stopped at nothing and were afraid at nothing – who didn't constantly require a fellow to chatter away about a lot of dead artists and authors and whatnot. As they rounded the corner and entered the gallery, his companion removed her mask to reveal her identity. It was, of course, Claire Kennedy; and as her eyes met Oakeshott's she realised that here was her true soul-mate – a man with whom she could travel to the ends of the earth, a man who would refrain from constantly scribbling away on bits of paper and boring her to death with stories of ancient Rome and mediaeval Italian poetry. Impulsively she stepped forward, and into Oakeshott's arms.

At precisely the same instant, the two couples – Northam and Heather, and Oakeshott and Claire – became aware of each other. Northam stared at Claire, taking in her embrace of Oakeshott; and the latter, staring at Heather, saw her hand in Northam's. A moment of stunned silence followed; but then all four burst out laughing, and ran together.

'I think, perhaps, that things have worked out for the

best,' said Northam. 'I will always love you, Claire old girl, but I suspect that Oakeshott here is the better man for you. He, at least, can keep up in the field, when you are riding with the Master on a strong scent!'

'And I'll always care for you terribly, Heather dear,' said Oakeshott, smiling affectionately at her. 'But I never could keep up with your art and your culture and all that. Give me a horse and a wide open sky – but Northam here is just the chap for you. He is your Lancelot, and you his Guinevere. Look – here's a waiter with some champagne, coming up the staircase – let's toast to the future, and to happiness – to horsemanship, and to art!'

'To horsemanship, and art!' they cried; and the vaulted gallery rang with their joy.

Lady Fiona, who had witnessed the essentials of the scene from below, smiled beneath her mask. The châtelaine's life may be a challenging one, she thought to herself – there may be seating-plans to arrange, difficult guests to accommodate, and a household to manage – but sometimes, just sometimes, it falls within her lot to add to the sum of human happiness. And on such occasions, thought Lady Fiona, it is the best and most wonderful life of all.

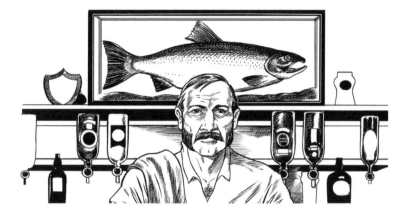

Trevithick's Story

IT WAS a blessedly warm day in the middle of May, when the undergraduates should have been cramming hard for the looming examinations; and so the river was filled to capacity with brightly-clad young men and women who had forsaken the cool interior of library and cloister for the delight of standing barefoot on the varnished deck of a Cambridge punt, and sipping champagne from crystal flutes, and gliding noiselessly amidst the soft exhalations of stone and bough and water. Their passing sent ripples dancing against ancient walls, and threw arrows of living colour amongst reflected balustrades and cornices, vivifying the immovable and blending it with youthful fluidity. The students stood on tiptoe and plucked flowers from secret gardens as they passed, placing them in their buttonholes or casting them on the river to float away like the long-forgotten exams. The Cam became a thread of bright hue amidst the spires and parapets, an apologue of unsanctioned release from the tyrannies of Livy and Homer.

Amongst the riot of truants were some intruders from the universe outside the university: a chauffeured punting tour making its way from the Mill Pond to Magdalene, and, proceeding in the opposite direction, a punt from Trinity

College, propelled by Harry Trevithick and containing the reclining figure of Buffy Porson. The two punts approached each other outside Clare College, with the tour guide's voice becoming steadily more audible to the two Sconcing Society members.

'The bridge we are now approaching is Clare Bridge,' said the guide. 'It was built in 1640 by Thomas Grumbold – but you will observe that a segment is missing from one of the stone balls on top of the bridge. Apparently the College neglected to pay Grumbold in full, so he took his revenge by leaving the bridge permanently unfinished.'

'And quite right, too!' called out Trevithick as they passed. The tourists laughed, but the guide looked rather annoyed.

'I think you stole his thunder there, Harry,' said Buffy as they went under the bridge.

'Well, he looked a silly kind of chap,' said Trevithick. 'I remember we once played a trick on a tour like that, when I was up' – Trevithick had read History at Trinity – 'by making a ball from papier-mâché, and dressing it to look like one of the real stone balls on Clare Bridge. We waited until a tour punt was underneath, and then pushed the ball off. It was one of the funniest things I've ever seen – the tourists scattered like ninepins, with half of them diving into the water, and the tour guide abandoning ship and striking out for the bank. They all thought it was a real stone ball, you see,' he concluded.

'Yes, thank you, Harry – I had managed to work that out for myself,' replied Buffy. 'What a rotten thing to do! Those poor tourists…'

'Oh, there's no excuse for tourists,' said Trevithick, pausing momentarily to polish his monocle.

'But I'm a tourist today, Harry,' pointed out Buffy. 'Are you going to try to get me into the drink as well?'

'Not unless you sconce me after my story, old boy! But I don't see that happening, as I have a pretty cast-iron tale.'

'I'll remind you that no-one has ever got away without a sconcing,' said Buffy.

'You just let me worry about who's going to be sconced,'

said Trevithick. 'I say! I think I can see the others – just there, standing on the Mathematical Bridge. I wonder what they're doing in Queens' College?' And he hailed Sharpe & Co. to ask them that very question.

'We've been waiting for you!' came Sharpe's reply. 'You're late – very late. Though it is confoundedly busy on the river, I'll give you that. Anyway, Henton here wanted to have a closer look at this bridge – though he was disappointed to discover that it is in fact held together with nuts and bolts, rather than gravity and ingenuity, as the myth goes.'

'Ha!' cried Trevithick. 'Another attempt by an Oxford man to run down Cambridge. Next you'll be telling me that Cambridge was founded by Oxford, rather than the other way round! Well, you'll be laughing on the other side of your face after my story.'

'That will be for us to decide,' called Penrose. 'Now look – just go through to Laundress Green and pick us up. Then the fun begins!'

'I see,' said Trevithick. 'Too cowardly to do the manly thing, and drop into the punt from the bridge. Just what I'd expect from Oxonians. Never mind – see you in the Pond!'

'Toodle-oo,' called Buffy, waving his boater at the others as the punt passed underneath the bridge and upstream towards Mill Pond. As might have been expected on such a day, the Pond was positively heaving with fellow Arcadians. So many punts were gathered there that it would almost have been possible to cross the Pond by jumping from deck to deck; and no sooner had this thought occurred to Trevithick than he thrust the pole into Buffy's hands, skimmed his boater ahead of him towards Laundress Green (where the others awaited), and jumped nimbly from punt to punt until he alighted on terra firma.

'I say, Harry,' said Penrose. 'That was a trifle hard on old Buffy – he seems to have got stuck between *Henry VI* and *Richard II* – punts from King's College, of course, named after monarchs – 'and he's making pretty heavy work of it.'

'He certainly is,' said Henton. 'In fact, he's gone in. No – he's out again. A bit sodden, though. I think he's clear of the

Kingsmen now – yes, here he comes.'

'Trevithick, you rotter,' panted a red-faced Buffy, as he guided the punt (now considerably damper than before) to the landing. 'I'm definitely going to sconce you now!'

'Oh, come on, Buffy,' said Trevithick. 'Bit of exercise'll do you good. Now look, let's get on – I'm ravenous after my punting exertions, and I fancy I see the makings of a picnic in your belongings, gentlemen – yes, a wicker basket, and another, and my goodness! A silver drinking vessel, and a large jug of what I presume to be ale. What a surprise! Well, if the sight of all the sconcing paraphernalia is intended to make me nervous, I'm afraid you'll be disappointed.

'Anyhow, before you get on, I think we should move onto the upper river. It will be quieter there, and we can picnic up near Grantchester – you know, the Rupert Brooke place. *Stands the clock at ten to three, is there honey still for tea,* and so forth. We'll need to manhandle the punt up the slipway round the corner, for the river is higher above the weir – but I'm sure that even four Oxford men will manage that, under my expert supervision, of course.'

Sharpe responded that the Oxonians would jolly well show the Cantabrigians what they could do, and indeed the punt was transferred from one level to the next with commendable alacrity. Having done so, the party looked enquiringly at Trevithick, at which point he remarked that he supposed even a pack of monkeys was bound to get things right once in while, and hadn't the monkeys better get on and load the punt with the picnic provisions before the whole day was wasted? This was soon done, and with a look of some concern (for the resulting freeboard was in the region of two inches) Trevithick pushed off from the bank and set the party off on the journey to Grantchester. Buffy popped the corks on a bottle or two of Pol Roger, and before long the noise and hubbub of Mill Pond died away and was replaced by the infinitely more agreeable sounds of conversation, birdsong, and the melodious chime of water rippling on wood.

When they passed under the footbridge and left the last traces of Cambridge behind them, Trevithick cleared his throat in a significant manner and said:

'I suppose I might as well begin my story – or, rather, to introduce my story, for there's a decent amount of background to get through before I proceed with the main event. My story's called 'Squaring the Circle', by the way – I'll explain why later on. In the meantime, just sit back and enjoy the scenery, while I do all the hard work – and I think I deserve some credit for punting you up to Grantchester (and against the current at that) at the same time as undergoing the most fiendish trial ever devised by man for the torment of fellow creatures – viz., a meeting of the Sconcing Society.

'The first thing you have to bear in mind,' he went on, 'is that this story isn't just mine; it's shared with a chap who was at the University with me – one James Purefoy. He's a philosophy don at St Andrews now, and a pretty respectable fellow when walking in the hallowed groves of academe; but it was a different story when he was an undergraduate, I can tell you. The scrapes he used to get into… I was hardly a shrinking violet when I was up, but Purefoy's antics made me look like the Bishop of Ely. There was the incident with the Vice-Chancellor's bicycle, which was reported in at least three national newspapers; and there was the Boat Race of '32, at which Purefoy's activities nearly precipitated a diplomatic crisis with Italy; but most of all, there was nightclimbing.'

'Nightclimbing?' asked Penrose, giving voice to the others' puzzled looks.

'Nightclimbing,' said Trevithick. 'It never really caught on in Oxford, doubtless owing to Oxonian pusillanimity, so I'm not surprised you chaps haven't heard of it. Put simply, it's just what it sounds like – climbing, at night. Nightclimbers leaven the dry bread of embryonic erudition by setting out under cover of darkness, with the intent of scaling various of the gates, chimneys, halls, libraries and chapels that Cambridge has to offer the upwardly mobile undergraduate.'

'Hardly the north face of the Eiger, old man,' said Henton, who was trailing his hand in the water. Trevithick's monocle fixed him with a steely glare, while its owner uttered the following:

'Our acquaintance, Henton, is of a recent vintage, so I will refrain from telling you what I really think of that remark. Presumably you have never done any nightclimbing yourself, but clinging to the battlements of Trinity Great Gate, with a cold breeze freezing your fingertips, or edging around the overhang atop the towers of King's College Chapel despite aching arms and a head spinning from the vertiginous drop below you... Well, it's no picnic.'

'You were a nightclimber, too, then?' said Sharpe.

'Indeed I was, in my own modest way,' replied Trevithick. 'It began in my first week at Trinity, when I found myself locked out of College at a late hour, and decided to make my way in over the Trinity Lane gate rather than face the wrath of the Proctors, Bulldogs, Tutors, Deans, coppers, beloved parents, & c. Anyway, rumours of my successful ascent (and descent) got around College, and before long I found myself invited to join an intrepid band of like-minded souls across the Varsity. Included amongst our number were several young Turks such as Christopher Kent, who now does something high up and secretive in the Foreign Office; Jonathan Nicholas, or (as he is now styled) the Reverend J.N., tipped to be the next Archbishop of Canterbury; and Eric L. Motley, now Dr Motley, I believe - an American chap from Montgomery, Alabama, who until recently was in charge of one of the departments at the White House. I understand he is currently serving in a management position in a major public policy institute in Washington, D.C.

'But while these gents were known far and wide for the extent of their daring, the famousest of all, as dear old nanny used to put it, was the aforementioned James Purefoy, who was by some way the most dedicated and daring nightclimber in Cambridge. At the time when I was still edging my way up the drainpipes on the bit of Gonville and Caius College facing Trinity Street, Purefoy was attempting the far more difficult pipes in New Court, St John's; and by the time I had persuaded myself to make an assault on the Old Library, my friend had shinned up the South Face of Caius and jumped the seven-foot gap between Caius and the Senate House.'

'Did you ever climb King's Chapel, Harry?' enquired Buffy, as Trevithick worked hard to navigate a tricky bend. 'Dashed sticky bottom along this stretch,' said their chauffeur. 'And the current doesn't help, of course. I've seen many good men lose hold of their poles just around here... That's it. What were you saying, Buffy? Oh yes – King's. No, I never had the skill for that, but Purefoy did, and he made the climb not once, but three times. Moreover, on the third climb he took up an oversized Egyptian fez, and left it on top of one of the towers. They had to send up a steeplejack to get it down again.'

'Sounds rather fun,' said Sharpe. 'I wish we'd thought of that in Oxford.'

This remark prompted a snort of laughter from Penrose. 'Having seen you cast a fly,' he said, 'and having deduced the steadiness of your hands from the result, I strongly suspect you owe your life to the fact that nightclimbing was never an Oxonian pursuit.'

'Penrose is probably right,' said Trevithick, ceasing from punting for long enough to mop his brow. 'Phew! This trip is always hard work, especially on a day like today. But worth it for the view - isn't it glorious!' And indeed it was a beautiful scene, the river winding through water-meadows to the accompaniment of woodpigeon and skylark, and with the occasional blue-and-orange flash of the kingfisher.

'Come on, Harry,' said Buffy. 'Your story is meandering more than the Cam. What does all this about nightclimbing have to do with matters of a sporting nature? You do remember that the tale is supposed to be about sport – unless you're going to tell us that you took a gun up on top of a college, and took potshots at passing crows?'

'All in good time, Buffy old man,' said Trevithick. 'I was merely trying to introduce James Purefoy, his character and his qualities, in as interesting and colourful a manner as possible, on the grounds that this knowledge will be useful later on. It is of some relevance to my story, for instance, to know that Purefoy was identified as the person who had placed the fez on top of King's Chapel, and as such was very likely to face rustication, or worse. It is also of some relevance to know that Purefoy only avoided this dread fate by arguing, most convincingly and eloquently, for the proposition that the University authorities couldn't be sure that King's College Chapel really existed, and, concomitantly, that the University couldn't be sure that he, Purefoy, had in fact been climbing it. The disciplinary committee were so taken aback that they commended Purefoy on the clarity of his thought, declared that he would be too great a loss to the University were he to be sent down, and threw out all the charges.'

'He used some variant of Berkeley, I suppose?' said Henton.

'Why, yes, he did!' said Trevithick. 'I see we have a student of philosophy in the party. I'm pleased about that, for I shall have occasion to refer to that gentle science a good few times in the course of the story proper, to which my remarks so far have merely served as a kind of prolegomenon.'

'Hark at him,' said Buffy. 'Never let it be said that an obsession with polo disqualifies a man from learning.'

'Of course it doesn't,' said Trevithick, 'no more than a passion for risking his neck on Cambridge's highest buildings means that Purefoy's a fool. But look here – this bit of meadow is probably as good a spot as any, for our picnic – let's moor up here, if you fellows are agreeable, and have some lunch while I'm talking.'

Trevithick manoeuvred the punt alongside the bank and moored by pushing the pole over the gunwale and deep into the river-bed. Soon the party had disembarked and set up their hampers, rugs, and supplies on the meadow; and when each man had a glass and plate in front of him, and some form of tobacco on the go, Trevithick began again.

'When Purefoy and I went down from Cambridge, we went our separate ways – him northwards to a life of scholarship, me to my rooms in Mayfair, to a life of indolence, indulgence, and, of course, polo. Our nightclimbing experiences had brought us into the same circle, but of course that would hardly continue to draw us together once we had left the Varsity. But a more enduring bond was formed between us when we discovered a common love of fishing – and, in particular, fishing for salmon in the great Scottish rivers. This shared passion has been the cause of many a happy rendezvous by stream, river, and loch, and, while fishing rarely matches nightclimbing for sheer spine-clenching terror, we have nevertheless enjoyed ourselves in our little expeditions together. It is one of these trips that forms the basis of my tale today.'

At this point Sharpe, who had been pretending to be asleep, made a great show of waking up with a start.

'I'm sorry, old boy,' he said, yawning cavernously. 'Your droning was so soothing, I couldn't keep my eyes open. Have you started your story yet? No? Well, I'm going to catch forty winks – wake me up when he really begins, won't you, Penrose?'

'Oh, shut up,' said Trevithick, aiming a vol-au-vent at Sharpe's head. 'I am just about to start the story, having completed the necessary preliminaries – that is, establishing Purefoy's philosophical skill and our shared love of salmon fishing.'

'But I always thought polo was your passion, not fishing,' interjected Penrose.

'Polo is indeed my life's passion,' said Trevithick. 'But I do love to cast a line, and I flatter myself that I am by no means the worst of amateur fishermen. Think of the artist Ingres, whose musical skill was so legendary that 'Le violon d'Ingres' became a byword for great accomplishment in a secondary pursuit. My modest hope is that, in time, 'Le rod de Trevithick' will supplant Ingres' violin as shorthand for superogatory brilliance.

'But to return to my narrative: I want to tell you about one trip in particular, which took place on the Tweed earlier this year – mid-March, to be precise. We met in Coldstream and journeyed to the Guards Hotel, where we were to stay for a week's fishing on the Holyrood beat. We arrived late in the evening, so we didn't seek out the river until the next morning – and you may be sure that we were out of doors and heading water-wards as soon as a glimmer of light appeared in the morning sky. There was a mile or two to be walked off before we could touch line to water, and to pass the time I decided to stir things up a little. So I said to Purefoy that it was rather a shame he didn't study a more useful subject from the point of view of sporting pursuits – botany or biology, for instance.'

'Goodness,' said Sharpe. 'I'll wager he took exception to that.'

'He certainly did – just as I had intended he should. It led to rather a heated conversation, from his end – but I must admit I found it most interesting. I had always thought of the ancient Greeks – Purefoy's speciality – as rather dull and primitive chaps in the philosophical line, when compared with your Kants and your Hegels – but it turns out they had quite a lot of good things to say.'

'Well, you learn something new every day,' said Henton. 'The Greeks were good at philosophy – I would never have guessed!'

'No, but you know what I mean,' said Trevithick. 'I read some Thucydides once and found it pretty heavy-going. But Purefoy has a way of cutting through all the nonsense, and getting to the nub of the subject matter – I suppose that's how he got out of being sent down.'

'Well, I wish you shared his gifts in that regard,' muttered Penrose.

'As I was saying,' said Trevithick, ignoring Penrose, 'my challenge to Purefoy was to demonstrate the utility of philosophy for sporting pursuits. And I must give the fellow his due – he damned well did it.

'He started off with a chap called Thales, whom (he said) had claimed that everything is made of water – a good start, for those of a piscatorial bent. Then he cited one Heraclitus, who seems also to have had water on the brain – he said that you both can, and cannot, step into the same river twice – that it might be the same geographical river, but the body of water is different all the time.'

'That's true enough,' admitted Buffy. 'Heraclitus must have learned that from fishing – I wish I had a shilling for every time I've tried to repeat a successful tactic on a river the next day, without luck.'

'Heraclitus also said that it isn't good for men to receive all that they wish for,' went on Trevithick, 'which Purefoy claimed was true enough in the sporting line – for when you've bagged a sixteen-pointer and a forty-pound salmon, what's left to live for?'

'Why, that's just what I said in my story!' cried Sharpe.

'There you are, then,' said Trevithick. 'But Purefoy added another line that I thought less congenial to the sportsman – from Epicurus, who said that the absence of pain is the wise man's goal.'

'Shame,' called Henton; 'I'll second that,' said Buffy. 'If we all signed up to that, there'd be no sport at all – for you can't have the good times without the bad.'

'That's just what I said,' replied Trevithick. 'The joy of hooking a grilse only exists because you can't do it every day – because you've gone countless days without wetting your net. I think Purefoy meant that perhaps a truly wise man would forego fishing altogether, which is probably true, after all.'

'You might have something there,' conceded Penrose, remembering a day on which he had contrived to get himself arrested for poaching, after straying too far from his beat in a desperate search for a fish that would take a fly.

'Anyway,' went on Trevithick, 'this conversation occupied most of the journey to our beat, but was soon forgotten when we set eyes on the Tweed once more.'

'So – sport trumped philosophy!' said Buffy.

'Yes, in a way it did – and what a day we had of it, too! Three fine springers to my name, and two to Purefoy – and not a fish under eight pounds. But the philosophical art had not finished with us – not yet!'

'You see,' he went on, 'the topic came up again as we tramped back to the hotel in a state of supreme contentment with ourselves and the world. I happened to mention to Purefoy how good it was to have fish in hand to show at the hotel, without having to invent any tales about "the one that got away", et cetera. I spoke facetiously, but Purefoy nodded vigorously, as if I had made a telling point in some scholarly debate. Then he said:

'"Well, of course, Hume would say that any such tales are more likely to be false than true."

'"How so?" I said. And Purefoy told me about Hume's theory of miracles – that any miraculous tale was more likely to be false than true, because it was so unlikely that sufficient evidence, or evidence of sufficient quality, could be found to outweigh the likelihood of men being dishonest, untrustworthy, malicious, and so forth. At least, that seemed to be the gist of what he said – he put it much more eloquently and rigorously than I ever could.'

'So Purefoy thinks every story of sporting adventure is more likely to be false than true?' asked Sharpe. 'It sounds like he would fit in perfectly at the Sconcing Society!'

'Indeed he would,' said Trevithick. 'As a matter of fact I did think of inviting him to join me today, but he was otherwise engaged – a meeting of the General Council at St Andrews, or some such. Damned shame, but there it is – and hopefully he will be able to join us in future on an occasional basis, like Buchan.

'Anyway, so there we were, walking back to the hotel with a salmon apiece, having put the others back to delight future fishermen. It was about eight, I suppose, when we sat down to supper (and dashed good it was too), and perhaps ten in the evening when we went through into the snug for a nightcap. Little did we know that Hume's theory of miracles – or, rather, fishy stories – was about to be verified before our very eyes.

'When we entered the little bar, our attention was immediately drawn to an enormous stuffed salmon above the bar – a magnificent creature it was, forty-plus pounds of fresh-run fish with powerful silver-blue flanks. A plaque on the case bore the legend:

Salmon – Forty-three Pounds Eight Ounces
Caught on Silver Stoat, on 12th March, 1922
By Colonel Arthur Locke

'We had just lit our pipes and begun to sip our whiskies when the door opened to admit an elderly gentleman, dressed in tweeds and filling an old clay pipe from a leather pouch that looked as if it had come across with the Conqueror. He patted down his pockets, and having apparently left his matches at home, asked us for a light. Purefoy obliged, and (by way of making conversation) asked the old fellow if he'd known the Colonel Locke who had landed the monstrous salmon above our heads.

"'Did ah know 'im?" he retorted in a broad Scots brogue. "Ah should damn' well think so – ah was 'is ghillie for twenty year. And I'll tell you anither thing, free o' charge – it was no the colonel that caught yon fush, but me – aye, auld Wullie McAllister, as ah'm standin' here afore ye."

'Well, of course we begged him to tell us what had really happened, and of course he obliged. The winter of 1922 had been unusually dry, he recalled, and the river had been low. The colonel had been fishing hard all day, but had had no luck. Finally, losing patience, the colonel had retired to the small fishing lodge a few hundred yards from the water's edge, there to sooth his weary soul, presumed McAllister – well, I paraphrase – with some strong whisky and tobacco. The colonel left his rod behind, exhorting McAllister to look after it, and to wet a line himself, if he had a mind.

'Now, McAllister didn't think much of his chances in the circumstances, and at first he took his ease on the bankside rather than "flog a deid horse", as he put it. After a while, however, it occurred to him that the river being so low, and the weather being relatively clement ("warm enow to curdle milk"), it might be interesting to hazard a dry-fly on the water. McAllister mentioned that he had heard of a ghillie trying this tactic with some success on the Dee, in similar conditions.

'Accordingly he put up a lighter cast, heavily greased of course, with a March Brown on the dropper and an Olive Quill on point – and it was the latter that proved the downfall of the great salmon, which took it on the second cast. McAllister fought the fish carefully, being on light tackle, and it wasn't until forty minutes or so later that he brought it to land.

'Unfortunately, that was also the moment that the colonel, having fallen asleep in the lodge, woke up again. Exiting the lodge and seeing his ghillie landing an enormous salmon, the colonel lost his temper, and threatened McAllister with all kinds of sanctions unless the latter agreed to the fiction that the colonel had hooked and landed the fish.

'"And it wasna until the auld villain passed awa'," McAllister concluded, "that ah could safely tell the truth aboot the fush. And noo ah'll bid you gentlemen a guid neet, and be on ma' way." And that was that.'

'So the colonel lied about the fish – that was a mean-spirited thing to do, upon my word,' said Buffy.

'It certainly would have been, if it were true,' said Trevithick. 'But the night's storytelling wasn't over yet – not by a long chalk. For no sooner had McAllister left the snug than the barman, who had been quietly polishing glasses behind the counter all this time, cleared his throat and said to us:

'"You'll pardon me, gents, for eavesdropping – but I've heard McAllister tell that story several times, and I'm afraid there's not an ounce of truth in it. I don't like to say so to his face, for a customer's a customer, as I'm sure you'll understand."

'"So the colonel did catch the fish?" asked Purefoy.

'"I'm afraid not," said the barman. "But it wasn't for any selfish reason that he claimed it, but as an act of kindness to a poor man, down on his luck, and trying to catch some supper for his family. And that man was me." Then he told us what had really happened.

'The barman, it turned out, had for several years led a life of some poverty. He had been a rag-and-bone man, a seller of jellied eels, a cobbler's assistant, and a window-cleaner, but had never managed to hold down a job for long. As such he found it difficult to make ends meet, as he said, and to keep body and soul together for himself and his large (and constantly expanding) family, with the result that he was often driven to acquire his sustenance in nefarious ways.

'"It's a shameful thing to admit to you gents," he said,

"but I took to poaching of an evening. Salmon, trout, rabbits, pheasants – it was all the same to me. We had to eat somehow, and that's how we did it."

'He then proceeded to tell us of one particular evening in 1922, when he had netted a superb salmon – "the very same fish that's above your heads, gents," he said. But no sooner had he brought the fish to bank than Colonel Locke came upon the scene, walking along the riverbank on the way back to the hotel after a fishing expedition. "I was caught red-handed," said the barman, "and had no chance of making a run for it – so when the colonel strode up to me with a stern look on his face, I thought I was done for."

'"But I'd mistaken my man, gents – and I've never been happier to be wrong," the barman continued. "Quick as a flash, he got his rod out and tackled up; then, looking over his shoulder, he gave me the tackle and got the fish out of the net. Well, gents, I couldn't make head nor tail of all this – but I cottoned on quick enough when the colonel rapped out that the keeper was coming – was just around the corner, and worse still, he had a local bobby with him."

'"Well, needless to say, the colonel saved my bacon. It turned out that the keeper and the bobby were doing the rounds of the local beats, because they'd had reports of poachers – poachers like me, I don't doubt. But of course with the colonel there, they thought I was his ghillie – and far from arresting me, they congratulated us on the colonel's luck with the salmon!"

'"That was jolly decent of him," said Purefoy.

'"I call it pretty sharp of the old cove," said I. "After all, he had probably had no more than a middling day on the river himself, and suddenly there he is, with a forty-three pounder to his name, stuffed and mounted here in the hotel – that's a fairly good deal, by my reckoning!"

'"Begging your pardon, sir, but you're wrong," replied the barman. "He was that unwilling to have the fish mounted, but knew he had to, to make the story credible… He was a sportsman, through and through, and hated taking the credit for my luck, even though I'd been poaching at the time.

What's more, he took the trouble of asking me why I'd been poaching, and when I told him about my family he gave me five pounds and recommended me to the hotel for a job – and here I am, to this day. That's sportsmanship, gents – that's sportsmanship." And that was the barman's story,' concluded Trevithick.

'So the mystery of the salmon was solved,' said Sharpe, yawning and raising his arms above his head.

Before replying, Trevithick got up and stretched his legs. He lit a cigarette, polished his monocle once more, and sat down cross-legged on the bank.

'Not quite, old chap,' he said. 'Not just yet! The barman was called away just after he finished his story – something to do with changing a barrel – and Purefoy and I were left alone for a little while. But soon another fellow came into the snug – a gentleman this time, with a wind-beaten look and an overcoat that had clearly seen much sport over the years; in his right hand he carried a wicker basket. He wished us good evening, and we fell into conversation.

'He told us he had been on the river himself that day, but ruefully admitted that he had had no luck – just a few small trout. "Well, you can't always catch a fish like that," he said, pointing to the salmon above us. "I caught him, sirs, fair and square, and I'll never see his like again."

'"Are you Colonel Locke, then?" asked Purefoy. "The barman has just been telling us about the salmon's capture, and your noble actions in giving the man a helping hand."

'"Oh, he's been telling his tales again, has he?" said the man, smiling. "I'm afraid Davies frequently imbibes not wisely but too well, if you follow me, when he is at work in the store-room, and is then all too apt to test the bounds of his audience's credulity. I expect he spun you the yarn about the colonel rescuing him from the keeper and the long arm of the law?"

'"Well, I'm not Colonel Locke," he went on. "My name's Kingsley, and that salmon wasn't caught by any under-hand poaching method, but on rod and line – my rod and line. I'll tell you how it came about." And the story he told us went as follows.

'Kingsley stayed at this hotel for some weeks in 1922, and one evening after dinner he made Colonel Locke's acquaintance over brandy. It was a sad story, he said; the colonel had recently lost his dear wife, Evelyn, to a long illness, and as he had already lost his only son in the War he was now quite alone in the world. He had returned to fishing, the passion of his youth, in an attempt to ease the sorrows of his maturity. His luck had been terrible, however, and despite fishing day after day for nearly two weeks, he told Kingsley that he had barely caught a thing.

'Anyhow, after talking for a little while, the colonel went up to bed, and Kingsley was left gazing into the fire. He felt desperately sorry for the fellow, but what could he do to help? "Nothing, that's what," said Kingsley, "and I felt pretty sick about it."

'But as it happened a chance for him to help the colonel came the very next day. "It all began when I hooked and landed the great fish you see above you," went on Kingsley, "and quite a while it took me, I can tell you, for he fought like the very devil. The pool I was fishing was a deep, dark glide with razor-sharp rocks, and to say that I had some nervous moments would be an understatement."

'"But I landed him, and after marvelling awhile at his sheer size and beauty I set off back to the hotel to have him weighed and packed off to the taxidermist before he was spoiled. On the way back, however, I came across the colonel fishing the next beat. I say fishing, but in fact he appeared to have fallen asleep – I should have mentioned that it was an unseasonably warm afternoon – with his rod resting on the bankside, and his line drifting unattended in the river."

'"I was just tiptoeing past the old man in order not to wake him," said Kingsley, "when I saw a leather wallet lying open by his side – and it seemed to me that I could see images of some kind within. Struck by curiosity despite my eagerness to get back to the hotel with my prize, and also thinking that perhaps I should wake the colonel up and tell him to look after his possessions more carefully (for his wallet was anyone's for the taking), I walked up to him for a closer look. I realised then that he had been looking at photographs of his wife and son – and while I am not usually a sentimental fellow, I don't mind telling you fellows that I had a lump in my throat. The colonel's fate was too pathetic for words."

'"Suddenly it came to me that I could, perhaps, do something to help the old man out, by cheering him up a little. It would mean the sacrifice of my own glory, but what was that compared to the colonel's sorrow? I made up my mind on the spot, and in a trice I had put my plan into operation. I ran to the colonel's rod and got hold of his line; then I took my salmon, still fresh from the river, and hooked it with the colonel's point fly. I waded out into the river with the fish and deposited it some forty or fifty yards upstream; then I rushed back to the bankside and began to reel in furiously, shouting to rouse the colonel and generally making a fine show of fighting a good fish."

'"Soon the colonel woke up and rushed to my side; I cried out that I had happened across his rod and noticed that it was moving from side to side, presumably owing to a fish on the line. Then I thrust the rod into his hands while wading into the river again (to disguise the fact that I was already soaking wet) with the colonel's net. I then made a big show of dropping the fish on a rock, to explain away its stillness; and I'm glad to say the colonel was completely taken in. I insisted on his claiming the fish as his own, and we took the fish back to the hotel together. It was a wrench giving it up, I need hardly say – but worth it, to my mind, to see the old man's face glowing with honest joy."

'"My goodness, is that the time?" he said, looking at his watch. "I really must be going. I thank you gentlemen for listening to my little story, which I'd appreciate if you would keep to yourselves. The colonel passed away some years ago, but he's still remembered fondly in these parts, and I'd give the world rather than diminish his memory. I'll wish you goodnight," and with that Kingsley was gone.

'Well, as you can imagine, Purefoy and I were more than a little bewildered – three accounts, and one salmon!' went on Trevithick.

'If you'll pardon the expression, it all looked rather fishy.'

'Just what I'd expect from one of your yarns,' said Sharpe, pouring himself a generous measure of Sauterne.

'Oh, this is no ordinary yarn,' replied Trevithick. 'It's the gospel truth, as you'll see. Just pass me some of that wine – thanks. Thirsty work, telling these tales! Anyway, to return to what I was saying, it all seemed rather odd to have these three chaps each claiming the fish as their own. In an attempt to clarify things, Purefoy decided to have a closer look at the fish itself – he thought he might at least be able to determine whether it had been caught in a net (as the barman claimed) or on rod and line. Muttering quotations from what I later learned was Hume's *An Enquiry Concerning Human Understanding*, Purefoy got up on top of a stool and peered more closely at Colonel Locke's infamous salmon. In doing so, however, he lost his footing – clearly he had failed to maintain his night-climbing skills – and grabbed at the case as he fell. Predictably, this resulted in the entire shooting match – Purefoy, glass case, salmon, and stool – falling to earth in calamitous fashion. The barman, hearing the uproar, came rushing back into the snug, and stood aghast – for the "salmon" lay in a thousand pieces on the floor. That fish was Plaster of Paris!'

'What – it was a fake?' cried Buffy.

'You're damned right it was,' said Trevithick. 'And judging by how Purefoy reacted when he realised that, you'd think he'd got a winning line in the football pools. He picked himself up, dusted himself down, and stood, smiling triumphantly, while he quoted a line from Hume: "No testimony is sufficient to establish a miracle, unless the testimony be of such a kind, that its falsehood would be more miraculous, than the fact, which it endeavours to establish… Of which principle," he added, "we have just received decisive demonstration. It should never be said," he concluded, and so this story also concludes, "that philosophy is irrelevant to sporting pursuits; for how else is the thinking man to prepare himself against the snares and deceits of other sportsmen?"' And with this final peroration, Trevithick leapt to his feet and bowed low to the ground.

'Damned good,' called Sharpe, applauding vigorously; 'Yes,' said Penrose, 'a superb twist in the tail.' 'Hear him,' cried the others, laughing. Trevithick, gratified at the reception afforded his story, grinned with satisfaction.

'Yes,' said Henton, 'you have squared the circle admirably – one salmon, three tales – but a fourth tale explains them all, and vindicates your friend at the same time. Only – the tale seems rather familiar – as if I had heard it somewhere before.'

'Of course you have,' said Sharpe. 'Don't you remember? It's the story of the Plaster of Paris trout from *Three Men in a Boat.*'

'Is it, old chap?' said Trevithick, lighting another cigarette with an airy, carefree manner.

'Yes, by Jove!' cried Henton. 'I remember now. Far too similar to be a coincidence.'

'You villain, Harry!' said an agitated Buffy. 'I've never seen anything like it, for bare-faced effrontery. To lift a story straight from a book – why, it's just not cricket. Look here, you fellows – get the sconcing vessel out, and fill it to the brim; I think that Harry has richly deserved a sconcing.'

The other members of the Society agreed, and Trevithick watched with some amusement as they fished out the silver tankard, unstoppered the jar of ale, and filled the vessel with cool, frothy ale.

'Is that for me, Buffy?' he enquired. 'Only I'm rather enjoying my Pol Roger, and while I like a sup of ale as well as the next man, I'm not sure the two beverages will mix harmoniously. I fear for my palate.'

'To hell with your palate,' growled Penrose. 'Now drink the ale down, as offended honour requires!'

Trevithick took the tankard, but set it down carefully on the grass. Then he reached inside his blazer and withdrew a small notebook, from which he plucked a newspaper cutting. This he unfolded and proceeded to read aloud.

'From the *Tweedsmuir Herald*, 10th April, 1931 – an article entitled 'Life mirrors Art on the Tweed', by reporter William Murray. The text begins: "Messrs James Purefoy and Harry Trevithick experienced a strange sense of déjà vu when they visited the snug at the Guards Hotel. Having made enquiries as to the provenance of the "salmon" of forty-three pounds, mounted in a case above the bar, the two Englishmen were successively entertained by three different gentlemen who each claimed the capture of the fish – only for it to be revealed that the salmon was in fact made of Plaster of Paris. The entire scene bore a remarkable resemblance to a story recounted in the well-known humorous book *Three Men in a Boat*, by Jerome K. Jerome, in which the protagonists similarly encounter tall tales about a Plaster of Paris fish, albeit a trout rather than a salmon. As Mr Purefoy remarked to our correspondent, there are few more powerful forces in the world than the mendacity of fishermen.'

Trevithick's declamation was followed by a brief silence, during which the various members of the Society digested the unpalatable fact that, for the first time, the speaker was able to defend himself against a sconcing. As usual, Buffy took slightly longer to catch up with proceedings than the rest of the Society.

'So, we can't sconce you?' he said. 'Nobody will be sconced? That's a pretty poor show – breaking with tradition, and all that!'

'Oh, I wouldn't worry too much about that,' said Trevithick. 'You seem to have forgotten the rules of your own Society. I was at Cambridge rather than the Other Place, and so was unfamiliar with the principles governing this particular method of becoming hideously intoxicated. But Sharpe was good enough to educate me in this regard, and I remember particularly well the punishment reserved for those who seek to inflict a sconcing without good reason – id est, they must be sconced themselves.'

'I'm afraid he's right, you know,' said Sharpe.

'Yes, indeed,' said Penrose. 'We must each drain the vessel, and Harry can punt our inebriated frames back to Cambridge.'

And so Trevithick leaned against a tree and smoked while each of the party took the tankard in turn, refilling it

217

as necessary to ensure that each man had his full three-and-a-quarter pints. When all four – Sharpe, Penrose, Henton, and Buffy – had drunk their draughts, Trevithick took the vessel and set about filling it again.

'We only have to – hic – drink it once, you know,' protested Buffy.

'I know,' said Trevithick. 'This is for me. I may have escaped a sconcing, but I'm glad to have been invited into the Society, all the same. You're jolly decent fellows, and you took your punishment – your richly deserved punishment, I might add – like Englishmen. So, if you feel you can drink another drop, please to charge your glasses – that's right – and I give you – the Sconcing Society!'

The others repeated the toast with a good will, albeit slurring the words slightly; and thereafter the upper reaches of the Cam resounded for some time with the boisterous sounds of perhaps the best, and certainly the most sporting, dining society in England.

The Assyrian King

ALASDAIR LOCHTON was the first to know, if intuition can be called knowledge. A shadow in the evening mist, a hint of massy bulk, a notion of steepling horns, nothing more – but it was enough. The elderly keeper withdrew inside the bothy that served as his home, and scribbled a hasty note in his crude hand. Early next morning, Lochton hobbled down the rough hill-path to the Lodge, and gave the note to the groom. The groom gave it to a maid, who gave it to the footman, who gave it to the butler; and the butler, having placed the note on a silver salver, gave it to Lord Dacre.

'A note, sir,' he said. 'From Lochton, the gamekeeper,' he added disapprovingly, for he saw it as cheek for a keeper to write to a lord.

'Ah yes?' said Dacre, ripping open the envelope and reading the note.

'Will there be anything else, my lord? Shall I – shall I send for Doctor Watkins?' – the doctor; for Lord Dacre had gone white as a sheet, and his health of late had been far from good. A weakness of the heart combined with general old age,

Doctor Watkins had said. The butler had been sorry to hear it, for the old fellow was a good employer, and his son, Lord Chalfont, would certainly replace him with his own man when the time came.

'Eh?' said Dacre, rising from a reverie of some depth. 'No – no, thank you, Benton. But send to the gun-room – my William Evans to be got ready. And look out my Harris jacket, will you?'

'You are going out, my lord?' cried the butler, alarmed. 'In this cold weather? I am sorry, my lord' – this in response to a fierce glare – 'I forgot myself. Shall I call Geddes, sir?' – the stalker.

'No, thank you, Benton. Just the rifle and my clothes.'

As Dacre set out from the Lodge, his heart was beating uncontrollably – 'Like a giddy schoolboy,' he remarked aloud. 'And yet perfectly understandable, under the circumstances.'

Under the circumstances: the surprising, the astonishing, return of the Assyrian King to the slopes of Glen Alder, after three – or was it four? – years' absence. Dacre had thought him dead – had mourned him, the noble beast, with a monarch's antlers and the jutting, dark-hued beard that had got him his name. Twice he had stalked him, and twice the stag had beaten him, seeming to fix him afterwards with a defiant, knowing gaze before disappearing into the trees. How Dacre had burned and raged! – for he had never before missed his shot. And now, in the twilight of his days, a third and gloriously unexpected chance.

'Even that old fraud Watkins couldn't begrudge me this,' grunted Dacre as he pushed his unwilling body up a steep, rocky incline. 'And if my heart gives up the ghost – well, I've had a good life.' His thoughts ranged over the course of his life, his successful, contented, and pleasure-filled life: Fives at Eton, a cricket blue at Oxford; his maiden speech in the House; useful years on the Imperial Defence Committee and fulfilling years at All Souls, Oxford; the joys of family life, diminished but not destroyed by the loss of his beloved wife, Cecily; and numberless days of delight with rod, horn, and gun throughout the kingdom and beyond. A good life: the very best kind of life. And if he had to leave it, what better way than on the trail of the Assyrian King?

'What was it John Buchan wrote?' Dacre muttered to himself, between breaths. '"To die on your feet – that's the best way for men and beasts." Or something very like that, at any rate. I think – '

But he did not give voice to his thought, for he had caught a glimpse of movement across the valley – there, just beneath the overhanging ridge, close by the tract of bracken. Dacre slowly lowered himself to the ground and took out his field-glasses. A closer inspection confirmed what he had already known at some primitive level: it was the Assyrian King himself. The same sixteen-point spread; the same mighty shoulder; and the same challenging look in his liquid, intelligent eye.

Yet the beast was clearly backward-going. The body was somehow thicker, weightier; the horns rougher; the coat sparse and grizzled. And Dacre was shocked to see the stag miss his footing and fall heavily against a boulder. Clearly he was declining fast – not unlike myself, thought Dacre with a wry smile – and it would be a mercy, as well as a cherished ambition, to claim his life.

At that moment, the beast caught wind of him. He drew up his head, casting around for the source of the scent. He seemed to catch a glimpse of Dacre across the valley – his eyesight must still have been preternaturally acute – and stood for some minutes (they felt like hours), apparently considering his course of action. Suddenly he bowed his head, and began to pick his way clumsily through the rocky valley floor towards Dacre's position. At first Dacre could scarcely believe his luck. With his heart thumping once more in his ears, he slid a cartridge into the breech, set his sights, and lined up for the shot.

The stag walked slowly onto a small hillock, and stood there with an air of expectancy. Dacre's sights were perfectly aligned, his breathing controlled; his finger tightened on the trigger. Yet he hesitated – something was amiss. The scene was not as he had imagined it; it was too easy: such a beast should not be shot in such a manner, uncomfortably akin to an execution. He lowered his rifle; and then, to his amazement, the stag snorted, tossed his royal antlers, and broke away, trotting with surprising vigour towards the northernmost end of the valley.

'Challenge offered, and accepted,' said Dacre. 'Could he hear my thoughts, sense my regret? He looked almost - glad. And so am I, upon my word; so am I.' He gazed after the animal in dazed wonder.

Suddenly he came to his senses. 'Well, come on, Dacre – after him!' he cried, pulling himself to his feet. The beast had made for the forest at the neck of the valley and was lost to sight amidst the close-planted trees. Good cover; but Dacre had a notion the stag was playing him, and would seek refuge elsewhere.

He considered three or four possibilities, rejecting each of them on different grounds: too distant; too exposed; too rocky. But what about the hollow, the raised, wooded hollow that lay between Ben Alder and the adjoining Bethell Forest? Difficult to come at without making a racket of one kind or another, and the wind had a way of funnelling one's scent through the narrow passes that led onto the verdant plateau. Accordingly, he had never seen a stag there, but Lochton swore he had – the old keeper was a superb stalker – and Dacre was suddenly possessed by a moral certainty that this was the place. That was where he would head for; and that was where the Assyrian King would be.

He decided upon his plan of action as he hurried up the valley. It was useless to approach the hollow from any of the usual paths, for the reasons mentioned above. No; he must take the approach Lochton had taken: up the southern side of Ben Alder, across the corrie near the summit and along the ridge for some distance, before cutting across the ridge and down to the upper rim of the hollow. It would not be easy: even a man in his prime might struggle on such a march. He stopped and looked up at Ben Alder's lowering bulk, and his spirit quailed within. He thought of his snug smoking-room and study at the Lodge; his Cotswold house and his bit of Hampshire chalk-stream; his favourite armchair at Brooke's; his son, his daughter, his grandchildren. So much to give up, should the climb exceed his strength! He wondered momentarily if the game was worth the candle, and almost he turned back.

But then he remembered that his father, and his father's father, had both died in battle; they had not held back, for fear of what they might lose. And what had they lost? Their lives, certainly, but with great glory. And, moreover, there was to be no long decline into senility for them, no slow settling into forgetfulness and weakness and everything he despised. His face took on a set, determined look: they had not held back; neither would he. He slung his rifle onto his shoulder, and set off across the heather towards the foothills of Ben Alder.

Determined or not, the climb very nearly killed him. The precipitous and treacherous paths seemed endless, as did the weary march along the summit's exposed backbone and the slow, careful descent to the hollow's upper reaches. By the time Dacre was able to peer down into the lightly wooded depression, his heavily perspiring face was mottled with puce and crimson, and his breath came in ragged, despairing heaves. Yet even so his heart seemed to stop when he saw a familiar shape. He had guessed correctly, and there was the beast he sought: the Assyrian King himself, moving now with a renewed and powerful grace among the slender trees.

Now for the dénouement, he thought, the coup de grâce: long-awaited, desperately sought, and redolent of destiny fulfilled. With trembling fingers he loaded his rifle, steadied his breathing, and took aim. A shot rang out and echoed from hillside to hillside.

He must have left his rifle then and scrambled down the scree-slopes to see the dying animal at close quarters, for that was where they found him the next day: resting upon the ground, his arm upon the beast's flank, a soft rain falling on his uncovered head, and a smile of infinite sweetness upon his face. Lochton and the stalker, Geddes, exchanged a look born of the hills and the moors.

'The best way, for men and beasts,' said Lochton.

'The best way,' replied Geddes.

FINIS